# IMMACULATE
# BLUE

# IMMACULATE BLUE

## A NOVEL

PAUL RUSSELL

Published in the United States by Cleis Press,
an imprint of Start Midnight, LLC,
101 Hudson Street, Thirty-Seventh Floor, Suite 3705, Jersey City, NJ 07302.

Printed in the United States.
Cover design: Scott Idleman/Blink
Cover photograph: iStockphoto
Text design: Frank Wiedemann

First Edition.
10 9 8 7 6 5 4 3 2 1

Trade paper ISBN: 978-1-62778-095-7
E-book ISBN: 978-1-62778-109-1


Library of Congress Cataloging-in-Publication Data

Russell, Paul Elliott
 Immaculate blue : a novel / by Paul Russell. -- First edition.
     pages ; cm
 Summary: "From the award-winning author of The Unreal Life of Sergey Nabokov comes the brilliantly conceived and precisely rendered novel Immaculate Blue, which explores the lives of four people - Anatole, Leigh, Chris, and Lydia - and their intermingled and unwinding desires. Set in upstate New York, the novel follows these characters as they achieve their aims in lives redolent with loss and hope, humor and sadness, union and alienation. Russell picks up the thread of his critically acclaimed novel The Salt Point 20 years later and tracks the lives of these friends, some of whom not only lost touch with each other but have also lost their way. Moving, at times shocking, and always memorable, Immaculate Blue points to where the personal and the political come together and shape our lives in unexpected ways. With this newest novel, Paul Russell reminds us of why he is one of the most important voices on the literary scene"-- Provided by publisher.
 ISBN 978-1-62778-095-7 (softcover : acid-free paper) -- ISBN 978-1-62778-109-1 (ebook)
 1.   Triangles   (Interpersonal   relations)--Fiction.   2.   Friendship--Fiction.
 3.  Poughkeepsie (N.Y.)--Fiction.  I. Title.

 PS3568.U7684I47 2014
 813'.54--dc23


                              2014025536

*For Eric Brown*
*and Ian Spencer Bell*

# ACKNOWLEDGMENTS

Many thanks to: Harvey Klinger, Frédérique Delacoste, Brenda Knight, Frank and Holly Bergon, Dean Crawford, Mike Alberti, Kiese Laymon, Gustavo Torres, Andrea Kalmbach, Tom Heacox.

I have made use of material from the following sources: James Ashcroft's *Making a Killing: The Explosive Story of a Hired Gun in Iraq* and *Escape from Baghdad*; John Geddes's *Highway to Hell: Dispatches from a Mercenary in Iraq*; Rajiv Chandrasekaran's *Imperial Life in the Emerald City: Inside Iraq's Green Zone;* Evelyn Glennie's "How to Truly Listen"; and Sebastian Junger's "Blood Oil."

## CHAPTER ONE

Friday early in June, and Lydia's come to Poughkeepsie's Main Street to sort out some last minute details at Floral Euphoria. Her friend Marla opened the little shop six years ago, a testament to somewhat better times, but the recent recession has undone many of the last decade's incremental improvements. Though as Marla likes to point out, marriages and funerals go on regardless, and Floral Euphoria goes on as well.

Lydia doesn't get downtown much these days, which is a shame; her life used to revolve around the pedestrian mall that replaced Main Street in the early eighties but had the unintended consequence of driving all the pedestrians away. With automobile traffic long since restored, the sidewalks are, if not exactly crowded, at least peopled. Still, some ghost image of the old mall with its dying trees and broken fountains remains affixed to the scene before her, like those annoying floaters her ophthalmologist tells her not to worry about, they're just a symptom of age. She'll be fifty-five in August.

She blinks hard, but the ghost image persists. She used to

work for a vintage clothing store in the building across the street that now houses a Mexican grocery; the coffee shop that jump-started her hungover mornings is now Sally's African Hair Braids; she and Anatole and Chris used to meet nearly every afternoon after work at Bertie's, the bar down that alley that closed a number of years ago. Two blocks east lay Chris's little record store—she can't even remember what it was called.

But there on the corner, still in its second-floor location, Anatole's Salon Reflexion perseveres, strangely linking present and past. He's working frantically today; on Sunday he and Rafa are flying to Spain for two weeks, and a host of ladies are distraught at the prospect of his taking a honeymoon from their hair.

Well, they can just wait, she thinks. After all, Anatole and Rafa have waited long enough.

They've been friends Since When, she and Anatole—that's always been their line with everyone—but there was a period when their friendship seemed completely finished. She hasn't thought of that ugly chapter in ages. When *was* the great rupture? 1985, 1986? It must have lasted three or four years, she muses as she enters the fragrant coolness of the flower shop. She can't even remember who reached out to whom, but she has a feeling it was Anatole, even though he was the one who'd felt more wounded by the whole stupid debacle.

So much in her life had changed during those years of their estrangement. She'd cut way back on the booze, banished the drugs and cigarettes. She'd gotten a "real" job as an administrative assistant at Marist. And of course, the biggest change of all, she'd married Tom Rylance. Mr. Steady, she calls him, both mockingly and in not-so-secret gratitude. He isn't a lawyer or doctor—he's a mechanic at Friendly Honda—but, as her mother said when they got engaged, "He's an *echt mensch*, and your poor father would be proud." Lydia wasn't at all sure what her father might have thought, but she was learning to pick her fights.

She'd refrained, for instance, from insisting that her mother take sides in her quarrel with Anatole; of course her mother was going to stay in touch with Anatole whether her daughter liked it or not.

She regrets not having kept a diary. So much has disappeared. There was something about those days—not the bleak time when she and Anatole weren't speaking but before that, when she and Anatole and Chris Havilland were the closest and most fabulous of friends.

Marla's made up a sample centerpiece, an astonishing confection of sweet peas, hyacinths, cyclamen, and peonies, all in shades of pink to fuchsia. There'll be fifteen tables of ten guests each. And for the attendants, elegant white rose bouquets.

"It all looks perfect, doll," Lydia tells her. "The weather forecast is good, the caterer seems to have everything under control, the DJ promises to rock us all out. But frankly, I can't wait for the Big Day to be over."

She's agreed to pick up Chris at the train station at two thirty.

*Finally,* as he likes to say. After twelve years with Rafael, isn't it about time? Of course, he and Rafa have actually been married for years, it's just taken the state of New York a while to catch up. Still, now that he's able, he intends to make the most of it. They've rented the clubhouse at Whispering Creek. They're going the whole hog. His clients, mostly women of a certain age, have proved surprisingly sympathetic—which means a hundred and fifty guests will be there. Nearly sixty wives and their Republican husbands. Mix them in with a handful of relatives and a cohort of gay friends and this promises to be a rather sensational event.

He never knew he was so conventional at heart. Part of that's Rafa's influence. Anatole left the church years ago, since the Holy Apostolic and Catholic Church made it perfectly clear that it wanted him no more than his parents had when they turned *their* backs on him. But Rafa has tempered his long-simmering resentment, and taught himself that there are thoughtful ways to remain Catholic. Rafa has even convinced him to go to Mass—occasionally!—at Holy Trinity. And of course Rafa's the one who's talked him into getting married at the great age of forty-nine.

Naturally, there won't be a Catholic priest to bless them, but Reverend Judy, the lesbian Episcopalian, is the next best thing.

Of all the guests, only Chris Havilland gives Anatole pause. They haven't spoken in twenty-seven years, more years than Anatole had even been alive when he knew Chris in the mid-eighties, before everything fell apart. Before Chris betrayed him.

A boy came between them. Can we even remember his name? But of course we can. At the time he seemed as auspicious as a wounded angel fallen out of Heaven. Our Boy of the Mall, Anatole christened him. How vividly he remembers that first glimpse, one September afternoon on the pedestrian mall. Leigh on a bench eating an ice cream bar. He wore jeans, a white T-shirt, loafers without socks. His profile was perfect.

Leigh won't be invited. Why should he be? He meant nothing, and besides, Anatole has no idea whatever happened to him. But Chris is different. Chris didn't just pass through; he took up residence, he was Anatole's best and most intimate friend. And then he too simply vanished. Anatole remembers calling him in desperation. How he let the phone ring endlessly, unaware Chris had already cleaned out his apartment and skipped town. For years Anatole assumed Chris and Leigh absconded together. For years he nursed that grievance. But the years bring other sufferings. One day his business partner at Reflexion gets sick, and life becomes the struggle to take care of Daniel, to keep him in the world, to resign himself to not being able to keep him in the world, to watch him waste away and then slip away. By then Chris and Leigh are just incidents from a distant past, the light of stars that burned out long ago.

Without Daniel, Reflexion should by all rights have gone under. He'd been the genius of the place, Anatole never more than the sorcerer's grateful apprentice. But maybe the genius of a place never entirely relinquishes its old haunts; improbably enough, Reflexion will celebrate its thirtieth anniversary next year.

It was Lydia who hooked him up him with Rafa. "You'll like him," she said. "He works in IT at Marist, and I know how much you love all things technological. Plus he's cute and smart and ethnic, and best of all he doesn't like girls."

"I don't know," he told her. "I'm still grieving. I think I'm suffering a case of Permanent AIDS Stress Syndrome. PASS. Have you noticed? If you want people to take something seriously these days, you've got to give it an acronym."

To be honest, though he'll never admit this to Rafa, the ethnic part put him off more than the IT part, but after some weeks of hemming and hawing he finally got in touch, they met for dinner at the Milanese, talked tentatively, then engagingly, then exuberantly through a martini, a bottle of wine, a final sambuca. They kissed chastely in the parking lot, separated; then, as if simultaneously hearing some otherwise inaudible cue, replayed that kiss, only prolonged and passionate, and by the time Anatole got home there was already a message on his answering machine saying, "Hey, fellow, that was probably the most romantic three hours of my whole life." Anatole wasn't sure he believed that, but as white lies go it wasn't a bad one. They saw each other the next weekend, and twice during the following week, and soon the past, that forlorn country of Chris and Leigh and Daniel, had come to be irrevocably past.

It's Rafa the IT wizard who tracks Chris down. It seems he works for an outfit called Sterling Global Risk Consulting.

His present location is unspecified, but he's reachable by email. "Really," Rafa tells Anatole with a self-satisfied gleam in his eye, "you'd be surprised how hard it is for anybody to disappear anymore. Though this one seems to have done his best. I tell you: it's the golden age of the stalker we're living in right now."

For weeks Anatole dithers. He composes and recomposes an email. How do you break such a long silence? Then one day—or rather one night, quite late—he hits Send. It's with not a little trepidation that he receives Chris's terse reply, saying that, as it turns out, some business compels him to be in the States the week of the wedding.

She wonders whether she'll recognize him. In his email to Anatole he wrote, "These days I'm fat, bald, dyspeptic, expatriate but otherwise exactly the same." So she's not prepared, as she catches sight of him ascending the stairs from the train platform, for how very little he's changed. He's still slender, but where there used to be something dissolute and languid in his posture, his body now is taut, fit, alert. He bounds up the stairs, small black travel bag in hand. His hair is much shorter, a severe buzz cut Anatole won't be happy with; his gaunt face is leathery from the sun, as if he's spent these years lying by pools or sailing on yachts.

He wears mirrored shades, a white short-sleeved shirt, sand-colored cargo pants, hiking boots. Practical, down-to-earth gear, not the kind of stylish attire he used to affect.

She waves, and seeing her, he removes his sunglasses and smiles—maybe a little warily. Well, why not? Despite her excitement, she feels a little wary too.

"Sorry to disappoint," she says, even as she opens her arms to greet him. "Anatole's got a hectic day at work, so he sent me."

"Lydia," he tells her, moving into her hug. "Still putting yourself down, aren't you? It's very good to see you."

Their embrace is a long one, and she releases him reluctantly. The past shines through, and yet it doesn't. "So, stranger," she says. "Where exactly are you coming from?"

"Denver," he tells her, lighting a cigarette, taking a long drag he's been craving for the last two hours. "I flew into New York last night. I was out there putting my dad in a nursing home."

"Tell me about it," she says. "The life of middle-aged children."

"Your mom's still around?"

"Hanging in there. She'll be ninety in October, if you can believe it."

"Dad's eighty-five. Been on his own for a couple of years. My mom died a while back, he remarried ten months later—very efficient, my dad, when he puts his mind to something. Next task: Find New Wife. Only trouble was, New Wife didn't last as long as she was supposed to. And apparently it's a bit harder to date in your eighties than it was in your seventies. Very frustrating for a guy who's used to getting everything he wants, though by the time I left I could see he was already starting to make some inroads on a couple of his new neighbors at the Home. I'm betting the odds of a Number Three before the final curtain call are pretty good."

His bitterness has the same light touch she remembers, and she laughs in spite of herself.

"Mom lives with me these days," she reports. "Us, I should say. Or actually, we live with her. Same house where I grew up. I'm married, if you can believe it, twenty-one years. I've even got a kid. Don't quite know how all that happened, but it did."

She regrets trying to match his cynical tone. Marriage and family are the best things that ever happened to her.

*"And you? What's your life like?"* she wants to say, but something constrains her. He always seemed so self-contained, even

when she knew him well. Anatole's told her their old friend works for some British company that does risk management— not that she's sure exactly what that entails.

"And before Denver?" she asks. "I take it you don't live there."

He laughs an odd little laugh she doesn't remember from before.

"Actually, this is my first time back in the States since 2003."

It takes a moment to sink in.

"So where do you call home?"

"Let's just say I've moved around a bit. Chris the Wanderer. I'm doing some work in Nigeria at the moment. Nothing too exciting." He laughs again, that half-nervous, half-embarrassed laugh, and looks around. "I can't believe I'm back in Pough-keepsie. I feel like I'm going to wake up in a minute."

"Welcome to the little nightmare some of us never left." That unwelcome cynicism again. "Actually," she revises, "it's not too bad. You'll see. Parking's impossible down at the station anymore. I left the car up by Reflexion and walked down."

"Reflexion's still there? Extraordinary. Anatole and Daniel—"

"I'm afraid Daniel passed some time ago."

"I'm sorry to hear that."

She makes a brave face. "But Anatole's absolutely thriving. There're now *three* Reflexions, if you can believe it. One in Kingston and another in Rhinebeck."

She realizes that she keeps saying "if you can believe it."

"Hey, I have a request," he tells her. He flicks away his ciga-rette butt, then looks around like he's worried someone will have seen. "Do you mind if we walk down to the river? I'd like to see it. I mean, obviously I saw it all the way up on the train, but that's like watching television. You should have heard the soundtrack. Some guy kept telling his girlfriend something about a Buddhist wise man who'd attained enlightenment, and one of his students was so upset that the wise man would never be reborn that, just as his teacher was dying, he said something that irritated the wise man and caused him to miss enlightenment. And so the wise man *was* reborn, and it took him another twenty-eight years on earth to make up for the three seconds of irritation he'd harbored just before he died.

"For some reason, the girlfriend didn't seem to understand the story, and so the guy kept repeating it, almost word for word, and I thought, if you tell this story one more time I'm going to fucking slot you. All the time I'm looking out the window and thinking, this river's one of the most beautiful landscapes I've ever seen."

"Slot?"

"Off. Kill. Exterminate. I work with these Rhodesian guys. Well, ex-Rhodesians. Whatever. I pick up their slang."

He's aware that he's just talking, but he's not sure what else to do. Truth is, being met by Lydia has flummoxed him a little. The years haven't treated her all that badly. At first glance she looked stout, even matronly, but then he's taken in by her brashly dyed platinum hair, the enormous, flashy handbag she carries, her too-bright lipstick, the even brighter orange shoes. Once a fag hag, always a fag hag, he thinks—not unkindly. Truth is, he hasn't thought of her in a long time. Before Anatole's email out of the blue, he hadn't thought of any of them. He's suddenly shy about meeting Anatole. Communing with the river's a postponement, but then so much in his life has been a postponement.

He wonders if Anatole's sent Lydia to pick him up as a way of postponing as well.

In the little park at the bottom of Main Street, old men and young mothers sit on benches, reading the paper, eating sandwiches, staring into space. A radio plays that catchy, annoying song he's been hearing at the drinking club in the Rumukoroshe compound for the last couple of months. In the old days he'd have known who the singer was, but now he has no idea. He lights another cigarette and stares into space as well: the brown, implacable, magnificent river, framed by the pleasingly Art Deco suspension bridge to the south, and to the north the great derelict hulk of the train bridge...

"...Is now the Walkway Over the Hudson State Historic Park," Lydia explains. "All paved and fenced in and safe. It's been a huge success. A half million visitors a year, or something like that. Hard to believe. I'll take you out on it. It's not scary at all—it's like being out on a big pier. And the views are to die for."

He notices now the protective fence, the festive flags. He used to find that ruin intensely poetic—a kind of symbol for everything that was wrong and beautiful about Poughkeepsie. He used to dare himself to sneak past the fences and venture out some night, but he never quite worked up the courage. Now tourists stroll there. It's OK: he went on to do far more dangerous and necessary things.

A weekend in Poughkeepsie's small potatoes compared to the life he's chosen. Still, he wonders why he's elected to put himself through it. He's staying at the Inn at the Falls, where he's arranged to have a rental car dropped off. Habits die hard: he's spent the best part of a decade relying on a set of wheels, a ready kit, some body armor, and sunglasses. Not to mention his own private arsenal.

He hears himself say, "Yeah, that might be fun to go out there. I mean, why come all this way and not be a tourist?"

When was the last time he said "that might be fun?"

At Reflexion, Anatole keeps darting back and forth to the big window over Main Street. A lady cop is writing parking tickets. A Hispanic fellow on a bicycle is having a jovial shouting match with a large, dreadlocked Jamaican; the man on the bicycle keeps circling back so he won't drift out of earshot. Each return provokes a new outburst. They both seem to be enjoying their quarrel so much they don't want it to end. Moving from car to car like a cat investigating a garden, the cop ignores them.

For thirty years he's been calling it his window on the world. It's a symptom of latent ADD, no doubt, but the truth is, he focuses better when he's distracting himself. Daniel used to joke he depended on that window the way other people depend on television.

Right now he's anticipating his first glimpse of Chris. Why this anxiety? Maybe he's still in love. (He popped a Xanax a while ago, but it hasn't helped.)

Nonsense, he tells himself, returning his attention to Carole Braunschweig and her unruly mass of hair. He's been candid with Rafa. *It's self-indulgent, I know, maybe just plain selfish. But I want Chris to be here. Maybe what I want is to let him know that I'm OK. I didn't get destroyed, I didn't get sick. I survived. Maybe I want to see if any of that matters to him.*

And Rafa has reminded him, calmly, as is Rafa's way, that he's got three, count them, three former lovers coming to the wedding. So surely Anatole can have just *one*.

Anatole's never told him Chris was not technically a lover—but since when is love about technicalities? It almost worries him that Rafa's so trusting. Most of the time that trust feels like maturity; only occasionally does it feel like—a kind of indifference? A kind of delusional self-confidence? But Rafa's neither indifferent nor delusional. He's just, well, Rafa—the computer geek with near-magical abilities, the good dancer with terrible taste in music, the fabulous cook who takes photos of his creations and posts them on Facebook, the avid bicyclist who's even found a way to automatically post his cycling stats from that day's bike ride. Why anyone would want to post such things is something Anatole's never figured out, but there you have it, Rafael Pujol's personality in a nutshell: generous, extroverted, a little exhibitionist, completely oblivious, totally adorable.

"I'm thinking of trying this new rinse," he tells Carole, running his fingers through her imperial mane.

Then once again to the window, and this time Anatole catches sight of his quarry. They walk unhurriedly, Lydia in animated conversation, Chris smoking, leisurely turning his head from side to side as if to take in everything. It's like seeing a ghost. Anatole tests his heart; there's a frightened rabbit cowering in his chest. They've disappeared from sight; they're coming up the stairs. He's sorry for Carole—her hair, rather. Little does she know how dramatically it's diminished in importance. And her husband's the assistant D.A.

Then they're in the salon. Heads turn. And why shouldn't they? A deeply tanned, strikingly handsome man, no longer young, stands before them all. Chris's hair's been brutally shorn—he used to have such beautiful locks—and Anatole instantly assesses the reason: he'd be showing a bald spot if his hair were longer. It's the way to go. Forget the comb-over. Just be fierce. Embrace baldness for what it is. Really short hair on men can be incredibly hot.

Chris is smiling—ruefully, it would seem, in acknowledgment of everything: his disappearance, the long silence, the missed years.

Anatole moves toward him. Chris puts out his hand, but Anatole's not having that. He blusters right into a hug that seems to catch Chris off guard. Chris, he reminds himself, never liked to get touched. There was a time when Anatole fantasized about what it would be like to make love to Chris. Lydia and Leigh had succeeded—if that's the right word—where he failed. For a long time he hated both of them for it, but now, as Chris pulls away from his embrace, he's perhaps glad that he never did. It somehow makes this easier.

"Long time no see, Kemosabe," Chris says in that deadpan

that used to keep them entertained at Bertie's. Anatole wishes he could meet it halfway, but he finds himself too flustered.

"I don't even know what to say to you, Mister," he sputters. "I'm just very glad you're here."

"Hey, no problem," Chris replies—as if he's just gone a block or two out of his way.

"We're not staying," Lydia says. "I know you're crazy busy. I just wanted you to see that the package has been safely delivered. Don't worry about a thing. I'll keep him entertained. We'll see you at your place at seven, okay?"

And just like that, they've gone. His head is spinning. But that has been the plan all along: work like a banshee till six, then a calm reunion dinner at the little house on Garden Street he and Rafa have been restoring for the last couple of years, and where Rafa is even now doing something wonderful with foodstuffs in the kitchen. Still, he can't help feeling a little bereft, as if he's stumbled back into a half-remembered dream where something precious is offered and then snatched away.

Anatole turns back to Carole. "Sorry about the interruption. An old friend in town for the wedding."

"Anatole, dear, you're crying," she says. And it's true. An annoying tear has crept down his cheek. He flicks it away.

"What can I say," he tells her, resuming his work. "I'm a sentimental guy."

"This is going to be a tremendous weekend for you," she says.

Anatole's put on weight. His once well-defined features have gone rubbery; the animated scarecrow's body Chris remembers as being in constant, hectic motion has gone slack. Not that he looks unhealthy or even unattractive—it's just disconcerting to see this disconnect between the present and the past.

"I didn't mean to hustle us out of there," Lydia says. "I know Anatole would've loved to throw down everything and join us.

But he's got work to do."

"Are you thirsty?" Chris asks. "Bertie's isn't still around by any chance, is it? I'd love to buy you a drink."

"Long gone," she tells him. "Besides, it's a little early for a drink, don't you think?"

He glances at his watch. Three thirty seems a perfect time for a drink. He's glad he packed a flask in his overnight bag. Always keep the escape routes open.

"You're right," he tells her. Her abstinence is nearly as disconcerting as Anatole's weight gain. "So here's what I want to do," he announces as a way of retaking charge. "I'd like to check in to the hotel at some point. Maybe grab a quick nap. Then if you give me directions to Anatole's—"

"Oh, I'll come pick you up. Not to worry."

"I can manage on my own. I've rented a car."

"You haven't changed," she tells him with a flash of the old Lydia. "Still skittish around the humans."

"Now prepare me," he says as they pass the ice cream and samosa stands that flank the entrance to the Walkway. A series of educational signs detail the history of the river, the considerable engineering feat of the bridge, the fire that ended its working life, the years of dereliction, its transformation into the tourist destination it is today. The Walkway is a ribbon of concrete, peopled by mothers pushing strollers, old couples, bicyclists. "Tell me about this Rafa. I like to know the lay of the land in advance."

You're just meeting Anatole's husband, Lydia thinks. You're not reconnoitering. But then he's seemed strangely on edge since his arrival. He keeps glancing around. Pay attention to me, she wants to tell him, though she's learned with her son that instructions like that tend to backfire.

"He's five years younger than Anatole. Grew up in Washington Heights, works at Marist, which is how I know him. His mom's Dominican, his dad was a French doctor who ran a clinic in the town where she lived. Passed away a number of years ago. I'm not sure exactly when they came to the States. Rafa can tell you all that when you meet him tonight. His mom'll be there too. Very creative type, old style bohemian. Paints, does ceramics, makes jewelry—this is one of hers." Lydia pulls back a sheaf of platinum hair to show off a gaudy orange and blue earring. "I adore her stuff. And she's still going strong at seventy-something. We should all be so lucky. Oh, and Rafa's got two sisters who'll be coming up with their families from the city tomorrow. What else can I say? He's the best thing that ever happened to Anatole. They've been together twelve years, if you can believe it. They're totally settled and domestic. And I'm not even being ironic when I say that."

Chris thinks of Anatole's binges, his frenetic fleeting crushes on teenage boys, his elations and depressions—everything that made him an anarchic and agreeable companion.

"Hard to imagine," he says.

"Oh, Anatole always wanted to settle down. Even back when you knew him. We both did. It's just that neither of us had any idea how."

"Funny, I don't remember either of you mentioning it at the time."

"We were way too cool to say what we really wanted."

"And then you figured it out."

"Thank God," she says. "One or both of us would probably be dead right now if we hadn't. We'd be like Daniel, poor soul. Getting drunk or high every night. Being hungover every morning. You run out of options at a certain point. You come to understand why everybody else is living the boring life. And it doesn't look so boring anymore."

The sun on the bright concrete reminds Chris that he's been in slight hangover mode all day, courtesy of a preposterously late night.

"Tell me more about Daniel," he says, as they pause, like any tourist, to take in the latest informational placard. "You know, I never liked him all that much. He seemed so…" He searches for the word.

"Gay?" she says.

"Not that. Just too…"

"Campy?" she tries out, and he suddenly remembers a night at Bertie's, he and Anatole drinking scotch, Daniel at the bar in consummate, platinum drag. And Lydia's younger brother Craig home from college—fall break it must have been. The details are hazy, but they involve his urging Craig to go talk to that dynamite blonde chick he'd been admiring from afar, and the two of them hitting it off, making out on the dance floor, then disappearing—to Anatole's prudent alarm and Chris's schadenfreude—then Craig coming back baffled, frustrated, Daniel as was his wont having ducked out before the inevitable and unwelcome discovery scene, the whole tawdry episode precipitated by nothing other than Chris's desire to play a punishing little joke—but on whom? On Daniel, whom he didn't care for (was he just a little jealous of Anatole's breathless friendship with him?) or on Craig, whom he'd found seethingly attractive?

Or had the joke been on Chris? Craig was as straight as they came, but what Chris wouldn't have given to overpower him in a dark alley in some other dimension where everything is possible, everything is allowed.

He winces to recall that he once slept with Lydia solely because the unattainable Craig Forman was her brother. In a life of many bad acts, that was one.

Lydia's been telling him the details of Daniel's illness. He senses that she's unfurled this narrative a number of times before. "He wasn't exactly the best patient," she recites. "He wouldn't give up the booze or the drugs, and he kept going off his meds because they made him feel lousy. Anatole was incredibly patient. He had to keep tabs on Daniel to make sure he wasn't doing something insanely self-destructive. 'Daniel's not house-trained,' he used to complain. They had some terrible fights. Daniel would scream, 'Just let me fucking die, asshole,' but Anatole wasn't having it. He was a saint, really. He saw Daniel through to the very end."

"Not to play the devil's advocate," Chris ventures, "and, of course, I wasn't there, so I don't know, but in the abstract at least, isn't it sort of selfish to keep somebody alive if they don't want to stay alive anymore? I mean, if I was Daniel, in that situation, I think I'd have wanted to make as quick an exit as possible."

She shakes her head. "Live fast, die young, stay pretty. Please: tell me you got that out of your system years ago."

She's adamant in the way of ex-smokers or drinkers. That tone in itself's a good enough reason never to give up anything, Chris thinks. "So I guess now you're going to tell me that I've grown old but I haven't grown up?"

He's nettled her. It's not what he wanted to do, but he's irritated by the sense she exudes of having finally figured things out.

Barely two hours into the weekend and they're at odds with each other. She envies Anatole, back at Reflexion, blissfully unaware of what he and his silly nostalgia have unleashed.

They've come to the edge of the Hudson, that river arising in Lake Tear of the Clouds in the Adirondacks (as a placard has informed them) and flowing south toward *Manahatta*. As they leave the shore behind, two hundred feet below them, and venture out over the water, the open vista invites their mood to expand as well. *Muhheakantuck. River That Flows Two Ways.* Chris seizes the chance to reset the tone.

"I want to hear about life, not death," he says. "Tell me about your life these days, Lydia. Your family. Who's this fellow you married? How'd you meet him?"

"How about the service bay at Friendly Honda?" She's aware she packages her stories, but that doesn't stop her from delivering her well-rehearsed account of the time she dropped off her Civic for "D" service and Tom was there with a clipboard to write down the mileage and ask about anything she wanted checked out. How he was there at the end of the day when she came back to retrieve the car, some five hundred dollars poorer. This was 1992, and he said, "Um, not to be too delicate about things, but if you haven't noticed this you might want to," pointing to her Clinton/Gore bumper sticker that somebody, unbeknownst to her, had vandalized to read Cunt/Gore. They had a laugh, these two complete strangers, and then two days later they ran into each other at ShopRite, and that was pretty much the end of the beginning, as she likes to put it.

"He's not the person I ever thought I'd marry. We don't see eye to eye on much of anything, which I guess is what keeps it interesting. He's pretty conservative. Dole, Bush, McCain—right down the line. He'll be pulling the lever for Romney in the fall. But hell, even I might be doing that if the economy tanks any more than it has. He's not Jewish, but he's very chivalrous toward my mother, which goes a long, long way with her, since obviously she was dead set on my marrying a Jew. Plus he's as pro-Israel as you can get.

"And one other thing. He's just a tiny bit homophobic, more knee-jerk than anything else, but sometimes that can be a bit of a problem."

From this vantage, Poughkeepsie's a forest from which slender church spires and squat apartment towers rise. To the south, the dark Hudson Highlands; to the north, the blue Catskills. A small plane is making lazy circles above the river. The sound of its engine fades and surges and fades again. Chris catches at a memory, but it recedes before he can grasp it.

"Will Tom be at the wedding?"

"Oh, of course. He and Anatole get along well enough. I

mean, without me they'd never be friends, but I have to give it to Tom, he's grown a lot, he's a lot more open-minded than I'd ever have thought."

"And you mentioned a kid," Chris says nonchalantly.

"Caleb. Our golden boy. Just turned seventeen. He'll be a junior at Arlington High this fall. He's been going through a rough patch, but who doesn't at that age? Life's been pretty tough on him at times, but all things considered, he's doing wonderfully. See, he was born with severely damaged nerve endings in both ears. He got cochlear implants when he was two, and that helped a lot. He even plays drums in a band, if you can believe it. Unfortunately, the insurance didn't cover a whole lot of the implant cost, so we've been pretty strapped. It's why we live with Mom. We've never really been able to get ahead. But it's been completely worth it. You'll see when you meet him. Anatole's helped out where he could. He's like a mentor to Caleb."

Once again, this theme of Saint Anatole. "I wouldn't have thought you'd let that old pervert get within ten light years of your son," Chris can't resist saying. "I mean, knowing what you know." He says it as a joke, or sort of a joke, or maybe not a joke at all.

Lydia's ferocity catches him off guard. "We were a pack of stupid, self-absorbed predators back then. All three of us. It's a disgrace. I can see that clearly now that I've grown up. And Anatole's grown up too."

"I'm sure Anatole—" Chris begins to say, but Lydia interrupts him.

"You want to know something? I came out on this bridge once. Back in its derelict days. I came out here with Leigh. Surely you remember Leigh. Leigh Whatever-His-Last-Name-Was."

She regrets her tone, but she's already said it.

"Leigh Gerrard," Chris says. "What did you think?"

"Sorry. Of course you do. Did he never tell you we went out here?"

"No," Chris says with a feeling of awful emptiness, "he didn't."

"We'd been up to the Vanderbilt mansion. I guess it was our first date, if you can call it that. A couple of bottles of wine and a baggie full of psilocybin mushrooms. Very glamorous. Anyway, we somehow ended up out on the bridge. I guess Leigh must have dared me into it. I was scared shitless we'd plunge to our deaths. I've never told anybody this, so consider yourself privileged."

"I take it Our Former Boy of the Mall's *not* invited," Chris says, knowing all along, without wanting to know it, that the secret spur to his accepting Anatole's invitation was the possibility that Leigh might be there. How wondrously strange it would be to see him across the room, drink in hand, all grown up now, handsome but still somehow in full (or even diminished, he'll settle for that) possession of whatever ineffable qualities had made him so absurdly compelling.

Lydia dashes any hope of that.

"Of course not. Nobody knows what happened to him. Unless you do."

"I don't, no. I cut my ties with everything and everybody when I left. It's what I had to do."

"Yeah, remind me. Smash all the china and then just leave. Though I give it to you; for a bull, you were pretty exquisite. But I just have one little question, after all these years. Mind if I ask it? You owe me a secret, after all."

He supposes he's glad they're having this out the way they are. "Shoot," he says.

"Let me put it delicately, okay? Did Leigh seduce you too? Or did you seduce him? That's always been the big question for us earthlings left behind. Did the two of you run off together, as the evidence, or at least the timing, would seem to suggest?"

Chris can hear perfectly well the question she doesn't ask: Were you as treacherous as we've had to assume? And if you were then, are you still now?

"No," he tells her. "I never fucked Leigh, if that's what you're asking. Trust me. I wouldn't have done that. My leaving had nothing to do with Leigh one way or the other."

"Then why?"

But Chris doesn't say anything. He lights another cigarette. He used to have a wonderful stylish way with his cigarettes, but now it just seems haunted and automatic. Overhead, the little plane is practicing stunts, showing off for the tourists on the Walkway.

"Whatever you might think," he says finally, "not all of us were predators."

She was looking forward to having Chris on her own for a couple of hours before Anatole got hold of him. Now she wonders exactly what it was she was looking forward to.

The house smells of incense. Rafa likes to light a few sticks an hour or so before guests arrive; he says it wakes the place up. Anatole's not so crazy about the practice. "Secondhand smoke. I don't really want to get lung cancer. Can't we just use Glade instead?" To which Rafa will usually point out: "Honey, you smoked for twenty-something years. The damage is done. And anyway"—he shoos the rising vapor toward Anatole—" this is *holy* smoke. Buddhist nuns made it from sacred trees."

Tonight the incense masks but doesn't erase other delicious odors. Anatole peers into the small kitchen and offers the obligatory but heartfelt "Smells wonderful!"

"Well I hope so," Rafa tells him. He's barefoot, in gym shorts and a paint-spattered T-shirt. He's taken the day off from work, hasn't yet shaved or showered. His shaggy dark hair is all a lovely mess, just asking to have a hand run through it. "I've been slaving in here for hours."

Over the years they've developed a parody domesticity cobbled together from a shared childhood diet of *I Love Lucy, Gilligan's Island, The Flintstones*; it overlays, not unlike incense, the real and mostly satisfying household routines they've fallen into.

"So has he arrived? Have you seen him?" Rafa asks as Anatole kisses him on the back of the neck, massages his shoulders, succumbs to temptation. "Hey, don't mess with the chef," Rafa warns. "Things have entered a particularly delicate phase."

"So what has the maestro conjured up? And yes, Lydia allowed me a single, tantalizing glimpse. He hasn't changed a bit, you know. Except for an atrocious haircut. So maybe he *has* changed. Oh my god: what if he's gone and lost his sense of style? That was his only real asset, you know. But it was a thoroughly impeccable asset."

"I tell you, Mr. Kitten, you're still in love. And I'm going to be the jealous husband all evening. Can you hand me that bowl of walnuts, please?"

"Are those beets?"

"It's going to be a beet and walnut puree. Traditional Georgian dish." He brandishes a tattered cookbook. "And I don't mean American Georgian. Perfect for this warm weather."

"It was like a vision," Anatole admits over the whir of the Cuisinart, "having him appear in Reflexion just for an instant like that. Then Lydia spirited him away. God knows what the two of them have gotten up to this afternoon!"

"Oh, by the way, she called to say they went out on the Walkway. And she deposited him at The Inn at the Falls. *And* he rented a car and will show up on his own. She gave him directions. She says he won't get lost. He's a world traveler these days. He lives in—Nigeria, I think she said."

"What?"

"That's what *I* said. I'm sure we'll ask him all about it. Now

I'm going to go take a shower and freshen up. If the timer dings, could you take the zucchini boats out of the oven?"

"You do understand why I'm anxious, don't you?"

Rafa turns and puts his arms around him. "Of course, Mr. Kitten. You loved him and he didn't love you back. That always hurts. But it's never the end of the world. You should know that better than anybody."

His room at the inn is comfortable, clean, and reliably air-conditioned, with a view of the eponymous falls. He splashes cold water on his face, turns on the TV, searches for Al Jazeera, but as in Denver the channel is nowhere to be found, so he settles on CNN.

Lying down on the bed is a mistake; his fading hangover decides to make one last stand.

He feels shredded by Lydia's attentions. Was she always so aggressive? Or maybe his younger self had more energy for that kind of sparring, maybe he used to feel emotions mattered more, that he and his friends were staking a claim to something important when they talked so endlessly about their feelings. But Lydia and Anatole never knew him, did they? Those secret trips to New York, the teenage boys on whose blank, bought bodies he'd enact those tawdry, stirring tableaux he'd scripted in advance and would savor for melancholy days afterward. Anatole and Lydia would have been scandalized, had they known. But they hadn't known. Truth be told, despite his genuine affection, he always slightly despised their cluelessness.

He hasn't been paying any attention to the background noise of news burbling into his room, but the phrase "Niger Delta" snags him. The flawless mannequin of a newscaster reports that two hundred people have died in an explosion in the troubled Rivers state. Ten seconds of inferno footage roll by. "The victims," says the newscaster, "were engaged in a practice known as bunkering, by which oil is illegally siphoned from the thousands of miles of pipeline that crisscross the region. Most of the victims, including many women and children, were incinerated instantly. The area has seen increasing strife in recent years as armed militias—"

He clicks off the remote and shuts his eyes. His hangover throbs. He sat far too long in that chic bar in Hell's Kitchen last night, a middle-aged out-of-towner methodically bunkering one scotch after another, as out of place as he could be and yet perfectly invisible to a roomful of callow young men chatting and flirting, oblivious to the sad old wolf lingering at the edge of the woods.

He can see too, on the back of his eyelids, the scene CNN hasn't shown, but which will have been broadcast in graphic detail on the Nigeria News channel—a jumble of seared human sausages, plump charred casings burst open, extruding tender pink meat.

He's seen his share of both corpses and boys. Too often they've been one and the same.

Half an hour of shut-eye, maybe forty-five minutes, he thinks, having long ago learned to catch sleep when he can. He'll be a little late to Anatole's, but that's also a lesson learned long ago: always keep them waiting a bit.

Selfishly, he wants a few minutes alone with Chris, since Lydia's gotten her share already. But it's not to be. Lydia's the first to arrive, and Anatole hides his disappointment as he hugs her, pecks her on the cheek, relieves her of the bottle of wine she holds out.

She can read him thoroughly. "I know," she says. "I should've held off a bit. I wasn't thinking."

"No, no," he tells her. "Chris and I'll have plenty of time to catch up." Though just when that plenty of time might show itself eludes him; he's realizing how heavily scheduled everything is, starting right now and going all day tomorrow till the chauffeured Rolls Silver Cloud spirits the newlyweds away from the music and dancing at Whispering Creek to their honeymoon suite at the Millbrook Inn and the next morning—Cinderella's carriage having metamorphosed into a pumpkin—via a more modest car service to Newark and their flight to Madrid.

"It's not like I've exactly caught up with him," Lydia admits. "I'd forgotten how good he is at extracting all sorts of information without giving up more than a shred in return. Maybe if we've both got him in our crosshairs he'll be a little more forthcoming."

"We'll get what we can get. Did he tell you anything about what he's up to in—did you say Nigeria?"

"Not a word. It's a little embarrassing, but he maneuvered me into talking about myself for practically the whole time. And you and Rafa, of course. He seemed to want to know what he's getting himself in for."

"I'm glad he's still Secret Agent Man. I'm glad he hasn't given that up."

"I don't think he's given anything up. He seems caught in a time warp. I don't think life's touched him the way it's touched you and me. Though that's just a guess."

Anatole understands he shouldn't be thrilled by that observation, but secretly he is. He wants Chris to have stayed exactly the same.

"Well, let's have a drink, shall we? Rafa's got dinner under control. Miosotis has had her nap and her tea, so she's good to go."

Lydia wonders if she should mention their talk of Leigh; now that she's conjured him, she can't quite dispel him. And she can't shake the feeling that it somehow has the potential to threaten the happiness of Anatole's weekend. She trusts Chris won't bring up Our Boy of the Mall, but who knows what happens when old friends get together and drink too much wine and the talk inevitably turns to the past? With any luck, Rafa and his mother will be a firewall against too much of that.

Miosotis is ensconced in the comfortable wing chair by the fireplace. She looks wonderfully regal this evening, dressed in a black skirt and purple blouse, over which she wears a vest embroidered with bright flowers. She's pulled back her long silver hair in a way that accentuates her high cheekbones and thin lips. At her throat rests a silver brooch of her own design. Rings encrust bony fingers. Only her feet seem incongruous, clad in those hideous crocs that are all the rage; hers are lime green—and comfortable as all get out, according to Miosotis. Lydia wouldn't be caught dead in them.

"Don't get up, my dear," Lydia tells her, crossing the room to bestow a kiss on her forehead. "You're looking very chic, as always."

"These days I just throw myself together any old way."

"Well, it always seems to come out beautifully. Now, what'll you have to drink? I'm going to have a nice white wine spritzer. Would you like me to make you one too?"

"Gin and tonic, please," Miosotis tells her. "Extra strong. Now, remind me, who's this man who's coming to dinner? I can't quite get him straight in my head."

"Don't worry. None of us can," Lydia says, thinking she should have put her foot down the first she heard of Anatole's invitation plans. One thing Anatole's never quite learned is how to protect himself.

Professional habits die hard: before setting out he checks, then double-checks, the oil, the tire pressure, the radiator fluid, the gas level. He takes a circuitous route that by degrees modulates from evasive to leisurely. Evening sun drenches the city. Clouds billow peach and salmon colored in the downpour of light, and for the prolonged moment Poughkeepsie seems nothing less than paradise. Unarmored, unarmed, he drives down leafy residential streets, past grand nineteenth-century houses, some still in good nick, others in sad decay; then along other streets populated by their more modest twentieth-century brethren. The orderly traffic is simply traffic. Intersections pose no hazard. Men lingering on street corners simply linger. A bit of trash in the gutter isn't worth a second glance. He hardly even bothers to look in the rearview mirror to see who might be profiling him.

It's a stranger who answers the door of the neat little house on Garden Street. "Come in, come in," he says, extending his hand. "You must be Chris. I've heard so much about you."

"And you must be Rafael. I've heard practically nothing about you. Except for what Lydia told me this afternoon."

"Lydia has such romantic ideas about me. But I'm not really a gangster, I swear."

"Then I'm disappointed," Chris tells him. "I guess I'll be going now."

"Well, maybe occasionally," Rafa says. "When things get boring."

Their banter, paltry as it is, nonetheless establishes a tone between them, and Chris is relieved. Despite Lydia's descriptive litany, he hasn't really known what to expect. Rafa's not unhandsome. Maybe a tad on the heavy side, with thickish wrists and neck, but a nice chin, large, attractive brown eyes, a noble nose. A dark stubble covers his lower face.

Handing over his bottle of wine, Chris follows his barefoot host into a cramped living room.

"So you found us," Anatole says. "I was starting to worry you'd gotten lost. I should've given you my phone number."

"Sorry I'm late. I wasn't lost at all. Turns out I still have a surprisingly accurate map of Poughkeepsie filed away in my head. The instant I turned on Garden Street, I recognized exactly where I was. I even remembered this house. Didn't it used to be blue?"

"Good memory. The place was pretty run-down when

we bought it. Which is why we could afford it. We've been working on it since—Rafa? When did we buy this house?"

"2005," Rafa says. "Why can you never remember that?"

"I have a mental block about lots of things. As you know!"

"This, by the way, is my mother, Miosotis," Rafa says.

Chris shakes the hand of the elegant older woman whose fine features have been blurred in her son.

"Here, let me give you the house tour." Anatole clutches Chris's arm. "Come. Follow me. This obviously is the living room. We've redone the floors. Rafa chose the apricot for the walls. I wanted something darker, but he was totally right. And here we have the kitchen, with these horrid tiles that need replacing."

It's the old Anatole, the awkwardness masking the nervousness masking the endearing enthusiasm. Chris relaxes into the moment, accepts the glass of wine Anatole offers, allows himself to be led through the dining room, a study cluttered with multiple computers, up the steep stairs to the blue-hued master bedroom with its four-poster bed that's too large for the space but which, Anatole explains breathlessly, they couldn't resist. Then here's the tidy guest bedroom where Miosotis is staying, and the bathroom which unfortunately is very small, and another room used mainly for storage, but if they ever decide to have a child—

Chris stops him. "No? Really?"

"That's a joke," Anatole tells him. "Well, sort of a joke. I mean, you never know. What do they say? First comes love, then comes marriage, then comes baby in a baby carriage."

"You're serious, aren't you?"

Strange that this is how they arrive at the first moment of intimacy they've shared in a quarter century. It's the moment when it all becomes real to Chris. Anatole and Rafa aren't playing. This is their life, which they take with exactly the seriousness with which people are allowed—even expected—to take their lives.

"Don't worry, I don't think there's a baby in the works. But then I never thought marriage was in the works either. We do keep a turkey baster downstairs in case some frisky lesbians stop by for a visit. Come, let me show you the garden. We'll take the back stairs. For some strange reason, small as it is, this house has two sets of stairs. Designed for hanky-panky, I guess."

Anatole has successfully deflected the serious moment, and Chris supposes he's grateful for that. At the bottom of the stairs, Anatole opens a door onto a flagstone patio with table and chairs, and beyond that the back garden in early bloom. Chris doesn't know flowers, but he knows enchanting profusion when he sees it. For the second time this evening a paradise—this one small, fenced in, amply protected—beckons him.

"Mostly Rafa's doing," Anatole explains. "But I've been learning. Turns out I've got a bit of a green thumb too. Chartreuse, you might say. I put in all these Siberian irises myself last fall, and just look at them now."

Delicate white blossoms float above slender foliage. White butterflies flitter among them, looking like blossoms that have detached themselves and become airborne.

Rafa has brought out appetizers—black olives in a bowl, several cheeses on a board, a basket of bread, a whole smoked trout on a platter, salsa and chips. No one ever minds that he overdoes it.

"Now that Anatole's bored you to death with every drafty window we've replaced and every bathroom tile we haven't, has he told you we're thinking of going solar? Sounds like a no-brainer, doesn't it? Though we'd have to cut down the big catalpa tree in front."

"Which I'm reluctant to do," Anatole adds.

"If we don't all go solar, and pretty soon," Lydia says, "there's no future for any of us, humans or trees or anything else. I know—it's a difficult trade-off."

"It *is* a difficult trade-off," Rafa affirms. "Anatole and I go back and forth. What do you think, Chris?"

Put on the spot, he laughs nervously—that hiccup he picked up in Iraq a few years back and hasn't been able to get rid of.

"Go with it," he says. "A tree's a tree. Lots worse happens in the world than a tree gets cut down. Sorry, Anatole. That's my two cents—for what it's worth. I'm actually surprised not to see more evidence of solar since I've been back in the States. Every fucking house in the country should have solar panels on the roof."

His lurch into vehemence surprises them. Surprises him as well. "Sorry," he says. "It's just that, in my line of work..." He hesitates. He knows he's a mystery. It's the one card he's always held. He's reluctant to let it go.

"So just what *is* your line of work these days?" Lydia prompts.

Chris barks that laugh. "These days? I work for an oil company."

"In Nigeria," Anatole says.

"Yep. Place called Port Harcourt. The Niger Delta. I've been there a couple of years. In my line of work I move around a lot. I was in Iraq for nearly six years. Way too long. After Baghdad, Port Harcourt's fucking retirement."

"I've never even heard of Port Harcourt," Anatole says. "Or the Niger Delta, to tell you the truth."

"Why should you? Port Harcourt's nothing but a hellhole and I should know, I've seen enough of the planet's hellholes. The delta's ruined these days, but it's still one of those truly grand things—a big river meeting the ocean."

Lydia's not so easily deflected. "You keep saying *my line of work*. But what exactly *is* your line of work?"

"Right now it's called Risk Management. Back when I was in Iraq, it was PMC."

"In English?" Anatole asks.

"Private military contractor. Basically I do security, whatever it takes to enable other folks to do their more important jobs. In Iraq that was Coalition contractors repairing the power grid. In Port Harcourt it mostly means making sure foreign engineers don't get kidnapped on their way out to the rigs and refineries."

"So you're some kind of glorified bodyguard?" Lydia suggests.

"I don't know about the glorified part."

"Tell me you weren't with Blackwater in Iraq," Rafa says sternly.

"Rafa spends all his time on the Internet," Anatole explains. "He reads, like, five newspapers a day."

"I procrastinate a lot," Rafa admits.

"I wouldn't be caught dead anywhere near Blackwater. Blackwater was everything that was sublimely fucked up about the occupation. No, in Iraq I worked for this little Brit company, Spartan, that specialized in covert profiles."

"I have no idea what any of that means," Anatole says, trying to suppress a panicked feeling that Chris has somehow gone and gotten himself in over his head. But that's ridiculous; of course Chris knows what he's doing. It's just Anatole's own ignorance, his lack of worldliness.

"It means, basically," Chris explains, "nobody can fuck with you if they don't know you're there."

"I can see how you'd be good at that," Lydia says.

"It's all about trying to blend in. You drive beat-up cars with local license plates. You wrap your head in a shemagh and hang prayer beads from the rearview mirror and slap on some Islamic bumper stickers. You keep your guns well out of sight. You don't swan around in a convoy of brand new, obviously weaponized 4x4s with a chopper escort overhead. You slip in, you deliver your guys to wherever they need to go, you slip out. You're long gone before the bad guys even realize you were there. So yeah, that's been my line of work for quite a while now. And I'm still mostly in one piece—*masha'Allah,* as my Iraqi brothers say."

Lydia's not sure what she expected, but it's definitely not this. She feels a little flummoxed, even betrayed, though she knows that's completely irrational. Whatever tiny claim she ever had on Chris and his future expired long ago; still, it's as if the languorous, world-weary glam and punk rock devotee she once cherished beyond words has been resurrected only in order to vanish before her eyes.

She's a little horrified to hear herself say primly, "Chris, this all sounds just terrifying. I can't believe it's what you've been doing with your life. I was imagining something so very different."

"Like what, I wonder?"

"I don't know. I mean, you go from owning a quiet little record store in Poughkeepsie to the most dangerous place in the world? How does that happen?"

As if owning a record store in Poughkeepsie hadn't been dangerous too, he wants to remind them, but what he says is, "You join the army, for starters."

"You didn't!" Anatole says.

"Yeah, I did."

"But wasn't your dad? Didn't you grow up on bases? I mean, didn't you just *hate* all that? Don't tell me my Alzheimer's is making this up."

"I did hate all that," Chris says. "And my dad was Air Force, so yeah, he ragged me no end about joining the army. And maybe I did it in part to piss him off. You know, demean myself by becoming the lowliest of grunts. Who even cares anymore? The fact is, I did it. After I left Poughkeepsie I went back to Denver, got a job working with a bunch of tattooed dropouts at a health food store, but pretty soon that was too dead-end even for me. So one day I let some recruitment guy at the local mall sweet-talk me into signing up, and before I knew it I was off to Fort Benning. It was all stupid as fuck, because almost everything about the army's stupid as fuck, but at the same time it was kind of intoxicating. I mean, here's this guy who can't run, can't jump, can't shoot. Who likes showers and clean clothes and independence and keeping to himself. I was fucking twenty-eight years old, and I gave all that up. How absurd was that? But I learned how to do all those things I never thought I could do. And you know what? I got really fucking good at them."

They're in the palm of his hand. Nobody's bothering to eat Rafa's appetizers—except Rafa's mother, who munches methodically, imperturbably, as if she's in another place entirely.

"Okay," Anatole says, "I'm impressed. I *think*. How does it go? Join the army, visit exotic places, meet interesting people, then kill them. You must have done all that, right?"

"I was basically everywhere you'd never want to be in the nineties," Chris hears himself saying. "Saudi Arabia, Kuwait, Somalia. Kosovo. That's when I got out. Thirteen years, and I'd had enough. I was forty-one. I didn't want to spend another instant of my life locating yet another mass grave full of massacred Muslims. And then of course 9/11 comes along. I couldn't care less about 9/11, to tell you the truth. We had it coming. By the time we staged Shock and Awe, I'd been out of action three years, I didn't believe in a single thing we were doing over there, but when an old buddy from the Rangers called me up and told me about the private military companies ramping up big time with all the civilian contractors coming in for the quote, unquote rebuilding process, well, I realized all I wanted was to be back in the thick of things. So I went. Just like how I'd gone off to Fort Benning in the first place. Because that's what I'd learned about myself in the army, for all its fucking stupidity. You can sit on the sidelines and be witty and critical and aloof, or you can be in the thick of it. The huge joke of my life is that I got myself all wrong for such a long time. I thought I wanted to be on the sidelines, running my little record store in Poughkeepsie, hiding out from the world, but I didn't, really. If you're going to live in the fucking world, then fucking *live* in it. Honestly, I've never felt so alive as when I was ferrying some scared-shitless civil engineer from the Jordanian border along that long, lonesome highway across the western desert, then around the fucking death trap of the Fallujah bypass and the Ramadi ring road, and on into Baghdad and the Green Zone."

He knows he's boasting—but hasn't he earned the right? Faced with evidence of their settled lives, doesn't his have its own peculiar, not unenviable shine?

At the same time he's embarrassed he's let his guard down, ashamed he's said so much. How to account for such a breach of discipline? How could the presence of old friends he's scarcely thought of in years melt his resolve like that?

Lydia and Rafa carry the mostly untouched appetizers into the kitchen. Chris excuses himself to have a much-needed cigarette on the front stoop while dinner's being put on the table. The peach and salmon clouds of earlier have turned the color of slate. Anatole joins him, sensing he's going to have to keep snatching moments like this. They're all he'll get. He hasn't realized how much he's missed Chris, how famished for him he's been, how complete a stranger he is now.

"I quit several years ago," he tells Chris. "But I still get that craving from time to time. Mind if I have a drag? We won't tell Rafa." There's something stupendously sexy in the idea of sharing a cigarette with Chris.

Disappointingly, Chris shakes one from his pack. "Go ahead—treat yourself." He flicks his lighter, and Anatole, with despair, inhales the familiar fumes.

"You're such a bad influence," he says. "I love it. I've had to get rid of practically all my bad habits since you last saw me."

"Because of Rafa?"

"*For* Rafa, I like to say."

"And is that what you think as well?"

"Definitely. I know it's a cliché, but meeting Rafa really did save my life. I don't think I'm exaggerating." He takes a deep drag. "Ugh. This is one habit I think I really *have* kicked. You know, I went through some pretty terrible times after you left, especially when Daniel got sick. I was absolutely convinced I was going to get sick too. I mean, how could I not? But the tests kept coming back negative. I was sure they were missing something, like I had a strain of the virus too subtle or new to show up. Things got so bad, I even said to one of the doctors, I don't think I can handle this. And you know what he did? He just looked at me and said in this stern voice, Cut out the booze. I mean, was it that obvious? Maybe I wasn't all that different from a lot of other gay guys he was dealing with. Hysterical faggots hitting the bottle because their friends and lovers were dying and there wasn't anything anybody could do about it. But you know what? I took his advice. I even went to AA meetings, though after a while I just couldn't stand that crap. Finding your inner power and all. Maybe the guys there weren't drinking anymore, but at what price?

"Anyway, I managed on my own. I limped along. I had good weeks and bad and I fell spectacularly off the wagon a few times. Then I met Rafa. There's something so measured about him. He has two drinks and that's basically it. And because I wanted to impress him, I made myself stop at two drinks as well, because whenever I went beyond two drinks I could see he thought less of me, and I didn't want that. I wanted to live up to some idea of me that would be lovable. I took a good hard look at my life and said to myself, You know, Rafael Pujol is your last chance. If you blow this one, there's not going to be another. And then I thought, this is why I've been spared. God wanted to give me the opportunity of Rafa. So I either seize it or I don't. Do you even want to hear any of this? It must seem so boring compared to where life's taken you."

"Of course I want to hear," Chris answers, his ears still ringing with his own ill-advised account of himself, about which Anatole hasn't said a word—the way you pretend not to notice an embarrassing incident. Lydia and Anatole seem to have agreed in advance on the "not just surviving but thriving" script for themselves. It's impressive but a little sinister. And he's really not sure how bearable the evening's going to be with the two drink limit Anatole is suggesting as the standard for earning Rafa's approval.

Not that Chris needs Rafa's approval. He long ago went past the need for anybody's approval.

Lydia sticks her head out the front door. "Hey, boys. Dinner's ready." Anatole flings his cigarette away, but not quickly enough. "Anatole," she clucks, shaking a finger at him.

"I know, I know," he says.

Once again, Rafa's outdone himself. There's Georgian beet and walnut puree, a radish and kohlrabi salad, zucchini boats stuffed with rice, onions and sausage with a sprinkling of paprika and parsley on top.

Dinner's an opportunity to reset the conversation, and they try. They make a point of bringing Miosotis in, coaxing her to tell stories about Rafa as a boy—which she seems happy to do, in fluent, lightly accented English. "Such a solemn little fellow, so serious," she says. "But imaginative. He had this made-up language all his own. He'd sing songs in it. He'd recite poems in meter that rhymed. His father asked him once, at the dinner table, what he called that language of his. And do you know what he said? He said the name of his language was Buffalo Latin. Do you remember that?"

Rafa shakes his head. "Mama's the one with all the imagination," he says.

"You just don't remember," she tells him. "Why would I make up a thing like that?"

"How could I *forget* a thing like that?"

"Buffalo Latin," she says grandly. "I was sure my little boy was gonna grow up to be a priest."

"You'd have killed me if I'd become a priest," Rafa teases her. "Anyway, I'm not a pedophile. I wouldn't have been a good fit."

She chuckles comfortably. Chris wonders what Anatole thinks of her; she must seem like some kind of dream parent after his own rejecting mother. Are those cruel parents of his even still alive? Did Anatole ever manage to reconcile with them? And he had a younger brother, didn't he? Who rejected him as well? He hasn't thought of any of this in years; now there's so much he wants to ask Anatole, but he's not sure when he'll have a chance. It's not a conversation all that well suited to the occasional cigarette break.

"Mama's always been *very* accepting," Rafa is saying. "Of *all* my creative peculiarities. The gay thing was just one more item on what by then had become a fairly long list."

Miosotis taps him fondly, flirtatiously on the shoulder. "Honey, I knew you were gay even *before* you were speaking Buffalo Latin."

The food is delicious—a million times better than Chris is used to eating. His wine glass, however, is empty already, though he sees everyone else's is still half full. Except for Miosotis's. Hers isn't yet empty, but it's getting there.

Usually by this time of the evening he's well into the scotch or Jack Daniel's or whatever he's managed to procure. He's not as bad as some of his colleagues, not by a long shot; he's cut way back since the Green Zone.

Miosotis comes to the rescue. "Rafa," she says imperiously,

extending her wine glass. "Pour me some more. And pour this gentleman some more as well. My son can be so damn abstemious," she explains. "I don't know where he gets it. Certainly not from me. Not from his father either. We used to have such parties. Up all night, listening to records, dancing. Making music ourselves. Americans don't do that, I've noticed. They depend on others to make the music for them. Not us! We Latinos invite all the neighbors so nobody will call the cops. Every house has a few drums, castanets, a guitar—you name it. Anything that'll make noise. And so we make beautiful noise till dawn comes. And nobody complains, because everybody's making beautiful noise together."

"When Chris lived in Poughkeepsie he owned this fabulous little independent record store," Anatole tells Miosotis as Chris gratefully sips his replenished drink. "Immaculate Blue. I always loved that name. Where'd you ever come up with a name like that?"

"I have no idea," Chris admits truthfully.

"So do you still keep up with the latest music? You used to be *encyclopedic*. I still have all the albums you made me buy. Only trouble is, the turntable broke at some point and I never got around to getting a replacement because who has a turntable anymore."

"I don't really follow music much these days," Chris says. "I guess I just lost interest." In the army, he made a decision not to stand out in any way, so he only listened to what the other guys listened to, which was mostly top-forty shit, and then rap came along, and hip-hop, none of which even seemed like music to him anymore. And the music he used to love—David Bowie and Psychedelic Furs and The Smiths and The Cure, all that glorious, fatuous, maundering self-absorption—by then it had shrunk to nothing in the scheme of things.

When he arrived in Nigeria, he heard for the first time the fiercely political, spiritual, sexual music of Fela Kuti, and for the first time in years something stirred in him. He doesn't imagine they've ever heard of Fela Kuti.

"I don't think I gave music up so much as I outgrew it," he says, even as a stray memory materializes: GIs in their barracks in the Green Zone, putting together and videotaping an elaborate dance and lip-sync routine set to Lady Gaga's "Telephone." He remembers two soldiers—eighteen, nineteen, handsome as all get out, kids bored and scared and very far from home—practicing their moves together with big, blissed-out smiles on their young faces. He despises Lady Gaga—the Taliban and Al Qaeda are exactly right to want to eradicate our decadent asses from the planet—but at the same time he was moved by the spirit that led those grunts to try to express whatever it was they were trying to express, a kind of inexpressible, young, sexed-up, anarchic energy. Three days later the prettier of the two, out on dismounted patrol in the Karadah district, which was supposed to be relatively safe, stepped on an IED that blew off both his legs as well as his genitals.

Anatole's down on his hands and knees rummaging among the CDs shelved in a little tower by the side of a bookcase filled with cookbooks. Having found what he was looking for, he brandishes a jewel box with a pink triangle emblazoned on a black background.

"Bronski Beat," he exclaims. "Remember them? 'Small Town Boy' used to practically be my national anthem."

The melancholy, beat-driven music emerging from the speakers takes Chris back, despite himself. It had been his national anthem as well, though he'd never have admitted it. But then his private life had been so much more complicated and problematic than Anatole's admirably public one. It was Anatole who proudly and unabashedly proclaimed, "I love boys!" It was Chris who took the train down to New York to pay teenage hustlers to have sex with each other while he watched. Jimmy Somerville's falsetto is a time machine transporting him back to that sweet, sad, vanished world. Is Somerville even still alive, Chris wonders, or did the tsunami of AIDS sweep him out to sea along with all the others?

Rafa pours Miosotis and Chris more wine—their fourth glass. Rafa even refills for himself and Anatole.

Lydia puts a hand over the mouth of her glass when the bottle comes her way. "I can't afford to be hungover tomorrow," she says. "And you boys don't want to be either, if you know what's good for you."

"By the way," Anatole tells Chris, "You're going to love the music at the reception. You'll see what I mean."

Chris desperately needs another cigarette. And if there's a way of getting to the flask of vodka he stashed in the glove compartment of the rental car, he'd love to manage that too.

"I'm afraid our friend's being a naughty influence," Lydia confides to Rafa. She scrapes the dinner plates and then hands them to him to put in the dishwasher. "Anatole's out there with him stealing puffs."

"Oh, let him," Rafa says. "Sometimes it's good to invite the bad habits back for a visit, just so you remember why you kicked them out."

"Let's hope."

"What does that mean?"

Lydia wonders whether to proceed. She doesn't want to be an alarmist. On the other hand, she'll staunchly defend her own; that's who she is, and Anatole and Rafa long ago became as much her own as immediate family.

"Anatole seems a little smitten with the past tonight. Don't you think?"

"I hadn't been noticing that, particularly."

Well, *she's* certainly noticed. Chris has deftly scooped Anatole up into the palm of his hand. Those stolen cigarettes on the front stoop seem just the tip of some dangerous iceberg.

She can't believe Rafa's not irked or rattled or distressed by it.

"Ugh. This is such a weird evening," she says. "I'm not at all sure I like who Chris has become. Though I can't tell whether he's just the same person he was all along, and *I'm* the one who's become something different. But this military stuff is just creepy. I mean, he was always an enigma, but now that I know what he's up to, he's sort of downright sinister. Don't you think?"

She hates her tone.

"I have to admit," Rafa replies, reasonably enough, "I don't completely get him either. And I really don't know enough about what he does to know whether it's something I approve of or not. It all does seem a little dubious, but then lots of people might say the same thing about the more arcane aspects of IT work."

"It's not even remotely the same."

"That was a joke. Relax, Lydia. You're very uptight this evening. You and Anatole both. I wouldn't call it 'smitten,' exactly, but I can definitely say this: Chris does something to the both of you."

"I'm just being protective. It's a mother thing. I don't want bad things to happen to people I care about. I mean, what's Anatole told you about Chris?"

He doesn't look at her. He methodically inserts dishes into the dishwasher. "He told me Chris broke his heart. And that it was a really, really long time ago. And that the world's in a different place now. *He's* in a different place. And I believe him. I don't really need to know any more than that."

She's surprised she never thought of it before, but now it seems clear. "You don't get jealous, do you?"

The last plate stowed, he shuts the dishwasher door, then looks at her with that serious, kind expression that makes her trust him, that makes her think he's decent and good and exactly right for Anatole. "No," he says, "I actually don't think

I do. I used to. You should have seen me twenty years ago. Now I don't believe in tempests. All I really believe in these days are tea pots. Are you worried Anatole's kissing Chris out on the front stoop right now? I'm not." Swiftly, unexpectedly, he throws his arms around her and plants a kiss on her lips. "There!" he says. "Don't worry. Tonight, everybody's kissing everybody!"

Miosotis stands in the doorway watching. "And I only came in here to see about dessert," she says. "And to see if there's another bottle of wine."

"I wonder what you make of all this," Lydia says.

"Don't worry," Miosotis tells her. "At my advanced age, I've become a great connoisseur of the human comedy."

The season's first fireflies are out, pulsing against the dark shrubs.

When Anatole points them out Chris says, "I haven't seen fireflies in years. None in Iraq. None in Nigeria either. I think I even forgot they existed."

His cigarette adds its own pulse to the night.

"I really shouldn't," Anatole says, allowing Chris to light one for him as well. He's a little perturbed how natural it feels to smoke again. "Lightning bugs, we used to call them. But they're not anything like lightning, really." He hasn't been able to keep his eyes off Chris all evening. At the dinner table he found himself on the verge of staring outright, though he contented himself with measured, abstemious glances. Crow's feet radiate from the corners of Chris's eyes, he's noticed; there's a crease in his brow that doesn't go away. Time hasn't diminished him, exactly, but it's passed a stern hand over him. A curious agitation has replaced that indolent, floating quality he used to adore—as if, even in the midst of this reunion with old friends, Chris is impatient to be on his way. But where to? What business could call him so urgently?

"Speaking of lightning," Anatole says. "Do you remember the first time we ever met? On the Metro North platform at Croton-Harmon. In a really scary thunderstorm. You were funny about it, you actually managed to calm my nerves."

"I honestly don't remember that," Chris tells him. "Sorry."

"You must've been pretty surprised to hear from me after all this time. I remember sending that email and thinking, He won't even remember who I am. But I was really, really in love with you, you know. There, now I've said it. And it's not just the wine talking."

He waits for a response. The ember at the tip of Chris's cigarette glows. The scattered fireflies throb. I should've turned the porch light on, Anatole thinks; then I could at least read his expression.

"Nobody should ever have been in love with me," Chris says. "I'm just sorry I didn't understand that back when I knew you. Things wouldn't have happened the way they did."

"What does that mean?"

"To be honest? It means I'd never have known you. I'd have closed that chapter before it even started. Instead of letting us get into the mess we did."

"But I'm *glad* I knew you. However fucked up things were. I wouldn't have missed what you call that mess for the world."

"Yeah, well, you were one of the lucky ones," Chris said. "At least you managed to survive. And look at you now. Getting married! And Lydia tells me Reflexion's become a local empire."

"I haven't done badly. But I don't know at all how *you've* done. I know, you've got a job that sounds exotic and dangerous and, frankly, a little perverse. But what've you been thinking and feeling all these years? As a matter of fact, what were you even thinking and feeling when you were living here in Pough-keepsie?"

"Poughkeepsie," Chris says. He wonders if he's ever spoken

honestly to Anatole before. He wonders if Anatole has any idea of the gift he's being given. "Poughkeepsie was just an accident. A place to hide and catch my breath for a while. It's all so long ago, and so fucking sad. I came to Poughkeepsie with a broken heart. My punishment for breaking somebody else's heart. I'd never have said this to you back when we were friends."

"But we're *still* friends. I've never considered you *not* my friend."

"Lydia thinks you're some kind of saint. And probably you are. But I worry about you, Anatole. Even now, from what I can see, you've got no defenses. Of all the people I've ever met, I think—with one major exception—you're the person with the least defenses of all. And I should know. I'm in the protection business, after all."

"That major exception wasn't by any chance Leigh, was it?"

Chris laughs. Of course Leigh will have to keep coming up. Now, as then, Leigh—or at least the memory of Leigh—is the star they orbit. He flings his cigarette to the ground and rubs it out with his foot. "Here I go, dirtying your front stoop. Sorry. And no. Leigh had plenty of defenses. He was quite the skillful little hustler, don't you think?"

Anatole hates to hear that word. He doesn't want to believe hustling was all those three months were about. Even now he clings to the notion there was something ineffably genuine— even pure—in Leigh.

"I'm sorry, but I never saw the hustler in him. What I saw was a sweet, confused kid stumbling toward some kind of oblivion. But then, weren't we all? It's just that we had more resources to draw on. We were adults. He was just a kid. Anyway, whatever happened to him?"

"I have no idea," Chris tells him. "No idea at all. You know he'd fallen in with this older guy toward the end of his stay here, right? Rich guy, drove a red Porsche, lived in a big Tudor-style mansion out toward Pleasant Valley. Owned a Cessna. When I exited the story he was proposing to take Leigh up in it."

"I didn't know that. I didn't know you exited the story. I always assumed you and Leigh took off together."

"Well, you and Lydia both, it seems. But that's not what happened. I withdrew. It was as simple as that. I walked away, like I've always walked away. It's not an admirable trait, but there you have it."

"You know," Anatole says, "till the very end he was still staying at my place. Even after he took up with Lydia, and then, I guess, with you. He didn't have much stuff, but he never came back for any of it. He even left his driver's license behind. For the longest time I thought he might come back for it. Strange where you place your hopes."

"Do you still have it?"

"I probably do. Somewhere. At the bottom of some box of old stuff I haven't looked at in ages. I never throw anything away. Wouldn't it be strange to come across it? I can't even really remember what he looked like. Isn't that crazy?"

But Chris remembers exactly how Leigh looked. He remembers exactly the expression on Leigh's face the last time he saw him.

"You should know," he tells Anatole, "what happened. If that'll put your mind to rest. It might be hard to hear, though."

"I'm way beyond all that now," Anatole assures him. "Do your worst."

But it's not to be done. At least not now. Lydia pokes her head out the door to alert them that dessert's on the table. "And Miosotis makes one mean dessert, let me tell you," she says.

There's something unnerving in these stolen interludes. A well opens up, the bucket goes deep, brings up all sorts of strange stuff. He's organized this weekend very badly. He can't shake the uncanny feeling that the wedding's no longer the real event;

that the real event consists of these snatches of conversation with Chris; that he's somehow sabotaging the wedding, even his and Rafa's future happiness. He's being egregiously unfaithful, in his way, though he knows—rather maddeningly—how understanding Rafa will be. Rafa doesn't feel threatened in the least by Chris, and though on one level he's perfectly right not to be, on another level he should be extremely worried. Because Chris makes their whole relationship seem suddenly like a sham.

He's not falling in love all over again. Nothing so simple as that. It's much worse. It eats at everything he thinks about himself, everything he thinks he's achieved over the years. Everything he's prided himself on.

He'd like nothing better than to get very drunk with Chris right about now.

Instead they eat Miosotis's *dulce de leche*, made the way her mother made it back in San Pedro de Macoris. It's delicious, as usual, but as she regales the table with a long, involuted story about her mother's travails on Hispaniola back in the 1930s, suddenly, for perhaps the first time, Rafa's wonderful mother begins to seem to Anatole a little insufferable.

The dessert's sweetness makes Chris shudder, though Miosotis herself rather charms him. She tells the story, clearly often told, of how her mother lost her virginity one night on the beach to a Soviet journalist named Tarkovsky, an acquaintance of her father's who'd arrived that morning from Mexico—where, she subsequently learned to her great horror, he had taken part in the first, unsuccessful, attempt to assassinate Trotsky. Part of the charm of the story, Chris decides, is its great unlikelihood. But never mind. He's certainly not one to condemn other people's fictions, especially if they're entertaining. And everyone seems content to listen to her, as if they've exhausted their own capacity for talking.

But what, exactly, have they talked about? For friends who

haven't seen each other in so long, the dinner table conversation's been, except for Chris's eruption, banal, even pointless. At some point Chris realizes he's not longing for a cigarette or even a furtive swig of vodka so much as a continuation of his interrupted front porch conversation with Anatole.

When Miosotis's recollections finally wind down, Lydia confesses, with a dramatic yawn, "I for one am totally zonked and ready for bed. I'm calling the hubby taxi."

"You didn't drive yourself over?" Anatole asks.

"I never drink and drive these days. And you guys are all too wasted to get behind the wheel, so don't even think of offering me a lift."

Her transformation's complete. Chris remembers that first night they met Leigh, and took him back to Anatole's apartment, and drank scotch by the gallon, and drew on the poor kid's T-shirt with crayons as he sat half passed out on the sofa, and how Lydia drove Chris back to his apartment, both of them so crocked they confessed to each other later they couldn't remember a thing after leaving their friend and his possibly underage acquisition behind.

She doesn't know—she'll never know—but for years Chris has presented her as his girlfriend, fiancé, whatever. Everybody's got a girl back home—that's just a given. And nobody's ever curious, nobody's ever going to check out the details. They just want that assurance—that you're not a fag. And Chris is most definitely not a fag. "Yeah," he'll say, "me and Lydia are thinking of tying the knot. Yeah, I'd love to have had kids, but after Lydia's operation... Yeah, Lydia'd kill me if she knew what I was really up to out here." The other guys say the same sorts of things, and he presumes they're actually telling the truth, but to be honest, he's not all that curious either. Where they go and what they do on leave is nobody's business, which is exactly the way it should be. And if he goes to Amsterdam or Berlin instead of back to the States, who needs to know that?

Strange that he randomly chose the name "Lydia." He's never really thought about that.

Within minutes the doorbell announces the hubby cab's arrival. In strides Tom—only it's not Tom, Chris thinks, it can't be Tom, all the while thinking, Oh my fucking god.

"Dad wanted to finish watching the end of his show," Caleb says in an oddly uninflected voice as Chris registers the two plastic commas behind his ears, the circular disc affixed to the left side of his skull. He somehow expected an awkward, even goofy-looking kid, complete with acne and thick-lensed glasses. And now the joke's on him. Only it doesn't feel like a joke; it feels much graver than that, as if a storm has just blown in. Caleb's tall, lean, ferocious-looking. His hair is cropped to quarter-inch stubble, military induction style. His lips are thin, his cheeks sculpted, his neck long, Adam's apple prominent. All his lines are spartan; there's not a single part of him that's superfluous. His eyes are steel blue. He's everything that tricks Chris's black, battered heart into leaping.

"Honey, this is our friend Chris," Lydia is saying. "From darkest Africa."

Caleb's handshake is perfunctory.

"Hey," Chris tells him nonchalantly. "Nice to meet you."

But Caleb is completely inattentive. "Let's go, Mom," he says. "I still have stuff to do before I go to bed."

"Okay, okay." Lydia pats his arm affectionately. "Now, you guys better not have a slumber party without me. And Chris. Lunch at our place tomorrow. Twelvish. Though feel free to come earlier. No need to call in advance. You remember the way?"

He doesn't. Maybe it's only a momentary lapse. Flustered a little—no, punched hard—he says, "Remind me of the address, okay? It's been a while."

★ ★ ★

Rafa has put Miosotis to bed. She's a bit drunk, which isn't unusual, but she's made sure to take her pills, plus two aspirin, and to put out her inhaler and a glass of water by the bedside. Also a novel she's reading and rather enjoying: *La Virgen de los Sicarios*. For the moment she lies under just a sheet, but there's a quilt folded at the foot of the bed in case she gets cold in the night.

Rafa sits on the side of the bed.

"I'm proud of you," he tells her. "I should tell you that more often."

"Nonsense," she says. "I'm proud of you too. And very happy for you and Anatole. And your dad would be as well."

"I know that. I've been very lucky that way."

"And I'm proud of Anatole. Whether they're in Heaven or Hell right now, his parents should be ashamed of themselves."

Rafa has to laugh. "You don't believe in either Heaven or Hell."

"Well, I hate to think of them as just being nothing, but I suppose they are. I wonder if they ever regretted casting him away like that."

"Who knows? At least his brother eventually came around. He won't be completely on his own tomorrow."

"He's not on his own one bit. He's got his own family now. His real family. You made that happen for him."

When she's drunk it can go two ways: either she turns sentimental or rises to a sort of brilliant, bitter irony. Tonight, he's relieved to see, is honey rather than salt.

"We all made that happen for him. Now, go to sleep. We've got a long day ahead of us tomorrow."

He bends down to kiss her on the forehead, but she stops him.

"I don't like that man downstairs," she says. "Why's he here?"

"He's an old friend of Anatole's. They go way back."

"He shouldn't be here. There's something wrong with him."

"What do you mean, something wrong?"

"I was looking and looking all evening, and I can't find it."

"Can't find what?" he asks.

"He has no soul."

Rafa laughs, though he's a little perturbed that he hasn't picked up on whatever Lydia and his mother seem to have detected. Anatole has a campy way of saying, in certain situations, usually when he's been right about something and Rafa's been wrong, "Feminine Intuition! Don't underestimate it!" Maybe there's something in Chris he's oblivious to. Maybe it wasn't a good idea for Anatole to invite him after all—though for the life of him, Rafa still can't make out why that might be so.

"He's not a good omen," Miosotis says with conviction. "He doesn't bode well."

"Mom! He works in Africa. It's not like we'll even see him again after this. And besides, he seems just fine to me. You're being superstitious—which is something you're not, remember? *I'm* the superstitious one. I'm the one who actually goes to Mass."

"I still don't know where you got that from."

"All gay men are superstitious, in my experience. Forget the sex; it's really the one thing they have in common."

"I never know when you're teasing me."

"I never tease," Rafa tells her. "You should know that by now."

"Whew! I think I could use a little nightcap after all that," Miosotis says.

"No, Mom. Now, go to sleep." This time he succeeds in kissing her on the forehead without any resistance. "You've had plenty for tonight. Besides, tomorrow is a drink-all-day kind of day. That's your favorite kind, remember? You'll have fun."

★ ★ ★

In Rafa's absence, and against his better judgment—but who cares? this night will only happen once—Anatole opens another bottle of wine. He and Chris sit on the stoop, drinking and smoking and watching the fireflies, the streetlights, the urban night. Somewhere down the block, guys are shooting baskets in a lit-up driveway. Their shouts, the ball's thump against the backboard sound faintly. Wherever Americans are gathered, Chris thinks, remembering the improvised courts that were one of the first things to go up in the Green Zone, amid the ransacked palaces and leafy boulevards, long before the Burger King and Pizza Hut went in.

"Ed." Chris says this after a long silence. "That was the guy's name. We'd met him in that dive bar on Main Street. What was it called? The one you never went to."

"Not The Congress?"

"That's it."

"Ugh. You took Leigh to The Congress? No wonder he left town."

"I think the idea was to avoid you and Lydia. Anyway, the guy bought us drinks, then invited us back to his house. I didn't want us to go, but for some reason Leigh was intrigued."

"Leigh was pretty easily intrigued, don't you think?"

"Always on to greener pastures, I guess. Besides, I was frustrating him. I didn't want to get any more involved than I already was, given how complicated everything was getting. I mean, first you and then Lydia. I really didn't want to be the next one on Leigh's list, but he'd already penciled me in. I wasn't having any of it. And so I left. That's the last I ever saw of Leigh. I hope he found whatever it was he was looking for."

"It sounds to me like he was looking for you."

"Well, it didn't happen. You don't have to believe me, but I tried to do the right thing. And maybe I did, and maybe I didn't. I'll never know."

Anatole sits in silence. Defenseless, he takes a gulp of wine. God, how he used to love to drink! It all comes back to him. He'd love to curl up with a bottle all his own right now, forget about Chris and Leigh and Rafa and the sobering fact that he's getting married tomorrow afternoon.

"I understand," he says. "Painful as it is. And I have to confess something too. Leigh and I never fucked. I know everybody assumed we did, and I know I let everybody assume that, but it didn't happen. So there. I've gotten that off my chest."

"Does Lydia know that?"

"We've never talked about Leigh. We weren't speaking for several years, and then when we reconnected, it seemed best not to reopen old wounds. Lydia and I've been very good for each other down through the years. I'm practically part of the family. As is Rafa, of course.

"But you have to tell me one thing, Chris. Who that one exception was. The other person you've known who doesn't have any defenses. Not that I think that's true about me. Anyway, I've got Rafa now. He can be a tiger on my behalf."

Chris empties his glass, Anatole refills for them both.

"I'll watch myself then," Chris says. "And I shouldn't have brought him into this at all. It was a long time ago, it was a very bad situation, and it ended even worse."

"You can't just tell me that and walk away. I'd like to think we can be honest for once. I mean, let's face it. When are we going to see each other again?"

There's a long pause. The fireflies must go on all night. And there's also the shimmery sound of spring peepers he notices now that the guys down the street have called it a night.

"Okay," Chris says finally. "There was a friend who killed himself. Actually he was my roommate, housemate, whatever. I was in love with his sister, and he was in love with me. At the end of that summer he killed himself. And I think it was because of me. I mean, you can't ever know something like that for sure. But whenever I wake up at three in the morning and stare at the ceiling, I'm always more or less completely sure."

"When was this?" Anatole asks gingerly.

"Cornell. The last school I dropped out of in my illustrious college career."

Actually John *had* left a note, but Chris didn't read it. He tore it to shreds without looking at it. But that part he still can't bear to say aloud.

"You never breathed a word."

"Why would I? I mean, how could I? I'm not even sure I should be saying anything now, except it doesn't matter anymore. I've paid my dues several times over. But it made me untouchable. It made me poison."

"You mean, it made you feel like you had to hole up in Poughkeepsie? But that's ridiculous, Chris. You can't live life that way. I mean, feeling like you're toxic."

"I've lived the life I've lived. For whatever it's worth. And I've made a ton of money doing it. Close protection work paid two thousand a day in Iraq."

"Please don't trivialize this."

"Sorry. You're right. Let's just leave the subject, okay? But now you know."

"If only we could have talked like this back when," Anatole says. "But what did we do instead? We tried to amuse each other to keep from being bored or despondent or whatever. What a waste. Gosh, I wish I could talk with you for hours. Now that at last we're really talking."

It's not rational, it's not even sane, but in all these years he's never really let Chris go. Part of him wants Chris to fuck him right now. Isn't that crazy? He's completely happy with Rafa, he wants to spend the rest of his life with him, but if Chris wanted to fuck him he'd bend over in an instant and though it would be the most totally fucked up thing he could ever do it would also be the most wonderful moment of his entire life. Does that mean he's insane?

"Anatole," Chris says, "why did you invite me to your wedding?"

Funny. For weeks Anatole's asked himself exactly that question without knowing the answer, but now suddenly he does.

"For this," he says. "For right now. I can't say it any better than that. If you don't get it, I can't explain. But I feel like something—wonderful's not the word, momentous isn't either, more like…" But he's right. He can't say it any better. All he can do is turn the question back on Chris: "So why did you accept my invitation?"

And maybe Chris's answer will hurt, or maybe it'll just disappoint, or maybe it'll mean the world to him, but at that instant Rafa appears.

"Ah, here are my kittens. I wondered where you were. I was beginning to think you'd eloped."

"Oh, don't worry, we're just making out. Isn't that what you're supposed to do on the night before your wedding? Anyway, you knew perfectly well we were out here indulging in bad habits."

"True. Lydia keeps a close eye on her kids. And she always reports to Papa." Rafa takes the wine glass from Anatole's hand and has a swallow. "Personally, I love kids misbehaving. Though I'll forgo the cigarettes, thank you very much."

"Cigarettes are nasty," Anatole says. "I'd forgotten how nasty they are."

"Don't let me shut this party down, but I'm going to bed. I'm getting married tomorrow. You too, if I remember correctly."

In France, Chris thinks—one of the many useless things he holds in his head—the bachelor party is called *enterrer sa vie de garçon*. Burying one's life as a boy. He watches the easy banter between spouses-to-be. It's completely alien to him; he doesn't even long for it. He's got "Lydia" tucked away safely on another continent. Where might she be right now, this "Lydia" who's served him so well over the years? He hasn't done right by her, not by a long shot. What he's loved is the easy, profane, butt-slapping, mind-fucking camaraderie with the young GIs in Iraq. Feckless kids mostly, dropouts, dead-enders, and goofy careless fuckups. Now in Nigeria he's among adults who don't interest him in the least. Currently he's hooked up with some Rhodesians—they'd never deign to call their former country Zimbabwe—who hot-footed it down to South Africa when Mugabe came to power, worked for a number of years with Executive Outcomes, the granddaddy of all PMCs, saw tough action in Angola and Sierra Leone. Cold-blooded killer types, really, but impeccably professional, guys you can trust to watch your back. He knew them first in Iraq when he worked for Spartan. For better or worse, Ian and Darby are family.

But there's also Jasper, Adam, Damien, Rolf, Kenny, the sweet, lost, benighted, not quite interchangeable hustlers at the Blue Bar or Jack's House of Boys or Paradise, who either will or won't be there on his next visit, and he's usually just as glad if they're not.

"I'll be up in a sec," Anatole tells Rafa, which is Chris's cue.

"I should be on my way. Thanks for the superb evening."

"Are you in any state to drive?" Anatole asks.

"I'm fine."

"You can always sleep on the sofa."

It's awkward now, the two of them alone together. Chris marvels at Rafa's equanimity. Anatole's more than lucky to have found him. It's clear that if there's a weak link in the relationship, it's not going to be Rafa.

"Chris, Chris, Chris," Anatole says, caressing his arm. "I really don't want you to go. I never wanted you to go. I missed you so much when you left."

"Be realistic. I'd outstayed my welcome. And I'd only have

made more trouble. You know that as well as I do. In fact, I have this feeling I've even been making a certain kind of trouble this evening. So yes, I have to go. Besides, at our great age, we all need our beauty sleep."

That quip should end it, but it doesn't. "But what's your life like these days? Do you have friends? Do you have lovers? Men, women? I don't really expect you to tell me anything, but still. I'm not going to see enough of you, and then you'll be gone. It's not like I can go sneaking kisses with anybody tomorrow."

Sneaking kisses isn't something Chris has contemplated, though these stolen conversations on the stoop haven't been without a certain illicit charge.

"You used to mean the world to me," Anatole continues. "I've always loved that phrase, but I have no idea what it means. I hope all this isn't too weird for you. I've always wanted to kiss you, you know."

"And you should know by now that I don't kiss."

"Nobody? Ever?"

"Nobody," Chris says. "Ever."

"Then I feel more sorry for you than I can say. But at least you're consistent. So drive safely, and I'll see you tomorrow. And, by the way, thanks for everything. It really has been wonderful—this evening we've had together. It's meant the world to me."

He extends his arms in an embrace, and Chris allows himself to be enfolded. Anatole goes a step further, and ventures a peck on Chris's stubbled cheek, and once again, Chris doesn't resist. Anatole tries to savor the moment for whatever it is. Nostalgia? Forgiveness? Hopelessness? They all have their stirring qualities, and he hopes Chris doesn't notice that he's a little aroused at their contact. But Chris seems, as always, oblivious to what he provokes in Anatole.

Breaking free—but gently, gently—Chris is surprised to find himself somehow moved by their contact. It's not anything sexual, though there's the minutest spark there—he has to be honest with himself. Bemusement? Regret? He's happy for Anatole, really he is.

At his car, he pauses to look back at the house. What he sees is a little lit cube floating in an immensity of black space. They have no idea how fragile, how precarious that little cube is. They're innocent, smug, ignorant, utterly unaware of the approaching catastrophe. He pities them; he feels entirely tender toward them; at the same time he thinks they probably deserve exactly what is coming for them.

Anatole never knew about this Ed. Not that it matters, it's all like looking through the wrong end of a telescope at this point. But he can't believe Chris cast Leigh to the wolves like that. At the time Leigh disappeared, he thought about putting up Missing Person signs all around Poughkeepsie, but that was too ridiculous, and he imagined coming home from Reflexion one evening to find the boy sitting on the sofa: *What the fuck were you thinking, putting up posters like that? I'm not your pet.*

After all, Leigh's leaving was a good thing, not a disaster. And besides, the story had been so clear in his head. In one final, grand betrayal, Chris and Leigh had skipped town together. They'd made a life together, however briefly and unhappily. But now that he knows it wasn't so, suddenly he's in a kind of panic. But how can you be in a panic over events that happened so long ago? And who's to say this Ed was a wolf? Maybe he'd been a perfectly pleasant fellow. Maybe Leigh had done well by him. Maybe Ed and Leigh are still living in Poughkeepsie, in that Tudor mansion…

"You're being restless," Rafa tells him. "Why can't you get to sleep?"

"I could ask you the same thing."

"Except I *was* asleep, and your fidgeting woke me up."

"Sorry. I'm just agitated. Something Chris told me has got

me agitated. Not that I can do anything about it. The past is the past."

"Was he being cruel to you out there on the stoop?"

"I don't think so. I think he was trying to be kind. I just have to turn all these thoughts off. You'd have thought I'd drunk enough wine to be able to fall asleep just like that."

"It's the cigarettes," Rafa says. "You shouldn't have smoked those cigarettes."

"I know. My mouth tastes filthy. And I probably reek."

"You do, a little."

"You're not annoyed with me?"

Rafa laughs. "Not in the least. Well, maybe a tiny bit. But I'm probably always a tiny bit annoyed with you."

"Is that true?"

"I was just joking."

"Don't joke about stuff like that. If I do annoy you, please tell me. I mean, before we go through with this."

"This is why I'm always imploring you to come with me to yoga. Yoga exists for exactly this kind of moment."

Anatole sighs. This again. "How about I start yoga once we're married?"

"It can't hurt, you know. And I'm pretty sure you'd like it."

"Gosh, I never thought I'd say a sentence like that. *How about I start yoga once we're married?* What's got into me?"

But it's worked. Rafa's talked him down from the window ledge, like he always does. "I love you, you know," Anatole says.

"I love you too. Now let's both just relax and try to go to sleep."

# NIGHT MUSIC

Night driving unnerves him. He's gotten out of practice. In the places he's been, once night falls all bets are off. In Baghdad he used to lie awake in the fortified villa he and his team rented on a blockaded street in the Karadah district and listen to the distant sounds of explosions and gunfire, usually from Sadr City to the north, the nightly battle that opened up between Coalition forces and the Mahdi Army—a kind of background music, oddly soothing once you got used to it, because it meant, at least for the moment, the storm was far off.

Port Harcourt's nothing like that. The Shell residential compound at Rumukoroshe enfolds you in its razor wire–wrapped arms, you're cradled. If you want you can wander the parody suburban neighborhood of bungalows and tidy lawns long after midnight, head out to the golf course, the only traffic a passing security 4x4. Beyond the compound's walls is another story. Sounds carry: stray gunshots, screeching tires, tendrils of music fading in and out like the unreliable AM frequencies he remembers listening to in his Colorado childhood, in bed at night, that little portable radio whose fickle, enchanting snatches of country music, Spanish-language announcers from south of the border, weather updates, slow-talking preachers and fast-talking used car ads, Motown and rock and roll all blended together in a sonic tapestry that stood for the huge world he longed for but that always seemed just beyond reach.

He regrets having talked to Anatole and Lydia at such absurd length about his life, regrets even more having done so with Rafa and Miosotis as audience. It all has the feel of a tawdry, self-promoting performance. But if he can't explain himself to Anatole and Lydia, then who can he explain himself to? And if he can't explain himself to anybody, or at least try, then what's the point of it all? He hasn't realized how much he's carried their friendship—the saving fact of their friendship—with him through the various unfriendly worlds he's made his home in.

He's had other friendships, of course, the kind you forge under fire—joshing, competitive, rough-and-tumble, uncomplicated military friendships. He never fully appreciated how much he cherishes the complexities and irritations and negotiations of mere civilian friendship.

As he glides along quiet leafy residential streets he realizes he's lost. WPN: Worst Possible Nightmare. Of course bad things are always on the verge of happening, kept at bay by skill and wits and (yes, admit it) dumb luck, but when you fumble your bearings it almost guarantees bad things will happen, Mike and Frasier getting sharked in Fallujah, inexplicably off-route, in a warren of streets they had no business in—he'll never know exactly what went wrong because they didn't live to tell. Their last frantic radio call haunts him, the agonizing race in nightmarish slow motion to GPS-locate them, by then two charred-beyond-recognition bodies in a burned-out vehicle on a sewage-swamped street with barefoot children staring curiously at the still-smoking wreckage, Ian howling Fuck, Fuck, Fuck in impotent rage, then letting loose a death blossom of automatic weapon fire, Blackwater style, aiming just over the kids' heads, nothing like putting the fear of God in those little sons of bitches and, of course, all for nothing.

He's not panicking, exactly, it's not like Poughkeepsie's morphed into Baghdad or Basra or Ramadi, though that's the recurrent nightmare: he'll be walking down a street in Berlin or Amsterdam and suddenly he's not on leave but somehow he's forgotten that, it's gotten lost in the shuffle, which is lethal, since you have to live completely differently in the red zone than you do back in a sane and sensible world.

He knows it's what some clowns would diagnose as a typical PTSD moment, though he scorns the notion that's what afflicts him. No, it's simple prudence, precaution, the skills that keep him alive. And for whatever reason they're coming unmoored in him.

As he turns onto one unfamiliar street after another, he begins to feel an unpleasant tightening in his chest. Then a couple of blocks up ahead he sees a stoplight at the intersection with the arterial. Once he's on the arterial, he loosens up. He'll loop around the convention center, take 44/55 heading east, then right on Raymond Avenue, left on 376, and on out to the Inn at the Falls.

But suddenly that prospect is just too disheartening. What's he going to do? Chug that pint of vodka?" Find some porn on the Internet and have a half-hearted jerk-off before passing out? Surely there's somewhere in Poughkeepsie he can go, mingle with strangers, postpone the inevitable sentence of solitude.

He shouldn't have brought up John Pembroke. That was just stupid; he knew Anatole for three years and never brought him up, so why now? And it's not like he even thinks much about John anymore. Or Leigh either, whom he still considers a catastrophe averted. And it's not like he broods about Gabir, now that Baghdad's just a fitfully receding nightmare. The situation in Port Harcourt's perfect, in its way. Africans don't attract him; he can admire their considerable beauty with cool detachment, but they're incapable of distracting him. It's probably racist of him, but who gives a shit? The heart and body want what they want. That's been the whole problem all along. And now that most of the families have been removed from the Rumukoroshe compound owing to the deteriorating security situation, the temptation European or American teenagers might pose has been removed as well.

Whatever dangers the MEND rebels and the bunkerers and the pirates represent are nothing in comparison.

He finds he can't quite stop thinking about Leigh. Anatole and Lydia's lack of curiosity perversely fuels his own. Nobody disappears completely anymore. The only thing that's disappeared is privacy, which is never coming back. And which is probably a good thing. Why should anything be private? No hiding, no guilt, no shame. Just a completely transparent world.

He hides everything from everybody, of course. So the world that would be heaven to him would also at the same time be hell. Which is just fucking perfect.

It's near midnight. Up ahead, two enormous raccoons lope across the three traffic lanes. He brakes instinctively, but a car in the lane beside him doesn't slow at all, plowing into both creatures with a sickening double thud. And then keeps going, the driver unfazed, apparently oblivious to what's just happened.

There's no other traffic in sight. Against his instinct, Chris pulls to the curb.

He looks back down the road. One of the raccoons lies motionless; the other, its back legs useless, is trying to drag itself to the curb.

In the world Chris normally inhabits, he'd never dream of stopping for anything. He'd floor the accelerator, hightail it out of there. But this is the dream world, the American world.

He's transfixed; he can't leave till he knows the fate of that crippled raccoon. It hauls itself slowly, slowly across the pavement. The occasional car swerves to avoid it, but it's just a matter of time till one doesn't. He should do it a favor: put his vehicle in reverse and run it down. But he can't.

Long ago, that fateful summer in Ithaca, he and John and Michelle adopted a stray cat. Or, to be more precise, it adopted them. Mr. Goblin, they called it—John's idea, because of its almost supernaturally black fur. He remembers how skillfully it insinuated itself into their lives, how at some point they stopped just feeding it, or teasing it with bits of string, and actually began to depend on its antic presence as a counterpoint to the paralyzed misery of a brother and sister in love with a housemate who wouldn't choose. Not couldn't but wouldn't. For reasons that to this day remain indefensible.

When it became clear that John would have to be the one to go (when it should have been me, Chris knows now, it should have been me), when they were barely on speaking terms, not out of anger but out of a sadness so heavy it was hardly bearable—John, in a desperate comic turn, would ventriloquize his increasingly hopeless sentiments through Mr. Goblin, trying in vain to ward off the inevitable.

And how skillfully, on another continent, in a different world, that other stray insinuated himself. For a time he was an occasional presence, then you began to see him more often, lingering outside the gate of the compound they grandly called The Mansion, hunkered down in that Iraqi squat Chris found supremely uncomfortable but that, according to those who grew up with it, is the most natural, comfortable position in the world. He'd wait patiently, for hours it seemed; watch shyly, cautiously, intently, a little scavenger hoping for the chance morsel to drop.

As the signs posted around the Green Zone warned: *There's nothing compassionate about compassionate feeding of strays. DON'T!*

Only they didn't have a stray cat at The Mansion; they had Gabir.

In reality, The Mansion was a huddle of three concrete block buildings surrounded by ten foot walls with a conveniently gated entrance and ample space for several vehicles in the courtyard. It was in a working-class, mostly Sunni neighborhood.

Folks don't generally kill their employers as long as their employers treat them well; Chris made sure to hire someone from every single family on the street. In turn, he could count on them to pass info about IEDs, impromptu checkpoints, planned ambushes. On the roof he and the Rhodesians sandbagged the corners, erected a cover-from-view screen to discourage snipers wanting to pick off a white-eyes, installed razor wire by the yard. The roof was where they'd make their last stand if it came to that, and they kept the battle box stocked with AK-47s, RPGs, medical packs, a stash of ammo, plenty of MREs, and bottles of water.

Downstairs, they sandbagged the doors and windows. They built a guard room for their Iraqi guards. They set up a weights bench and punching bag. And the Rhodesians somehow managed to acquire a flat-screen TV so they could watch their beloved football matches. Their setup wasn't cozy or even comfortable, but it was secure.

At first the guards tried to shoo the stray away, but Gabir was persistent. "Family all dead," the head guard Ali explained when Chris asked what was up with the kid. "No place to go." He was smart, a survivor. In no time he became a mascot/errand boy for the guards. They'd send him off to get cigarettes or glasses of tea or plates of kebabs and rice. He invariably wore, dirtier with each passing month, a pair of gray sweatpants, those slide sandals all the Iraqi kids wear, a red jersey with CARLSBERG inscribed in gold across the chest. When winter came the guards let him make a rat's nest in a corner of the guard building where he could spend the night. Hard to tell how old he was: probably younger than he appeared. He had the gaunt, haunted look of so many Iraqi street kids. Chris's best guess would be fifteen or sixteen. What particularly struck him were the boy's blue eyes and dark blond hair—bronze, really, puzzling in an Iraqi till Ian reminded him that Alexander the Great and his Macedonians had left traces in the gene pool when they conquered Babylon. "All the way to fucking Kandahar you see these blond, blue-eyed relics. Pretty fucking amazing, if you ask me."

Any prospect of direct communication was thwarted by Chris's rudimentary Arabic (*As-salaam alaykum. Chayf aalik? Fii amaan il-llaah*) and Gabir's English, which mostly consisted of phrases he'd been taught by GIs whose idea of fun it was to coach Iraqi kids to say things like *You're a fucking douchebag. Suck my dick. What's up, nigger?*

And then there was the phrase, which the GIs presumably hadn't taught, which was in the DNA of all the street kids: *money, mister; scatter me some money, mister; money, money.*

So Chris got into the totally inadvisable habit of giving the stray money from time to time, sometimes for services rendered, but more often just on impulse, dollar bills Gabir would kiss reverently but also with a beguiling hint of mockery. "Thanks, Amrika!" he'd say. And then look at Chris with those Macedonian eyes.

Across culture, across language—was it possible the kid recognized something in him? Maybe it was as simple as sizing up this particular white-eyes for an easy mark. Maybe more ominous, like detecting a chink in the Coalition's formidable armor. Maybe (though this seems highly improbable) he looked at Chris and saw the same kind of ticket out of hell those canny Iraqi girls working in the Green Zone saw whenever they looked at young, not-so-bright American fellows in uniform.

Or maybe it was something else. Maybe what he recognized was not that different from what first John and then Leigh had recognized so long ago, something Chris had spent most of his life hiding away.

He knew he should be careful. More than careful—suspicious, wary, always on guard. Ian liked to say, darkly, "Just remember: all of them fucking hate us. Even the ones we pay salaries to. Even the goddamned babies still sucking their mothers' poisoned milk. Shia, Sunni, Kurd: it doesn't matter. Saddam may have been a nightmare, but we're an even worse nightmare. Forget all this shit about the Coalition of the Willing. We're the fucking Crusaders, and we're occupying their country."

Ian was right, of course. Chris had said as much himself on

more than one occasion, invariably pissing off the army morons in the Green Zone canteen chowing down—in the former Presidential Palace of an occupied Muslim country—on BBQ short ribs flown in from Kansas. It was one of the reasons his team had moved their operations to The Mansion. They weren't going native or anything like that. They were just trying to get the hell away from the idiots who still thought Saddam had been behind 9/11.

And so in spite of himself—or no, let's be honest, *because* of himself—he developed this ill-advised, one-sided attachment. Invisible to everyone but himself. And just possibly Gabir.

Sitting in a pulled-over SUV idling on the Poughkeepsie arterial, hazard lights flashing, watching in his rearview mirror a raccoon in its death struggle, Chris wonders whatever happened to Mr. Goblin. He'd like to think that Michelle adopted him permanently, but on purpose he lost touch with her so completely he'll never know.

He knows all too well what happened to Gabir.

The other guys never blamed him. Why should they? What eventually happened had nothing to do with what went on covertly inside his skull.

Which doesn't for an instant keep him from blaming himself.

Once again.

Against all odds, the broken-backed raccoon has succeeded in heaving itself to the curb. OK, good. And now what? If he had a gun he'd put it out of its misery. He feels totally naked and useless without a gun. Far luckier its companion: the equivalent of an IED blast, everything over in a split second, definitely how he'd want to go. But he also knows even the wounded raccoon is lucky in its way.

We should all be merely animals. As humans, there are miseries nothing can put us out of.

CHAPTER TWO

Caleb is off rehearsing with his band. Tom's giving the back lawn a mow. Ravioli, the white toy poodle, is perched on the sofa, standing on his hind legs, looking out the front window and yapping for no good reason. Lydia's trying to do some last-minute tidying up. As she's always telling her mother, the house isn't dirty, it's just messy. Not that her mother ever believes her, but what can you do? Eleven thirty, and she hasn't yet emerged from her bedroom—but that's not unusual. Lydia delivers a breakfast tray every morning at eight thirty; she's been doing it for years, a benign ritual that manages to prolong as long into the day as possible her mother's cherished solitude. She's had a morbid fear of crowds, congestion, public places ever since her husband's death—at least Lydia surmises that's when it began, since she doesn't remember a trace of it when she and her brother were still kids, and the four of them were apparently content in their little house. It shouldn't be any different now—there're no more bodies in the house than used to be—but somehow it *is* different, and Lydia often regrets that she's inflicted this punishment on her mother. Still, what's the alternative? She and Tom were living in a nice apartment when Caleb was born; it was only after the medical bills started to pour in that they couldn't keep up with the rent anymore. And besides, her mother hasn't been capable of living on her own for several years now.

It's not an ideal situation, but there you have it.

Her mother's what passes for a good sport. She may linger in her room till late in the morning, and nap there in the afternoons, and retreat to its safety or solace early in the evenings, but she's not sulking, she's not brooding. She assures Lydia of that, and Lydia chooses to believe her.

It hasn't been great for any of them, she admits as she catches sight of cobwebs in the corners of the window frames that she doesn't have time to tackle, but neither has it been a disaster.

She's not looking forward to spending more time with Chris. As she told Tom this morning. "I kept looking for the old Chris, but it's like the parts of him are arranged differently than they used to be. It's hard to describe." Will her mother remember him? She claims never to have met Chris, but that can't be true. Anyway, Chris will remember; Chris will be able to set the record straight.

And, of course, Chris and Craig knew each other, a little. Craig and his wife are coming to lunch as well.

All morning she's half expected Chris to appear at the door; she regrets having told him to show up anytime, but now that it's clear he's not going to come before noon, she's relieved. She wonders whether he'll expect a drink. Well, tough. There'll be plenty to drink after the wedding: an open bar at the reception and continuing through dinner, and bottomless wine with the meal. She's helped with the arrangements; she's appalled how much it all costs, but, of course, it's Anatole and Rafa's money, they can do with it what they want. She doesn't begrudge them a thing.

She and Tom were married here, in the backyard, a small but perfectly fine ceremony. They hung paper lanterns from the crab apple trees and strung Tibetan prayer flags along the back deck. Though Floral Euphoria was still years in the future, the ever-inspired Marla had collected roadside wildflowers to make lovely bouquets for the bride and bridesmaids." To her mother's delight, and everyone else's amusement, Mr. Derschowitz from the Jewish community center played old tunes on his accordion. Tom fired up the grill for steaks and hot dogs and hamburgers, which was perfectly fine. They'd both agreed even back then, before everything changed, that there were much more important things to spend hard-earned money on than a gaudy wedding.

A brisk knock on the door is followed by Ravioli's barking scamper down the hall. "Hey, anybody home?" a voice calls. It's an old routine Craig somehow finds funny. Behind him, Jenna fends off the little dog, who is bouncing waist high in his enthusiasm.

"Ravioli! Stop!" Lydia commands, to no avail.

"It's okay," Jenna says, a little breathlessly. "It makes a girl feel welcome to be greeted so warmly."

"His behavior gets worse and worse," Lydia apologizes, shooing Ravioli away. "I don't know what's wrong with him these days. It's nice of you to come all this way. You certainly didn't have to." Though she's touched, for Anatole's sake. They've driven down this morning from Boston; they'll stay tonight at a motel before heading back tomorrow.

"We wouldn't miss it for the world," Craig says, and she flushes with secret pride at what a thoroughly decent person her brother's turned out to be. Jenna too. She likes them both, and wouldn't mind seeing them more often than she does, which is usually Rosh Hashanah, Thanksgiving, Passover, and the Fourth of July—the sacred holiday quartet for secular Jews, Craig once joked. It's a shame, really; Boston and Poughkeepsie aren't that far from each other in terms of miles. But she knows there are other kinds of distance as well.

Craig and Jenna don't have children, though they've tried. Countless doctor visits, consultations about *in vitro* (too expensive, and too much of a long shot); at one point they were very close to adopting a Romanian orphan, but for obscure reasons it fell through and they've never told her the details. She tries not to feel sorry for them, but she does. Despite all the difficulties, she doesn't know what she'd do without Caleb. Without him there'd be no reason not to screw up, run off the rails, abandon Tom and sobriety and career and simply revert back to her old, doomed, selfish, half-feral self.

It's not something anybody will ever know—though she has, to be honest, intimated as much to Marla on occasion.

"Make yourselves at home," she says. "Craig, you might want to go roust Mom out of her bedroom. She's been in there long enough this morning. And Jenna, would you mind helping me set the table? It's nothing fancy. Tom's going to make his famous grilled cheese sandwiches."

Ravioli's frantic barking signals Chris's arrival.

"Ugh. Ravioli. Now, stop! I'm telling you for the last time. Sorry," she apologizes as the dog swirls hysterically around Chris. "You'd never guess he's nearly nine. More or less our age in dog years. And he gets more hyper every year. Sometimes I think he's stealing his years from me."

"I never thought of you as a dog person," Chris says.

"I'm not. Caleb was the one who desperately wanted a dog. He made this elaborate presentation to us one evening, complete with poster boards. He must've spent weeks working it up. He specifically wanted a toy poodle. It was very cute. This was when he was maybe six or seven? The deal, though, was it's his dog, his responsibility. Of course, he never pays any attention to it now. I guess you didn't really need to know all that."

"What kind of boy wants a toy poodle?"

"Tom's reaction exactly. You really want to know?"

"Sure," Chris says. "Why not?"

"Well, you'll like this. Our Caleb was a pink boy."

Chris looks puzzled—though at the same time, Lydia can see, he's assiduously assessing the space he's just stepped into. It's a little sinister, really. "Never heard that term," he says.

"No, I guess you probably wouldn't have. You've been here before, haven't you? You must've been."

"Actually, I don't think I ever was. I'd recognize it if I had. But anyway, what's this thing about a pink boy?"

She's not sure why she even brought it up, she wishes now she hadn't, she regrets putting her son on display like this; at the same time she feels it's a badge of honor, a tribute to her parenting skills, her general enlightenment, her ability to be capacious. "He's our golden boy now, but when he was younger all he wanted to wear were dresses. And he wanted his toenails painted. And he played with dolls. We were a little freaked out, Tom probably more than me—well, definitely more than me—but we got counseling, which helped a lot. The counselor told us he'd probably grow out of it, so we should indulge him within bounds. We set certain rules. He could wear whatever he liked at home, but he couldn't go to school dressed like a girl. It was really for his own protection. We didn't want him to be the boy in high school who used to wear dresses in elementary school."

"And did he grow out of it?"

"Completely. You'd never guess he went through that phase. He's totally normal now. I mean, whatever totally normal means. He's got lots of guy friends. He's in a band—in fact, he's rehearsing with them right now. But he should be back soon. So that's probably a lot more information than you want. But for better or worse, it explains Ravioli."

"I thought Caleb was deaf. How does he play in a band?"

"Everybody asks that question. You should ask him directly. He's actually got some really good answers."

Ravioli's found a new source of excitement. He charges down the hall, then spurts back into the living room, barks frantically, reverses himself, and repeats the sequence.

"It's Mom," Lydia explains. "She always makes a grand entrance."

The approaching clack, clack, clack reveals itself as a walker, employed by an ancient, bent-over woman. Behind her, hovering solicitously, is a man Chris recognizes—through context alone—as Craig. He'd be a complete stranger if he passed by on the street. His looks are gone, lost in the rubbery mask of American middle age. His hair's receded and thinned, his lacrosse player's body gone to seed. Only his eyes are still bright and boyish. He grins when he sees Chris.

"Dude," he says. "It's been years. You're looking good."

"You as well," Chris tells him.

"And you remember our mom."

Chris isn't sure he does, but Mrs. Forman smiles warmly and says, "Oh you. I remember you."

And now Tom has come in, sweaty and flushed from mowing the lawn; the day promises to be warmer than usual for early June. Unselfconsciously he strips off his T-shirt, wads it into a bundle, sniffs it, makes a sour face, and hands it off to Lydia—who makes a face as well, as if to say, in fondest exasperation, See what I put up with?

"Sorry," Tom tells Chris, extending a meaty hand. "I meant to finish up before you got here." His grip is firm. He's one of those guys who gives you a knowing wink after certain sentences—a gesture Chris has never understood. How do you ask somebody, What does that wink mean? But Chris imagines it might go over well with the customers at Friendly Honda.

"It's nice to meet you," Tom continues. The most striking thing about him is the enormous holes in his earlobes. Chris tries not to stare, but he can't *not* stare. "Another mystery man out of the wife's past. Just kidding. I'm cool with everybody. Lemme go up and grab a shower and I'll be down in a jiffy, okay?"

"That was my husband," Lydia says once he's bounded up the stairs.

"You didn't mention he must've had *enormous* plugs," Chris says, marveling, a little squeamishly, at those telltale holes.

"Still did when I first met him. I'm not even sure why he gave them up. I guess at a certain age—like with everything else. But yeah, it looks a little strange."

Chris laughs. "I'm glad it was you and not me who said that." And suddenly, for the first time, they're on the same wavelength, they're back in Bertie's being deliciously catty, no time at all has passed.

"At least he's not covered in tattoos," she continues, "like some of his old buddies. He's got a fairly tasteful skull with roses, and that's it."

"No 'Lydia' in gothic letters across his back?"

"Sorry, no. He's not *that* romantic. Though he used to sport a purple Mohawk. There're pictures to prove it." She often teases Tom about his punk past, the Ramones and Butthole Surfers and Black Flag he's never quite given up on, though he doesn't play those old CDs much anymore. Besides, it's not the kind of music Caleb has any interest in. "Boring!" is his considered judgment on his dad's Jurassic musical tastes.

Anatole isn't prepared for the onslaught of Rafa's full family: two sisters, their husbands, five children ranging in age from an impossible four to an impossibly handsome sixteen, two aunts and an uncle, plus a very rambunctious Siberian husky with unnerving ice-blue eyes and the ridiculous name of Marley (as in Bob Marley). The big mistake is letting Marley charge into the house along with the humans; during the first half minute before the sixteen-year-old brings him under control, Marley manages to knock over a floor lamp whose glass globe shatters, wolf down half the cheese and nearly all the pepperoni slices

Rafa's set out for the guests, and send one of the pretty Turkish rugs sailing beneath his scampering paws across the bare wood floor till both dog and magic carpet crash into the far wall.

*The Dominicans came down like the wolf on the fold*, Anatole thinks, though he knows better than to inflict that bit of lame wit on Rafa at the moment.

"Paloma, honey, you might have left the dog behind," Rafa suggests. "I don't think we can take him to the ceremony. And on the basis of the available evidence, leaving him here would be a death sentence for the house."

"Elian," she addresses her sixteen-year-old son, "could you take Marley out to the car? Make sure the window's cracked open a bit. We'll leave him in the car. He just wanted to come in and say hello."

"*Some hello*," Anatole doesn't say.

"I'm really, really sorry about the lamp."

"Don't worry," Rafa reassures her. "It's just a lamp. We can get a replacement globe, no problem."

No we can't, Anatole thinks. We bought that lamp in an antique shop. It's one of a kind—as in *irreplaceable*.

"Besides," Rafa goes on, "you can't just leave Marley in the car. It'll be hours. He can stay in the garden. It's fenced. I don't think there's any chance he'll get out."

"He'll howl," she tells him. "That's why we brought him. He drives the neighbors bonkers."

Great, thinks Anatole. He'll drive *our* neighbors bonkers. And destroy the garden to boot.

"Well, so he'll howl," Rafa says. "We'll take the neighbors a bottle of wine."

The youngest two children have invented a game which consists of clambering up on the arm of the sofa, yelling themselves silly, then throwing themselves down onto the hardwood floor.

Rafa ignores them. "Please sit," he tells everyone. "Pick

among the wreckage. There's champagne. Diet ginger ale. Would anybody like anything else? Mom?"

"Gin and tonic," she says. "Extra strong."

"Go easy. It's going to be a long day."

"All the more reason to get started on the right foot," she tells him.

Anatole's relieved to accompany Rafa into the kitchen for a moment alone. He paws urgently, affectionately at his sleeve. "Talk about getting started on the right foot. Aargh, mi amor! Your superabundant exuberant family is *smothering* me."

"Oh Mr. Kitten. Honey. I'm sorry to inflict my family on you. We could've invited your brother to stop by, you know."

"No, thanks. There's more than enough family in this house right now. Anyway, I'm better now. I just wanted to scream a little back there."

"And now you've screamed."

"And now I've screamed."

"And it's been duly noted." Rafa uncorks the champagne and begins pouring it into flutes set out on a tray. Anatole busies himself with Miosotis's G and T.

"Go light on the gin," Rafa advises.

For months they've joked to each other, "We'll break up the morning of our wedding; you just wait and see." But now they've had their fight. And it's not even been a fight; it's just been a ritual they had to get out of the way.

Still, Anatole can't quite let his annoyance go.

"Even your mom's being super critical this morning. I showed her our cravats. I thought she'd like them. You know what she called them? *Tacky*! Please, I told her. They're not tacky—they're *opulent*! She just gave me this look."

"Mom's just anxious."

"But why?"

"She wants everything to be for the best. For both of us. She really does believe in us, you know."

"I'm not even sure what that means."

"Yes, you do. These old women: my mom, Mrs. Forman. They know what counts. It's like they instinctively know what folks like us are up against. How they know that, I don't know. But they just know. Trust me on that one."

"What choice do I have, darling? I trust you on everything."

The living room bursts unexpectedly into applause as they reenter carrying the drink trays, Rafa's loaded with champagne, Anatole's with ginger ale for the kids and that weak G and T for Miosotis.

"A toast," says Paloma's husband, plucking a champagne flute and lifting it high as the other adults follow suit. "There'll be plenty more, but it's never too early for a toast on a happy day like today. To the grooms!"

Anatole knows Nikauris as a blustery, good-hearted fellow who never has anything the least bit interesting or surprising to say.

"To the grooms!" everyone responds.

"Here," says Chiara, the other sister, ambushing them with an iPhone. "Picture time. Come on, you two lovebirds. That's it. Now, a kiss."

"We're not supposed to kiss till we're married," Rafa tells her.

"As if you haven't kissed a million times."

"Today we're playing by the rules. We'll kiss when Reverend Judy tells us we can kiss."

What he doesn't mention is that he and Anatole haven't had sex for two weeks. They agreed it was important to make this little sacrifice, though neither of them can exactly articulate *why* it seems important. Just as neither of them can fully explain why, after twelve years together, knowing everything they do about each other and the fragile, imperfect, enduring relationship they've forged against all odds, it's seemed vitally important to enter into this absurd, shopworn contract of marriage. Maybe the best either of them can come up with is this: The world's a terrifying place. And this flimsy little fiction is the best humans have managed to make it seem less so.

"There's no gin in this drink," Miosotis announces, squinting suspiciously at her glass.

"There's plenty," Rafa tells her. "Trust me. I don't know why you're not tasting it."

She makes a face at him and takes a long swallow. "I can't taste any gin in this at all."

"There'll be lots more," he reassures her. "Just hang in there. By the way, everybody, we've hired both a photographer and a videographer. So everything's going to be recorded. You don't have to go crazy with your iPhones. Just enjoy it all as it happens. And we'll post everything afterward on Vimeo and Facebook."

They've settled in the cluttered living room, where Lydia's had to move a few stacks of magazines and DVDs to make room for everyone on the sofas. Mrs. Forman is parked in a fraying armchair by the upright piano, on whose bench Craig and Jenna perch, a little uncomfortably.

There are photos of Caleb everywhere, Chris notices, on end tables and the mantel, hanging on the walls; they trace his progress from nondescript infant to chubby toddler to gap-toothed first-grader to lithe little leaguer to the exceptionally striking youth of the present. Chris hasn't been able to get him out of his head, though he refrained, last night at the Inn, from masturbating to reckless fantasies. Actually, he corrects himself, he didn't so much refrain as simply pass out from exhaustion the instant he climbed under those lovely, fresh-scented American sheets.

Tom's as good as his promise, back in no time, wet black hair sexily slicked back, barefoot, in khakis and a white shirt he's not yet buttoned up. He's not handsome, though his face has a homely integrity to it, nicely dressed up by dark, soulful eyes. And the earlobes, oddly, seem like war wounds—badges of some primitive honor, of a time when such gestures seemed defiant and necessary.

Chris finds it quaint that Lydia's married a former punk rocker. It means she didn't completely settle down after all.

"Where on earth is Caleb?" she's asking Tom. "I've sent him about a million texts, and as usual he's not replying. You need to get on him about that. He's *got* to answer his texts. That's part of the deal."

"He'll turn up," Tom tells her.

"Our son the delinquent," Lydia explains.

"He's a good kid," Craig says.

"He's all right," Lydia admits. "Sometimes a pain in the butt. But we love him all the same."

To change the distracting subject, Chris says, "Hey. I have a question. I guess I've been away too long, but what's the sign on your front lawn mean? I've been seeing them all over town."

"*Don't frack with New York*," Lydia tells him.

"Yeah. I mean, I get there's a pun there. But what exactly does 'frack' refer to?"

"Hydraulic fracturing," she explains. "Fracking for short. It's this way to get natural gas from shale. A very nasty process. It's been a total environmental catastrophe down in Pennsylvania, where they're already doing a lot of it."

"The gas gets into well water," Craig says. "I know this guy who lives outside Lancaster, he says if you run the faucet and strike a match next to it, there's a big whoosh of flame in the kitchen sink, like a mini fireball."

"We're fighting to stop it in New York. It's supposed to reduce our dependency on oil, but you have to ask, at what price?"

"Oh, I see," Chris says. "NIMBY, in other words."

Everyone looks at him blankly.

"Not In My Back Yard," he prompts. "Has that expression totally gone out of use? I mean, it's why we're in Iraq. Why drill here when we can drill there? It's why we're fine with what's happening in the Niger Delta."

"My sentiments exactly," Tom says. "I'm all for domestic drilling. And fracking, and nuclear power, and everything else. Drill, baby, drill."

"As you can see," Lydia says, "we've got some disagreements around here."

"The wife's a huge environmentalist. Is that a surprise? The kid too. We've had a regular activism factory going here for several years now. We're the Poughkeepsie hub of frickin' Greenpeace. Besides banning fracking, we're saving the whales, and the wolves, and the coral reefs, and the prairies, and the snail darter. Am I forgetting anything, darling? Oh, and I hope you noticed the hybrid in the driveway."

Chris hasn't.

"Courtesy of me, by the way," Tom adds.

"You're an idiot but a sweetie," Lydia tells him.

Chris is once again conscious he's come into a conversation that's been going on for a very long time without him. They used to talk about exciting things, didn't they? But about what, exactly? He can't quite remember, but surely it wasn't about hybrids.

"My birthday present a couple of years ago," Lydia explains. "It's a Civic. Somehow Tom got a used one—"

"Preowned," he corrects her.

"— through an employee discount he's never been fully forthcoming about—"

"I wanted her to think I spent a fortune."

"I was upset *because* I thought you'd spent a fortune."

He gives Chris a look of soulful resignation. "As you can see, I can't win."

"I just want you all to know I've been having a terrible time of it this morning," Mrs. Forman announces. "Since nobody's seen fit to ask."

They all turn and look at her. She widens her eyes and stares back at them with comic pugnacity.

"Why's that, Mom?" Lydia asks.

"These two little flies got me all riled up. They kept landing on my food, and then on my water glass. Just walking around the rim. I kept trying to catch them, but I couldn't. They're still in there. It's very annoying."

"You should've called me," Lydia tells her.

"You're all so busy. I didn't want to bother anybody. But I got very peeved. I just wanted you to know, thanks for asking."

"I'll go see what I can do," Craig says.

And Chris remembers: what they used to talk about was desire. Impossible, longing dreams. Delirious, aching confusion. That was the vital element they lived off—at Bertie's after work, in their apartments till late into the night—because it was the one thing that mattered. Not things, or achievements, or politics, or fracking or anything else: just sweet naked blameless unending desire. So this is what's become of them all: they've descended into dreariness. Except Anatole, bless him, still silly and needy and hopelessly romantic. Still hoping to be kissed. No doubt he's woken up this morning hungover and embarrassed. Not to worry. Chris has no intention of reminding him. Besides, he knows Anatole was right: it wasn't just the wine talking. Beyond the wine, something else was talking.

That's why he's longing, however preposterously, to see this Caleb once more.

Attuned to frequencies inaccessible to the rest of them, Ravioli suddenly hurls himself, with a frenetic clatter of claws, toward the front door.

"Finally," Lydia says. "The prodigal returns."

"Hey, everybody." Caleb lopes into the room, executing a

half-hearted wave in their direction while doing some fancy footwork in order to avoid Ravioli's dervish dance of adoration. He carries a pair of drumsticks in one hand, a couple of mallets in the other. He's wearing tight, black, very low-slung jeans, a lime-green T-shirt that doesn't quite reach his metal-studded beltline, sneakers in a black-and-white checkerboard pattern. He's passed through the room and up the stairs before Chris can half take him in.

"That's my cue," Tom announces.

"I hope you weren't expecting anything too fancy-schmancy," Lydia says. "Tom's grilled cheese sandwiches are a Saturday ritual. And you get a choice: American or Swiss? White, rye, or whole wheat?"

"So how was your practice?" Lydia asks.

Caleb mumbles something, his mouth full of sandwich.

Chris just wants to look and look. The cochlear implants make Caleb seem somehow customized, otherworldly, a creature from the future, a cyborg.

"His band's called Mother Spook," Lydia says when Caleb doesn't answer immediately. "How's that for a name? I'm trying not to take it personally."

"Modder Spook," Caleb says patiently.

"That's what I said."

"M-O-D-D-E-R," he says, his voice harsh and tuneless.

"But what's that mean?"

"It doesn't mean *anything*. I keep telling you."

"Whatever," Lydia says.

"Dial it back, honey, okay?" Tom tells her.

"I was just trying to invite Caleb into the conversation. You know, Caleb, Chris used to own a record store here in Pough-keepsie. A funky, wonderful record store called Immaculate Blue. That's about as mysterious as Modder Spook, when you think about it, isn't it?" She knows she's acting badly. She's trying to show Caleb off. But the truth is, her son frustrates her. On the one hand he's exquisite, and brave, and the place he's making for himself in the world, despite his hardships, is amazing. But then he seems to withdraw into a cave made all the more inaccessible by his deafness. Not that's he's *deaf*. With the implants he can hear plenty, though what the sounds he hears actually sound like she'll never know. Dr. Manx has explained that Caleb's implants aren't a hearing aid, they don't restore hearing, they only provide what he calls "a useful representation of sounds." To this day she's not sure what that means. Caleb's music, she imagines, is the closest she'll ever get to understanding what the world sounds like to him.

"Why don't you go grab the laptop? Let Chris hear one of your songs."

"We're in the middle of lunch," Caleb says.

"We're finishing up. Go on. Don't be shy."

He throws up his hands, shakes his head, makes a strange animal sound, but complies. He's barely left the room when she says—to Tom? to Chris? or just to herself?—"I'm sorry. I know I'm bragging here. But I get to brag, don't I?" Then Caleb's back, tapping the laptop keyboard. "Sorry. There's no video," he explains. "Just audio. Okay. So this one's called *Spooklear Deterrent*."

But it's not just audio. Black-and-white stills of the band—there are four of them, Caleb by far the handsomest—fade in and out as the music plays. It's very percussion heavy. Caleb plays a variety of drums with reckless abandon. The keyboardist sticks more to jangling chords than to melody, which he leaves to the not-untalented kid on the marimba. The bass player is fairly deft as well. It's high-energy stuff, all four going in different cacophonous directions at once until, dramatically, they all coalesce, in sync with each other, pounding out irregularly spaced eruptions, lacerations punctuated by silence. They take turns howling, reciting, humming, shrieking, whispering, occasionally singing in unison. They're not good, necessarily, but they're at least semioriginal, The Swans meet Spiral Jetty (Chris hasn't thought of those bands in decades). He's kind of impressed—though he wonders how impressed he'd be if he just randomly came across their stuff on YouTube.

"Awesome, my man!" Craig gives Caleb an encouraging pat on the back. Jenna claps her hands daintily.

"What's all that noise about?" asks Mrs. Forman.

"Shh," Lydia tells her. "It's Caleb's music we're listening to."

"Is it from the computer?"

"Yes, Mom. It's from the computer. It's like magic."

Mrs. Forman shakes her head sadly, though she isn't half wrong, Chris thinks; there's definitely a large noise component at work.

The next track is called *Funk Spookifies the Cat.*

*Spook Plumbbob* follows.

"I'm detecting a pattern here," Chris says, but he instantly regrets his ironic tone. These are four high school kids making up a world. Noise, music, just being alive—whatever. He has no trouble thinking of it as celebration.

*Spook Plumbbob* wends its chaotic way through chord bursts and drum attacks and sweet floating marimba lines before finally settling into a sustained diminuendo, over which the boys chant, singsong, sinister—can he be hearing this right?— "Anatole is dreaming, Anatole is dreaming." Then silence.

"Yeah, you heard right," Lydia says.

"Shout out to Uncle Anatole," Caleb explains in his affectless way. "You used to be a friend of his."

"Well, I hope I still am," Chris feels compelled to say. "How did Uncle Anatole, as you call him, end up in your song?"

"You'll love this," Lydia says.

Her comment threatens to silence Caleb, but after a semisulky pause he says, "I don't know. One time he was telling me about these dreams he used to have. Atomic bomb dreams. They sounded really scary. So I went online and had a look around. There was this thing, Operation Plumbbob, where they exploded atomic bombs over soldiers to see how they held up. Short answer: not very well. Lots of them got really sick."

Lydia's beaming. "This was back in the fifties," she explains. "File under 'Nefarious Military Doings.'"

Caleb doesn't seem to hear her—or if he does, he pays no attention. When he speaks, Chris notices, it's more like a speech than simply speech. "It's supposed to be a kind of dream blog," Caleb continues. "Except not my dream. Somebody else's. That's all."

"Okay," Chris says. "Impressive. I like your stuff. It's different. It's imaginative. So what did Anatole think about you putting him in a song?"

"We don't know," Lydia says. "Caleb just sent him the link yesterday."

"It's a wedding present," Caleb explains. "All Modder Spook's crazy about Uncle Anatole."

"Really?" Chris says slowly, more a comment than a question.

"Anatole helps them buy studio time, instrument upgrades, that sort of thing. He's incredibly generous that way," Lydia says. Her smile isn't exactly a smile: it involves pursing her lips and raising her eyebrows, which conveys, well, what? Chris isn't sure.

"Now, enough Modder Spook," Caleb announces. "The deaf boy's taking a shower. Time to go to a wedding."

"You've already had one shower today," Lydia reminds him. "You don't need to waste so much water."

"I get sweaty at practice." He sniffs an armpit, reacts, like his dad, in mock horror. "I'll stink up the wedding." And with that he marches up the stairs.

"That's one habit I can't get him to break," Lydia says before he's even out of earshot. "What do teenage boys do for such a long time in the shower?"

"As if you have to ask," Tom says.

She just looks at him.

Tom's a lot easier on the kid than she is. Why is that? Chris wonders.

"Good sandwiches," he tells Tom, then excuses himself to smoke a cigarette outside.

Tom's put on the sort of jacket befitting a guy who clearly doesn't dress up a lot. Having slathered on enough lipstick and eye shadow to make a drag queen proud, Lydia's slipped into a canary-yellow dress and lime-green jacket with padded shoulders. Her pumps are ruby red. It's just like the old days.

Mrs. Forman is telling everyone and no one that it might be best for her to stay behind; she'll just be in the way.

"Nonsense," Lydia tells her. "Anatole and Rafa are expecting you."

"Who's Rafa?" Mrs. Forman asks.

Lydia rolls her eyes at Chris. She's doubled her mom's dose of Xanax for the occasion.

Thoroughly scrubbed down, Caleb's donned a white shirt, gray trousers, and, as if he's somehow intuited Lydia's report from earlier, a pink tie. Except for the tie, his appearance is that of a schoolboy at a conservative prep school. With the tie he looks—Chris thinks—weirdly smashing.

He's always secretly shared Anatole's tendency to go worshipful around exquisite boys. He'll never admit it, he'll pretend not to notice, nobody can seem more indifferent to the boy in the room than he. But really, he's just as shamefully and grovelingly devout as Anatole used to be. But is Anatole still that way? Or has his cult of the teenage boy vanished? Did he wake up one day and find himself no longer susceptible? Did some moral scruple turn him into the adult-marrying Anatole of today? Or did it just go underground, a black intoxicating river liable to burst free under the right circumstances?

He regrets what a waste last night was, how many topics they never broached, how much they simply sidestepped—but wasn't that always the case?

Rafa's superabundant clan, including Miosotis, has departed—they plan on stopping by McDonald's to get a bite to eat before the ceremony. Marley, bereft, is crooning in the garden. The Rolls Silver Cloud is scheduled to pick Anatole and Rafa up at three, leaving them a blessed hour and a half alone.

They've planned this parenthesis between family and ceremony. In the bedroom, Rafa lights sticks of incense and they undress each other, wordlessly, the way they did that first unforgettable night they made love—October 2000, the exact date lost to memory. Off comes Anatole's pumpkin-colored shirt, then Rafa's faded *Obama '08* T-shirt. Rafa peels off Anatole's khakis, Anatole takes care of Rafa's relaxed-fit jeans. Rafa prefers boxers, Anatole briefs. It all seems a little silly. And also intimidating. They see each other naked all the time, of course, but it's usually casual, accidental. Somebody hops out of bed to get in the shower. Somebody's getting dressed for work. It's not like this: strangely, grandly ceremonial. Now, as he faces Rafa's nakedness, as Rafa faces his, Anatole feels entirely exposed and vulnerable. He feels scrutinized. But how can that be? They've lived together for nearly a decade. Whatever changes have happened, have happened slowly. They're not the sexy youngsters they once were. They've thoroughly entered the middle of middle age.

When Rafa puts his hands on Anatole's shoulders, Anatole returns the gesture and, braced like that, they meet each other's gaze. Anatole knows it's a cliché, the windows of the soul and all that, but still, there's something about staring into a person's eyes that's just beyond words—though if you ever could put it into words it would somehow, he feels, solve everything.

He tells himself he has no illusions. He knows their problems, their shortcomings. He knows there's never one hundred percent fidelity in any relationship, that life is a series of larger or smaller betrayals, and if anybody begs to differ, well, they're either hypocrites or in serious denial. Despite whatever crazy feelings Chris's reappearance might have provoked, he's entirely sure what he and Rafa are about to undertake is exactly the right, flawed, reasonable thing. He's not even going to ask Rafa if he feels the same way, because if Anatole knows anything in this confusing world, he knows that.

"Come." Rafa takes his hand, leads him into the bathroom. They hardly ever shower together, but now they leisurely soap each other's arms, thighs, calves, between fingers and toes, around whorls of ear and cleft of chin and hollow of collarbone, shampooing each other's hair (Rafa's luscious black curls!), scrubbing each other's hairy and hairless chest with the loofah, laving cocks and balls and asscracks. They both sprout hard-ons—but they refrain from groping or horseplay. It's deliciously maddening, but their decision to abstain these last two weeks adds something like a holy gravity to everything (their cocks don't rise, they just grow heavy, blood-thickened, pendulous).

Back in the bedroom, they dress each other in the formal clothes they spent a fun couple of evenings bidding for on eBay some weeks ago: preowned floral vests, bold cravats, and retro tuxedos from Raffinati and Jean Yves. Sure, they're going to look like two Edwardian dandies—but then, gay marriages aren't supposed to be dull!

It turns out transportation arrangements, even in Poughkeepsie, are complicated. Lydia's arranged to pick up another couple—"to encourage carpooling, and designated drivers," she explains. The plan, tediously enunciated, is this: Mrs. Forman will go with Tom and Lydia in the hybrid, because it gets much better mileage than Tom's macho Ridgeline but has very little trunk space, which means Mrs. Forman's collapsible wheelchair will have to share the backseat with her, and Craig and Jenna in their gas guzzling Explorer will pick up Marla and Bob. So would Chris mind ferrying Caleb?

"You're right about him," Tom says as they pull out of the driveway. "He's an odd bird. I was expecting him to be gay. He's certainly no Anatole."

"Not all my friends back then were gay."

"Just most of them. But this one—no, I don't think so."

"Well, there you have it."

"You've never really talked about him, you know. Was he by any chance a boyfriend?"

"We *are* nosy today."

"Just curious."

"Well, no, I wouldn't say he was my boyfriend, exactly. But we all had our moments back then, didn't we."

"Tell me about it," Tom says.

*Was* he ever her boyfriend? Not in the least. Then why does she still want to bend the truth a little? They got drunk one night, they fucked, he lost his hard-on halfway through, they never repeated it, never even referred to it again, though she remembers, humiliatingly, saying something to the effect of *You know where to find me if you're ever in the mood.* And obviously he was never again in the mood. But that's fine. She never fell for him the way Anatole did; she tells herself his reappearance rekindles nothing.

She also realizes that she's still much more angry with him than she has any reason to be. So what's that about?

"Speaking of curiosity," Tom says, "why'd you suggest Caleb ride with him?"

"You mean, beyond logistics?"

"Sure. Beyond logistics."

"Well, I think Caleb wants to talk to him about something."

"Really? About what?"

Lydia has to smile. "I think our golden boy is preparing to spring an ambush on poor Chris."

It's been so long since he's talked with a boy who's not for hire that he's a little out of his depth. (Whether Gabir was ever for hire—and by whom—will always be the bottomless question.) Paying boys may be phenomenally efficient, but Chris worries it's stunted him, made him unfit for normal, open-ended human interaction. He's used to transactions, not interactions—which might account for how discombobulated he's felt ever since arriving back in the States.

An innocent, amiable conversation is all he wants, now that he has this strange, extraordinarily attractive boy to himself for twenty minutes or so.

But Caleb's clearly not one to start a conversation on his own. He peers out the side window; he has a curious way of turning his head to follow something that's caught his eye, then facing forward again.

Chris can't help but feel irrational panic. They're going about this run out to Whispering Creek all wrong. Soft vehicles, no bulletproof vests, no weapons of any kind? Not even the most elementary essentials like towing straps or extra fuel? The lead vehicle should be in constant contact with the others about potential threats. He's feeling not so much vulnerable as insanely irresponsible.

He takes several deep, measured breaths, his spasm subsides, he says, casually, "So what exactly is this Whispering Creek place we're going to?"

"Golf course," Caleb says.

"Anatole's getting married on a golf course? Does this mean he's taken up golf?"

Caleb seems amused. "He and Rafa play with me and Dad sometimes. I mean, not at Whispering Creek. That's way too expensive. We usually go to College Hill, which is only nine holes. Anyway, they're terrible, Rafa and Anatole. Especially Anatole!"

*Well, of course*, Chris wants to say but doesn't.

"The clubhouse at Whispering Creek is beautiful. You'll see. I've been to one, two"—he counts them off on his fingers—"three weddings there."

"That's a lot of weddings," Chris says. "And you're how old?"

"Seventeen."

"I don't think I'd been to a single wedding when I was that age. Let alone three in the same place."

"It's a popular place to get married," Caleb says.

"And is this your first, um, gay wedding?"

Caleb nods vigorously. "We're very proud of Anatole and Rafa."

There's something rote in that, and Chris can't help but think it's the kind of line a politically correct straight kid would have gone and memorized. But that's fine. All he really wants is some semblance of ordinary banter, and in that regard things aren't going all that badly. He can't quite believe how easy it is to converse with a deaf boy. Caleb doesn't even seem to be lip-reading.

"So your mom said I should ask you about what it's like to be a deaf person who makes music," he ventures.

Caleb smiles the enigmatic smile he seems to specialize in. "Yeah," he says. "Mama likes people to ask the deaf boy questions. She thinks I need to be in social situations more."

*You're doing just fine*, Chris considers saying, but he has a vision of how Lydia overmothers her son, suffocates him with love. He doesn't want to make it worse for the poor kid. He's about to say *You don't have to answer that* when Caleb continues, in that toneless way of his (and yet he's a musician; Chris has heard the evidence. It's extraordinary, isn't it? He's really sort of enchanted with those Modder Spook songs), "You know how when you eat some really good food?" Caleb pauses as if expecting an answer.

"Go on," Chris says.

"It's not just the taste all by itself, right? It's the smell too. It's whether it's warm or cold. What it looks like on the plate. The texture you feel in your mouth." He accompanies all this with gestures. "The five senses—they aren't these separate things. They're like this." He meshes his fingers together. Chris sees that Caleb's nails are shapely, well-groomed. He was a pink boy, Lydia said. Is he still? Chris's gaze lingers on those fingernails. He catches himself, looks back at the road, half expecting to have missed something crucial in that lapse of a second or two. But Lydia's Civic is still in front of him, Craig's Explorer still behind. There's not a hint of suspicious activity anywhere.

"You know, people—hearing-abled people—somehow think, if you cover your ears, that's what deafness is like." He shakes his head vigorously. "That's just silly. Like right now— you feel the car's vibration. So that's part of hearing the car. You hear music the exact same way. I mean, I think most hearing-abled people have no idea they hear that way in addition to the way they think they hear. But they do. It's like your body has all sorts of ways of listening that don't just involve hearing."

This all seems wonderful, Chris thinks as he slows, follows Lydia to the curb; the Explorer eases in right behind him. He can see in the rearview mirror the couple who've been standing in the driveway clamber into the backseat of the Explorer. Lydia must've called ahead on her cell phone.

"Your mom's got this all very well organized," he says. "I'm impressed."

She waits for a couple of cars to pass, and then their convoy is off again without incident.

"There's this really great Scottish lady," Caleb is saying—maybe he hasn't heard Chris compliment his mom. It doesn't matter. Chris is allowing himself the luxury of thinking the kid's a sort of genius.

"Evelyn Glennie. Maybe you've heard of her."

Chris shakes his head.

"Really amazing lady. She does solo percussion with symphony orchestras. And she can't, quote unquote, *hear* a thing. But there she is. Making really complicated music with a whole symphony orchestra."

*You don't think they're all pretending?* Chris wants to say, but that's the Chris of Port Harcourt, the Chris who's wickedly skeptical of everything. That's not the Chris he wants to be at the moment. He feels strangely humbled in Caleb's presence. Part of him keeps thinking, *You're not a musician. You bang on drums while your guys cover for you. Who are you kidding?* A much bigger part of him thinks, *A lot of people are going to have crushes on you. In some other world I might even be one of them.*

What he says is, "How fascinating."

"And of course there was Beethoven," Caleb tells him, as if that clinches it—and maybe it does.

"Yeah, Beethoven," Chris says. Beethoven's always been a bit of a stretch for him.

"But now can I ask you a personal question?"

"Sure." Chris is touched and a little thrilled. There's something weirdly gorgeous in the mood of the moment. Life unfolds its bounty in startling ways. For the first time since arriving in Poughkeepsie he's genuinely glad he chose to come. "Go ahead," he says. "Ask me anything."

"Okay." Caleb pauses. He frowns. He twists his interlaced fingers with those well-tended nails. He's wearing several bracelets on his left wrist—plastic, braided cloth, leather, beads—just the way Leigh used to. In twenty-odd years, certain things haven't changed. Chris loves this sheer proximity of boy. "So here's my question," Caleb continues. "And I'm not trying to offend you or anything. But how can somebody like you justify doing what they're doing?"

Chris laughs that abrupt laugh he hates but can't control. Adrenaline kicks in. The lead vehicle may as well have radioed, *Bad guy at three o'clock.* He looks over at his passenger. "What do you mean, 'doing what they're doing'?"

Caleb meets his eye. "Mama tells the deaf boy everything."

"Whoa," Chris tells him. His mind races through possibilities, things Lydia surely wouldn't divulge to her son, deaf or not. "What the hell are you talking about?"

"I mean, Mama was kind of upset on the way home last night. So before I went to bed I did some Googling. You know, Amnesty International has tons of stuff posted about Nigeria. Royal Dutch Shell. I mean, that's who you work for, right? So you must know all about the stuff that's going on there in the Niger Delta. I have that right, don't I? The oil spills. The— what's it called—with the methane—"

"Flaring," Chris says.

"Yeah, flaring. This one statistic said flares in the Delta make up like forty percent of all the greenhouse gas emissions on the whole planet. I mean, that's insane. And then there was that guy, the activist, he was a poet—"

"Ken Saro-Wiwa," Chris says wearily. "Long before my time there."

"Yeah, that's him. Shell got the military to arrest him because he was being inconvenient about human rights and the environment and they hanged him, right?"

The ambush always comes when you least expect it.

"You seem to be way more up to speed on all this than I am," Chris tells him. "I just work there. But before *you* get too worked up, first off, you shouldn't believe everything you find on the Internet. There's lots of misinformation out there.

Second, Amnesty International's a group that's known for having its own very particular agenda—"

"I know all about Amnesty International," Caleb says. "I started a chapter at our school. Besides, the deaf boy's web savvy. He's learned a lot from Rafa. He's pretty good at filtering out the junk."

"How can you know how to filter out the junk when you don't even know the facts?" Chris isn't losing his temper, but neither is he as cool as he should be. They've left Poughkeepsie and are driving through sparsely settled country toward Pleasant Valley. Though he's stayed close on Lydia's tail, Chris notices that Craig's allowed another vehicle to intervene between him and Chris. Where did that marauder come from? It doesn't matter, he reminds himself, this is America, there's nothing whatsoever to fear, but still he's annoyed at Craig's negligence. "And you *don't* have the facts," he goes on in spite of himself. "I mean, the on-the-ground facts. Fact number one, most of the oil spills are the result of bunkering—do you even know what that is? It's not because of Shell's supposed negligence, which is what folks like Amnesty International and Greenpeace would have you believe. There's this ass-backward misconception that bunkering is just this small scale stuff—guys siphoning off some oil from the pipes. Sort of hit and run. But that's not what's happening at all. These are large-scale, professional criminal operations; we're talking about massive bribes to government officials, the army, you name it. It's a fucking nightmare. And there're thousands of miles of pipeline to protect. As for Saro-Wiwa—did bad stuff happen with him? I'm sure. Is there a shitload of corruption in Nigeria? You bet. Is everything basically fucked up there? Definitely. But like I say, you don't have the facts to sort that out. Hell, I'm right there staring it in the face and even I don't have the fucking facts to sort it out. What I've got is a job. Listen to me. It's a very simple job. I protect people who are doing their legitimate work from other people who want to kill them in order to keep them from doing their work. Simple as that.

"And the truth is—I'm just being frank here, okay? I'm talking like this because I want to take you seriously, Caleb—you've got it great here in Poughkeepsie. This whole fucking country's got it great and doesn't even know it. Why? Because the price for having it so great gets paid somewhere else, by somebody else, where you don't have to see it. Out of sight, out of mind. That's the fucking key to the whole shit system. Stay blind, stay deaf."

"Blood oil," Caleb says.

"Oh yeah, you found that phrase, huh? Nice phrase. Call it blood oil if you want to; you're certainly happy enough to enjoy all the benefits of blood oil back here in America. What do you think is fueling this car we're riding in? What heats your house in winter and air conditions it in the summer? What makes the plastic that's in everything you use? Even your mom's precious hybrid's running on blood oil when it's not doing its hybrid thing."

Chris knows he's bullying the deaf boy, as Caleb annoyingly keeps calling himself. He's no better than a Blackwater convoy charging through an intersection, guns blazing. At the same time, he's strangely excited Caleb's so outgunned. The deaf boy twists his hands together, his face squinches in a mobile frown, and for the moment he's completely tongue-tied. Bullying the deaf boy sort of stirs Chris. It's some kind of revenge—for what, exactly, he doesn't care to know. And it's giving him the beginnings of a hard-on.

"It just seems like," Caleb stutters—in confusion, in full retreat—"I don't know, don't we need to try really hard to think about the consequences of what we're doing in the world?"

Already Chris's excitement begins to falter. He hates it that he's gone after the boy so brutally. "Look," he says, "I couldn't agree more. We all need to take more responsibility. I didn't mean to get into an argument here."

He's annoyed with Lydia for having filled the kid's ear with half-truths, and even more annoyed with himself for having said too much at dinner last night.

"I guess I'm a little jumpy," he goes on. "As you grow up, you'll discover things are always a lot more complicated than you think they are. There're always more sides to a story than you can ever even guess."

"The deaf boy can take it."

"Why do you keep calling yourself that? It's just weird. In fact, I find it sort of manipulative, if you want to hear the truth."

"I can hear the truth just fine," Caleb says.

They've been following rural back roads for several minutes; a right turn leads them to the entrance to the golf course. They ascend a hill. Manicured links stretch out on either side. Golf carts and golfers dot the landscape. A few artfully placed clumps of trees and strategically located lesions of sand punctuate the rolling greenswards. He never goes anywhere near the pitiful golf course at the Shell compound. He hates amenities meant to foster the forlorn illusion of home. At the same time he understands how necessary they are, the Burger Kings and Pizza Huts of the Green Zone, the nine holes in the Rumukoroshe Residential Area. But this is a real golf course, not a simulacrum, and his gut instinct is to hate it as well.

Their chauffeur, an elderly goateed fellow elegantly turned out in a black suit with white gloves and a classic driving cap, opens the door for them with an impeccable nod and a crisp "Gentlemen! You're both looking splendid this afternoon."

Once they're underway, he asks, "Music, fellows? I suggest some Vivaldi to set the mood. And, obviously, you should help yourself to some champagne."

A half bottle sits on ice. Two flutes await.

"Sure," Rafa says. "Why not."

Sprightly music floods the Rolls. They float along Pough-keepsie's streets, a movie with a soundtrack. Anatole's second glass of bubbly, and already he's feeling giddy. Whether this bodes well or ill he isn't sure, but it does calm the swarm of butterflies fluttering in his stomach.

"Just so you know," their driver says. "This is a historic occasion. My first gay wedding."

"Ours too," Anatole tells him.

"Touché. The name's Bill, by the way. And don't get me wrong. I'm straight as straight can be. Happily married for thirty-seven years. Three beautiful kids. But as far as I'm concerned, it's an honor to be doing my part for this marriage equality thing. It was a great day for New York when that law went through. Okay, there, I've had my say. I'll let you ride in peace."

"We're happy to talk," Anatole tells him. "I mean, we've been together twelve years. It's not like we have any last-minute secrets to confess to each other before the wedding."

Rafa touches his arm. "Oh, yes, we do. I was intending to tell you."

"What?"

"Just kidding."

"Don't scare me like that."

"I was just going to say, I've never ridden in a Rolls-Royce before."

"Some ride, huh?" says Bill.

"Some ride," Rafa says, knocking back the rest of his champagne. He's nervous too, Anatole thinks. Good. I'm not the only one.

"You know," Bill tells them, "I had a buddy in the army who was gay—queer, we used to say back in those days. But we didn't think a thing of it. A really decent guy. We were all just like brothers. A family, you know? I never knew what happened to him afterward. This was Nam. Lots of good guys died there. But this is your wedding day. I don't mean to darken it or anything. This is your happy day, and you've got my heartfelt blessing. Not that that means anything—just ask my wife!"

Even Bill's a little bit nervous.

She can tell, as Caleb and Chris emerge from Chris's rental, that there's no rapport between them whatsoever. They come toward her, Chris strolling, hands in his pockets, with a look of distracted indifference, Caleb loping in that coltish, agitated way he has. She's not surprised: when Caleb goes on the warpath, as he so clearly intended to do, watch out. She admires that about him, though it causes more than its share of strife around the house. She'd like to think he gets that headstrong streak from her, but she suspects she's just trying to console herself for the wistful realization that Caleb gets along with his dad much better than he does with her. Tom tends to indulge his son, while she's probably unnecessarily hard on him.

"So," she says, "I see everybody's arrived in one piece. How'd you two make out?"

"Fine," Caleb reports with a shrug that says everything.

"Come here," she tells him as he begins to wander off. (She's perversely pleased with him.) "Your tie's crooked." He squirms. "There," she says. "Now you look presentable."

"Mama, I want to go check out the golf course."

"Don't go too far. The wedding's going to start soon."

Actually, they've arrived a bit on the early side—only a handful of others are milling about, a few she knows, most she doesn't. Anatole's clients have never struck her as a particularly interesting lot. She finds it hard to believe that he actually likes many of them, but he protests he does, and maybe he's telling the truth.

She can't help but feel the slightest twinge of envy at the sight of rows of folding chairs neatly aligned on a flawless lawn facing the white pergola under which Anatole and Rafa will be united in matrimony against an impeccable backdrop of rolling fairways.

Stop, she tells herself. Her own wedding was everything it needed to be and more. Besides, how many gallons of herbicide are needed to produce this unnatural landscape? How much water does this waste? Her wedding with Tom left a *much* smaller carbon footprint.

"Well, that was just strange, Lydia," Chris says. "So why'd you put him up to it?"

"I didn't put him up to anything."

"But you know what I'm talking about."

"Caleb's an intense young man. As I'm sure you found out! Imagine what it's like being his mother."

Tom and Craig are settling Mrs. Forman into her wheelchair. "If I'd known I was going to live this long," she tells them, "I'd have taken better care of myself."

"You're in great shape," Craig reassures her.

"You've got a problem with me, don't you?" Chris addresses Lydia, speaking quietly. "I did something to you that you haven't forgiven me for."

"This really isn't the time to talk about it, okay? So Craig," she says brightly, "you'll be okay with looking after Mom?"

"Ready to rock and roll," he proclaims, grasping the handles of the wheelchair and swiveling it.

"Stop that," warns Mrs. Forman. "You're making my head swim."

"It's time for Craig to do his part," Lydia tells Chris confidentially. "Tom and I have to deal with her on a daily basis."

"But we *will* talk about all this at some point. Yes?"

"We'll see," she tells him. "What a weird weekend this is, don't you think?"

"No weirder than the rest of life."

"Speak for yourself. Now let me introduce you to my friends

here. This is Marla Wong, and her husband Bobby. Marla's done the flowers for the wedding. She's the Emeril Lagasse of flowers."

Chris has no idea who that is, but there's no chance to ask.

Rafa's sisters have arrived—Paloma and Chiara, both great beauties, their handsome husbands whose names Lydia can't quite remember, and their exquisite, well-behaved children whose names she hasn't even tried remembering, but it's OK, the sisters thoughtfully introduce them: Jeremias, Yesenia, Elian, Nikauris. And of course there's Miosotis, artfully turned out, and still wearing those god-awful crocs.

Chris isn't quite sure why, but he's grateful for Miosotis's presence; for some reason he thinks of her as an ally.

He notes that sixteen-year-old Elian is something of a stunner—dark-eyed, dark-haired, an adolescent aristocrat in bearing and demeanor, worthy heir of his grandmother's fine features. At least the landscape won't be entirely bereft of vistas.

In the distance he can see Caleb wandering alone on a carpet of monotonous, uninflected green. And thinking what?

Chris is feeling thoroughly burned.

From a hundred yards away, the gathering looks strange and comical. Cars pour into the parking lot. People greet each other, or stream toward the Clubhouse. Caleb relishes the silence out here on the fairway. He'd rather be playing than attending a wedding. New situations worry him. He's taken this opportunity of solitude to brace himself for what's coming. His dad understands, his mama doesn't always. She pushes relentlessly for him to be normal, but the fact is he's not normal and never will be.

He's feeling aggrieved by any number of things.

He's aggrieved that Chris talked down to him the way he did. Maybe bringing up Shell Oil and the Niger Delta wasn't such a good idea, but what was he supposed to do? Pretend he didn't know anything? Adults don't realize the world's gone transparent. There's no hiding anymore, and he can tell that this Chris character's all about hiding.

Though he knows it's totally irrational, he's aggrieved his mama has a past that manages to stay maddeningly opaque in this Internet age. *So who was this Chris?* he asked on the way home last night. A friend, she said. A close friend who let your mama and Anatole down very badly a long time ago and still won't own up to it.

When he asked *How?* she patted his knee and said, There's things you don't need to know about your mama.

He's also aggrieved that Modder Spook isn't playing at the wedding. His bandmates haven't even been invited. They sent Anatole the YouTube link to their spooklear wedding song yesterday, and he hasn't even responded. Maybe they should've sent it earlier, but then they didn't finish it till yesterday. Maybe if they'd sent it earlier he'd have loved it so much he'd have begged them to play at the wedding, instead of some lame DJ spinning tunes nobody much cares about. But Caleb senses this isn't the way things work in the adult world. (He can see Anatole and Rafa, trailed by a photographer, as they stroll hand in hand over the little wooden bridge, where they pause, pose, then resume their slow progress, now with the photographer in front, walking backward, clicking away.) This is the big, ongoing problem: figuring out how things work in the adult world. It's not just deaf boys who have this problem; he has a feeling his bandmates are often at a loss as well.

Stop, he tells himself. He concentrates on listening to the sound of a bird calling. He doesn't know what kind of bird it is, but if he listens carefully, he can differentiate its call from everything else in the confounding mesh of distant, vaguely unpleasant noises.

He'll never forget that moment when he was first able to say to himself, about a sound he'd been hearing for years, *So that's what people mean when they talk about a bird singing.*

Chris can't get the image out of his head: Lydia insisting on straightening her son's tie. And Caleb, still partly feral, which is what he loves so much about boys, resisting. He wonders when Leigh would have lost that feral touch.

Last night, safely returned to the Inn at the Falls, he went online to scan the latest headlines at Nigeria News. Same old, same old—*Man Electrocuted Vandalising Installations of Power Holding Company; Boko Haram: Nigeria Will Know No Peace Till Christians Convert to Islam; Lawmaker Promises to Surrender N93m Bribe; Student's Head Slashed Open, Brain Spills Out as Cultists Take Over Enugu: Graphic Photos!* When he'd had enough of that, and having mostly finished the vodka, he Googled "Leigh Gerrard."

Thank fuck for somewhat unusual names. Many Leigh Gerrards out there—Jessica Leigh Gerrard, Brittany Leigh Gerrard, Annabel Leigh Gerrard, all female. But intriguingly, he found a Leigh Gerrard living in Newburgh, New York, twenty miles south of Poughkeepsie.

Age 44. Social Worker. Likes Madonna, Pet Shop Boys, Lady Gaga, Scissor Sisters, The Funky Knickerbocker Café, Harvey Dark's Homespun Tattoos, Barack Obama, Queers for Economic Justice.

Could it be that Our Boy of the Mall has been hiding in plain sight?

The rows of chairs have filled. The speakers on either side of the pergola have begun to dispense Anatole's longtime favorite, Pachelbel's *Canon*, something of a cliché, but can anything so beautiful ever really be a cliché? Feeling very much the outcast, Chris sits with Lydia and her family. Caleb's at the far end of the assemblage, out of his sight line, for which Chris is wistfully grateful. From her wheelchair Mrs. Forman keeps asking, in a too-loud voice, "What are we doing here? Why are we doing this?" It's a question Chris is asking as well.

The two rows in front of them are occupied by Rafa's large family, and Chris has a nice, side-angled view of Elian.

Though he's had enough of boys for the moment.

And now the wedding party, preceded by the photographer walking backward, processes down the center aisle: first the minister, a short-haired, round-faced, beaming dyke in a white and gold cassock and glittering cat's-eye glasses, then the attendants, Paloma and Chiara in long matching turquoise skirts, accompanied by their thoroughly outshone husbands (though Marla's marvelous boutonnières, Lydia thinks, lift them out of the entirely ordinary), followed by Anatole's slightly uncomfortable-looking brother Declan and his mousy wife, Tabitha. One of Rafa's pretty little nieces has been designated ring bearer, and she precedes the two grooms, who stride forth boldly, arm in arm, both grinning as if to say, *We own this day.* Their outfits are over-the-top amazing; they look like they've stepped out of one of those steampunk novels Tom likes to read; Lydia loves it that they're managing all this solemnity with a dash of irony and flair.

Chris thinks they look like a pair of middle-aged peacocks. This ceremony set amid the pampered emerald swales of a golf course—he sees it as if from above, a drone's-eye view. As Reverend Judy, that's how she's introduced herself, begins the opening prayer, he remembers the last wedding he attended— Baghdad, 2008 or so, nice kid named Johnny. Chris and his guys had gotten Johnny's patrol out of a fix once, an impromptu shoot-'em-up near the Dora refinery, and after that Johnny always seemed to feel he owed Chris one. Tennessee boy with an endearing gap-toothed grin and an enormous tattoo on his left arm, one of those abstract, black, faintly menacing talismans favored by scared kids trying to show their toughness.

He's always found tattoos repellent, in large part because he imagines how they'll look in thirty years (also because his dad has one, vintage USAF Korea, now blurred and sad). But of course when you're in a war zone you aren't exactly worried about thirty years from now.

Noor was one of those lucky young women with a job in the Green Zone and a single purpose: to procure by whatever means possible a one-way ticket out of hell. She arrived on the chosen day with luggage in tow, and after the briefest of civil ceremonies in one of the wrecked, grandiose state rooms at the Presidential Palace, she was whisked along with her American catch via armed convoy down Route Irish, that deadliest stretch of highway in the world, to BIA and their flight to Amman.

Two weeks later Johnny was back from leave, and Noor was ensconced with his bewildered parents in Murfreesboro—while her own distraught family cursed the Yankee seducers.

Paloma is reading from Corinthians. She's got a great speaking voice, Lydia thinks, and the passage is lovely:

*If I have the gift of prophecy and can fathom all mysteries and all knowledge, and if I have a faith that can move mountains, but do not have love, I am nothing.*

Lydia can practically hear her mother thinking *goyische schmaltz* and realizes that, except for a four- or five-year hiatus back in the eighties, she's lived with her mother her entire life. How pathetic. She knows her mother's every last tic and eccentricity. Doesn't getting to know someone too well reduce them to exactly that? Why put yourself through such exacting knowledge? Why marry Tom, and bear Caleb, only to end up knowing them too well? Wasn't that Leigh's allure—she hates to be thinking of him, now of all times—that you could never get to the bottom of whoever he was? But that's ridiculous. She knew him for three months. The shine would have worn off soon enough. And it's a tribute to Tom's rock-steadiness that his admittedly somewhat dull luster has remained just that—dull, but a luster nonetheless. For which she's grateful.

She's touched almost to tears to see Craig holding their mother's hand. Though Mom seems to have dozed off in the warm June sun.

*And now these three remain*, Paloma reads aloud: *faith, hope and love. But the greatest of these is love.*

As far as Anatole's concerned, this passage is like the Pachelbel: nothing's more flawless. He wonders how many in the audience remember that he read those same verses, fifteen years ago, at Daniel's memorial service. Many of Reflexion's loyal ladies are here today, just as they were then.

He'll never forget that final afternoon in the hospital room at St. Francis: Daniel shrunken, delirious, shitting blood. His dad had driven down from Rochester. They hadn't been in touch in years, father and son, they'd had a catastrophic falling out shortly after Daniel graduated from high school, and through the course of his illness Daniel hadn't shown any interest in getting back in touch. *I hope he's dead*, was all he'd say when Anatole brought the subject up. *As I'm sure he hopes I'm dead. Well, at least one of us is getting his wish. But then maybe he's beat me to it. Oh happy world. We both get our wish!* Daniel had never been particularly bitter, but he turned bitter toward the end. Who could blame him? Certainly Anatole didn't; he blamed the virus, the drugs, the failing body, the increasingly flickering mind, but not Daniel. Still, it was dispiriting. *I wonder whose virus I caught?* Daniel would say, cranky and bored. *I hope it was somebody good-looking, not one of the way too many trolls I woke up next to. No, what am I saying? I hope it was one of the trolls. I don't want the good-looking ones to have gotten it. They're already an endangered species as it is.*

In the end, he changed his mind about seeing his dad. *Go ahead, get in touch with him. Let him know what's happening. He can come down and see me if he wants. He can gloat. It'll do his heart good to see me like this.* And his dad made the trip down—arriving, as it turned out, with only hours to spare. If Daniel was the most fabulous creature who ever sashayed through an open door, his dad was the grayest, most retiring shade imaginable. His suit sagged. He wore his meager hair in the most pathetic of comb-overs (Daniel had long ago lost his golden mane to the chemo). He seemed way too mild-mannered ever to have said or done the things Daniel claimed of him.

*Whether he'll recognize you is anybody's guess,* Anatole warned Daniel's father. *He's been going in and out of a coma for a couple of days.*

The timid little man drew close. Daniel lay on his back with his eyes—huge and haunted—wide open, staring at the ceiling.

*Daniel,* his father said. *Can you hear me? It's your dad.*

Daniel turned his head slowly.

*Hey, old buddy,* said his dad.

A grin Anatole can only describe as devilish appeared on Daniel's lips. He reached over and grabbed his dad's crotch.

Be in the moment, Anatole scolds himself. This isn't the time to be remembering all that. For a moment he panics, almost a feeling of free fall, the sudden anxiety that he's completely lost his place in the ceremony's script—but he hasn't spaced out for long, it seems. Chiara is reading Rafa's favorite Neruda poem, first in Spanish, then in English. Neruda's poems always leave Anatole a little cold, not that Rafa hasn't tried patiently to explain why they're so beautiful and full of meaning—just as he's tried patiently without much success to teach Anatole some Spanish. *Just speaking English is enough of a challenge for me* is Anatole's excuse. To which Rafa always responds, *You have no idea what you're missing. English is a head language; Spanish is a heart language. I've always thought of you as a heart language kind of person.*

Anatole's having a very hard time staying in the moment.

★ ★ ★

Bernardo's come, and Lanny, and Josh. As Rafa looks out at the assembled throng, he's grateful they're here. One of the blessings of his life is that he's still friends with each of them, Bernardo with his passion for dancing (even around the apartment, with no music on, folding the laundry or stir-frying vegetables, always dancing to some rhythm in his head), Lanny with his flamboyant suits and his lovely, purring sluttishness in bed, shy bespectacled Josh with his serious photography hobby (and, no, Rafa doesn't regret posing nude on several occasions, though he does hope the video they made on a lark one Saturday afternoon remains forgotten in whatever closet it ended up in). He's had a terrifically lucky life. He's slipped past tragedy where others got caught. He doesn't think about Jupiter Nuñez much anymore, but he used to all the time. For years Jupiter was the shadow he couldn't get out from under. Maybe all first loves are like that. But not all first loves end so badly. He knows he should be paying more attention to the service—it's his *wedding,* for God's sake!—but this is important too. This taking stock, this solemn summing up of the past. This homage. It's a very serious and holy thing, marriage, but this secret ceremony, the one in his head, is just as important as the one his friends and relatives and husband are witnessing, and he wonders what secret ceremony is unscrolling in Anatole's head at this very moment. He'll ask him later, because one of the great things about their relationship is that they can ask each other the silliest or most serious questions without embarrassment.

Oh, Jupiter, Jupiter. My stupid amigo. Señor Throw It All Away—and for what? Nobody was more handsome, with your movie-star face and muscular arms and runner's legs and swimmer's waist, and inside all that a soul so sweet and lunatic. But who knew that, when we were sixteen and seventeen and eighteen and used to go up to Bennett Park after school to smoke a little dope, shoot the breeze, take in the view south to the George Washington Bridge gleaming in the light and west to the frowning brow of the Palisades across the river, and you, always the history buff with so much fantastic knowledge stored in your good-looking head, would tell me in mesmerizing detail about the *chevaux de frise* the Americans laid across the Hudson to block the British ships (*chevaux de frise*—by what right did a seventeen-year-old kid from Washington Heights know such words?), how in the end the British captured Fort Washington with the help of Hessian mercenaries, how the American prisoners—thousands of them!—were interned on prison ships in New York Harbor, where most of them died.

Then maybe they'd make out a little, nothing too serious, some kissing, some groping and fondling, the occasional blowjob—they never got around to actually fucking, which Rafa sort of regrets but sort of not. Those idyllic pre-fucking days—days he can't return to.

Of course they drifted apart. It was inevitable. By the mid-eighties crack had taken over the neighborhood; the Red Top Gang ruled; guys their age were getting gunned down in the streets. Miosotis absolutely insisted he go away to college, while Jupiter chose to remain in the city ("You're not about to get me to move to the country!"), attending CUNY and wandering deeper and deeper into the gay club scene downtown; if drugs hadn't killed him, AIDS would have. Rafa's always credited SUNY New Paltz with saving his life.

"The text of this afternoon's sermon," Reverend Judy announces, "is drawn from the seventh chapter of the Gospel of Matthew. Jesus said to his disciples, 'Therefore everyone who hears these words of mine and puts them into practice is like a wise man who built his house on the rock. The rain came down, the streams rose, and the winds blew and beat against that house; yet it did not fall, because it had its foundation on the rock. But everyone who hears these words of mine and does not put them into practice is like a foolish man who built his house on sand. The rain came down, the streams rose, and the winds blew and beat against that house, and it fell with a great crash.'

"Here I like to think Jesus is just speaking of what he knows—after all, he was a carpenter by profession. But, of course, he's not just talking about good building practices 101..."

Chris is drifting off. He can only suffer so much of this. One of the few things he gives his self-absorbed parents any credit for is that they never inflicted religion on him when he was growing up. Their own religion, if you can call it that, consisted of Sunday morning tennis followed by cocktails at noon (martini for him, highball for her). He never even set foot inside a church till he was in high school and a boy he found intriguing (that was the word he used as a teenager when examining his inconvenient feelings) invited him to come to Mass with him at St. Andrew's. Not that it led to anything the least bit intriguing.

He's surprised Anatole's chosen such a religious wedding, but he guesses there was always some religious impulse at work in him, however disguised and even sacrilegious—"Our Boy of the Mall" and all that.

"So yes," Reverend Judy is saying, "it's important to live in a well-built house that's not situated in the floodplain, but there's another dwelling that's even more important to our overall well-being than just the physical roof above our heads. Which brings me to the reason that we're gathered here this beautiful and joyous afternoon."

Lydia can see her mother's come awake, but that doesn't mean she's listening to the sermon. She's taken a piece of paper from her sweater pocket, unfolds it in trembling hands, with excruciating slowness, as she does everything these days, and reads it over intently, pausing to look up now and then and mouth a few words before returning to her perusal. Lydia's curious. Has her mom copied out a Hebrew prayer to guard against this *goyim* nonsense? But that would be giving her too much credit. She has trouble even remembering it's Anatole and Rafa's wedding they're attending. Who knows what nonsense is scrawled there.

"This strong relationship has weathered storms in the past, severe storms, and there'll undoubtedly be storms in the future." Reverend Judy's half-heard words, accompanied by a knowing murmur in the audience, bring Chris back to attention. "Pain and suffering," she continues, "come to each and every one of us. Life is turmoil and tumult. Make no mistake about it. You can't avoid the storms in a relationship"—the grooms' tense brilliant unwavering smiles give nothing away—"but you can make sure your relationship, your love, is built on solid rock rather than shifting sand. And that is what I have witnessed these two beautiful men work at building, year after year after year, steadfast carpenters skillfully, diligently, *reverently* laying the foundations of their present and future happiness."

Well, Chris thinks. The things I don't know.

Then, finally, the moment they've all come to witness. Everything else was just prelude. Now the grooms move to the fore. They stand on either side of Reverend Judy, facing each other. There's no drama, per se, but there *is* a barely perceptible heightening. You can feel it ripple through the audience. There's an expectant hush. People sit up straighter, they lean forward a bit. This is the part no one wants to miss (except perhaps Mrs. Forman, still preoccupied with that piece of paper and its contents).

What will Reverend Judy say? Lydia wonders. I pronounce you husband and husband? Everyone will get an illicit little thrill out of that. They'll feel a lingering qualm (Tom, Declan, probably most of those Republican husbands), or they'll feel a warm splash of self-righteousness (Rafa's sisters, the Republican wives: how progressive we are!); none of them will feel (except maybe Caleb) they're witnessing a moment that's entirely normal or ordinary. Maybe in ten years, or twenty, but not in 2012. At least that's what Lydia tells herself.

Chris, meanwhile, is longing for a smoke and a drink. Would it be wrong to light up a cigarette? They're outdoors, after all. In Iraq there'd be no question, but then in Iraq they'd celebrate the conclusion of the wedding by firing their Kalashnikovs skyward with joyous abandon.

Really—it's an abomination, he thinks. There's nothing so pathetic as two grown men getting married. On a golf course, no less. Is this what Anatole's once adventurous life has come to?

He can't take his eyes off Elian's profile. The contemplation is purely aesthetic. Sure, he can fantasize, but the wolf isn't stupid; the wolf knows how to behave among the humans. The wolf has had years of practice.

With a bit of urging from Rafa, the pretty little ring bearer comes forward.

"These wedding rings," Reverend Judy explains, "crafted with love by Rafa's amazingly talented mother, Miosotis, represent unity, wholeness, the perfect unending circle. They symbolize the journey Anatole and Rafa have begun today. It will be a journey marked by laughter and sorrow, wonder and tears, celebration and disappointment, joy and grief. But wherever the journey takes you, Rafa and Anatole, always remember that it's Love that brought you to the beginning of the journey, and it's Love that will feed and power and sustain you on your way. Never forget that Love is the only thing that makes possible the rock that makes possible the house that survives the storm.

"Anatole Prowse and Rafael Pujol, as you have consented together in lawful wedlock and have pledged your faith to each other, and have declared the same by the joining of hands and the giving and receiving of rings, by the powers vested in me I now pronounce you married for life. You may kiss each other to seal this unbreakable bond."

And kiss they do, prolonged and deep and theatrical (they're loving it, for the most part the audience is loving it too, though some secretly cringe), two middle-aged guys in their dandy getup with their complicated and not untroubled pasts, at last living entirely in the moment as the photographer insatiably clicks away until that moment comes to an end. "Wow!" Anatole has to say, a whisper meant only for Rafa's ears. "Just wow!"

"You wait till tonight, Mr. Kitten. Just you wait."

There's still some silliness to be gotten through. The unity candle is lit, its flame invisible in the bright afternoon sunlight (though clouds are piling up to the west). Then one of Rafa's nieces plays a mercifully short violin piece. (Caleb can't really make out what it's supposed to sound like, but he's still pissed that nobody even thought to ask for Modder Spook.) Everyone begins to stir a bit. Surely it's over now? Cocktails and canapés await in the clubhouse. But Anatole has something to say. He clears his throat to focus everyone's attention.

"This is such a joyful day for both of us." His voice trembles. "The best day of our lives. But we didn't think we could end without remembering our loved ones who are no longer with us. So if you'll bear with us for a moment, Rafa and I would like to ask you to honor them now." People look at their programs. This isn't listed. It injects a note of uncertainty into the ceremony's well-oiled machinery. Even Reverend Judy in her cassock and cat glasses looks surprised.

"Daniel Francoeur," Anatole says gravely.

"Jupiter Nuñez," Rafa intones.

"Holden Wright."

"Dominic Sorge."

"Tommy Palmer and Eric Naughton."

"My father, Bernard Pujol. Uncle Elian."

"Peaches."

"Aunt Hallelujah."

"Roger Wu. Benjamin Rosenthal. Susan Watson Kemp. Emily Travis. Nushawn Hobbs."

"The Araujo and Travares families and everyone else who perished aboard American Airlines Flight 587."

Daniel's is the only name Chris recognizes, though, on second thought, wasn't Peaches that flamboyant African American who used to hang out at Bertie's, along with that other drag queen, what was her name, Flame Azalea? And it's not clear whether Aunt Hallelujah was a relative of Rafa's or yet another drag queen.

The length of the list startles him. Many are doubtless dead of AIDS. He hasn't fully registered the war that's been going on in the years since he left.

Two names, Lydia notes grimly, are conspicuously missing.

"Let us all pray," Anatole and Rafa say in rehearsed unison, "for their beautiful and loving souls to rest in eternal peace."

The audience, which has caught its collective breath for the duration of this detour, exhales. The loudspeakers play a brassy recessional, and a serious-looking Anatole and Rafa, as if conscious of the solemn note they've ended on, file down the grassy aisle followed by a beaming Reverend Judy and the mostly giddy entourage of attendants (a stricken-looking Declan is the exception), and that's it, Chris thinks, it's over.

Or as Reverend Judy would have it, the journey begins.


Inside the clubhouse, Chris steers clear of the long line of people waiting to sign the guest register and instead heads for the open bar, where he orders a double Stoli on the rocks. Attractive young waiters bearing silver trays tempt him. "Goat cheese crostini topped with pesto & eggplant salad," murmurs one. "Asian marinated beef–wrapped asparagus tips," purrs another.

He wonders whether any of them might be amenable to making a few extra bucks after all this is over. Wouldn't that be rich? I went to Anatole's wedding and all I got was this handsome waiter.

That one whose name tag reads QUINN, for instance, is a real gem.

He tells himself he's having these thoughts because, frankly, he's bored out of his mind.

Side tables are laden with cheese and fruit and antipasto. Platters of crudités beckon. The raw bar offers jumbo shrimp, oysters, and clams on ice. The guests, many of whom could afford to lose twenty pounds or so, heap their plates full.

He escapes to the outdoor patio, where he finds Lydia and her family ensconced at a table. She and Caleb are drinking soda, but Tom's having a beer and Craig, who used to be so handsome, is sipping a martini. Mrs. Forman dozes in her wheelchair.

"I thought that was a very nice service," Lydia says. "I imagine you found it very dull and bourgeois."

"Lydia," Chris tells her. "That's not really fair, now is it?" Though she's hit the mark with uncanny precision. "I'm delighted for Anatole and Rafa. Why shouldn't I be?"

She looks at him narrowly, and sips her soda through a straw.

"Just checking," she says. "I'm still getting my bearings, you know."

"You two," Tom says. "Were you always like this?"

"You had to be there," Lydia tells him. "It all played out differently in 1985. Even the light was different. Everything was in Technicolor back then. Emotions, most of all. Now, if you'll excuse me, I desperately need to pee."

Actually, she doesn't, but Chris has flustered her. She has no idea why she's just said what she said. Tom's right, of course: it was completely uncalled for. If Caleb were to do such a thing, she'd call him on it in an instant. Then why can't she control herself?

Chris is a reproach, somehow. A reminder that she hasn't always been who she's become.

It turns out she has to pee after all, which at least makes everything a little less of a sham than it might otherwise be.

On her way back from the ladies' room, she pauses to peer into the empty banquet hall—just to make sure everything's ready, not that it isn't all completely out of her hands. The central dance floor is an expanse of polished blond wood; on the carpeted perimeter, fifteen round tables are gleamingly set for dinner. At the center of each, Marla's bouquets provide bursts of summery color. It's a stage set awaiting the arrival of the actors who will give it life and meaning, but for the moment she savors the soothing emptiness. She notices something out of the corner of her eye. She's not sure what it is, a flicker of movement, and then she sees: a bird has flown into the room and can't find its way out. A small brown bird—a sparrow, she thinks. It flutters wildly, trying to fly through windows whose panes rebuff it with a disconcerting thump. She keeps expecting it to knock itself out but it doesn't. It tests window after window with the same result. Part of her wants to pretend she hasn't noticed; just to leave and let someone else deal with it—it's not exactly her responsibility, after all, and there was certainly a time in her life when she'd have done just that. But she's not that Lydia anymore.

In the corridor, the banquet manager is giving last minute instructions to the wait staff. His mustache is the kind nobody's sported since the seventies, though he himself looks no older than forty. She finds it oddly endearing.

"Um, there's a bird trapped in there," she tells him.

"Oh great," he says. "It'll be in a panic. It'll be shitting all over everything. But don't worry. These things happen. We'll take care of it. Thanks for mentioning it."

"No problem," she tells him. She doesn't believe in omens or signs or anything like that, and besides, what would a bird fluttering around an empty banquet hall be an omen of anyway?

She remembers, the morning of her own wedding, she found a dead hummingbird lying on the back patio. This doesn't even rate as a coincidence, but she's vaguely disquieted nonetheless. She thinks back to the house built on rock, the house built on sand. Anatole and Rafa have had their problems, Reverend Judy even alluded to them (was that really necessary?), but Lydia's not going to feel qualms, not today. It's not the past that matters; it's the future.

Then why does Chris agitate and irritate her so?

When she gets back to the table, she can sense he and Tom have been struggling to find something to talk about. Chris is telling her husband, quite emphatically, "Look, the AK-47 is the best assault rifle out there, bar none. Its aim is true, it doesn't break down, you can treat it like shit and it's still there for you at the end of the day. Sure, the M4's good, but it's finicky, it just doesn't pack the same kind of punch. That old Soviet philosophy: you don't want to just take your guy out, you want to blow a hole clear through him so you can take out the guy behind him as well."

Chris, who used to talk caressingly about the twelve different live versions of a David Bowie song.

"The AK's only drawback is the muzzle flashes," Chris continues tediously. "Those can give your position away. Otherwise, it's about as perfect a machine as human beings have designed."

"Mama," Caleb says, "I'm going for a walk, okay?"

"Sure, honey. But we're having dinner soon. Don't go far."

"It's a golf course," he tells her. "Wherever I go, you'll be able to see me."

He needs to be alone for a while, he thinks. All these competing complicated sounds are confusing and distressing.

Plus he doesn't like this Chris. The way he brags, the way he's all about hurting other people. Including his mama. It's nothing overt, but he can tell. Chris has hurt his mama badly in the past, which is something his dad doesn't seem to be able to see for some reason. It's dispiriting how much adults miss about each other.

"It's too crowded here," observes Mrs. Forman, as uninterested as Caleb in the stream of information issuing from Chris's mouth. "It's worse than the mall. I don't see how Anatole can stand it. All these strangers at his wedding."

"Mom," Lydia reminds her, "they're not strangers. Believe it or not, Anatole and Rafa know every single person here."

Mrs. Forman looks at her with that narrowing squint which means she doesn't really believe her daughter.

"Well, I'm freezing out here."

"Do you want to go inside?"

"Please. I hope they've got a nice fire going in there."

"It's *June*, for God's sake."

Indoors is noisy and crowded. People have spilled out of the bar. A group clusters around the register, signing their names. After a quick reconnoiter—the empty banquet hall won't do; her mom hates big open spaces as much as she hates crowds—Lydia decides to park her in the Grooms' Suite (the sign on the door having been thoughtfully converted from "Bridal Suite"). "Really, I'm not punishing her," she explains to the banquet manager. "She suffers from acute agoraphobia. She won't mind the seclusion one bit."

"Just checking," he tells her. "I got to keep my eye on everything around here. Crazy stuff happens. One time a raccoon wandered in. You can imagine how that went over."

"And the bird?"

"Oh yeah. The bird. Don't worry. José took care of it."

"Took care of it," she says. "Meaning what?"

"Whacked it down with a broom. No, just kidding. Not to worry. We opened some of the windows and the little fellow flew right out. Happens all the time."

Elian's playing a game of tag with his sisters and cousins out on the lawn beyond the patio. He's "it," apparently, and the girls run from him in giddy panic. It's clear they adore him, and Chris notes how the boy almost tags them, but then barely misses on purpose in order to prolong the chase, their squealing ecstasy. He's discarded his tie, and his shirttails have come undone in his exertions. Already he's rehearsing the heartbreaker he'll become. It makes Chris feel very old, very used up. At the same time it gladdens his heart.

Now that he's finished talking about guns, and there's been a full-scale desertion of their table, he's at a loss for what to talk to Tom about next.

Where's Lydia when he needs her?

"I think I'll wander off and have a cigarette," he tells Tom. "Somewhere where the smoke won't bother anybody."

As Lydia passes through the bar, Anatole's brother accosts her. He's holding a plate heaped high with goodies. "Can we talk?" he says. "I don't want to make a scene, God forbid, but that was just hurtful, don't you think? I mean, not to even mention our parents there at the end."

She's not sure what to say. *Your parents threw Anatole out of the house. They turned their backs on him.*

Declan was only in junior high at the time, he's not to be blamed for having towed the family line, and to his immense credit, once he graduated high school he reached out to his pariah brother. She's never liked him much but she has to admit he's a decent person. Years later, when their father's will left the black sheep nothing, Declan offered to split the inheritance—which Anatole declined, saying he'd respect his dad's desires even if his dad had never respected *his*. By then Reflexion was thriving, which made it easier to stand on principle.

"Our parents weren't bad people," he continues. "They did what they thought God and the Church wanted them to do. I know it was harsh, but they loved Anatole. He was the apple of their eye. I was just his dull gray shadow. They weren't ever the same afterward. They weren't ever happy again. They missed him every day for the rest of their lives."

*Then it's their own damn fault,* she wants to say. *They were fucking morons.* But what good would it do? The sins of his parents don't carry over to him—and yet they obviously do, which is why he's suffering.

"I don't know why I'm telling you all this. I know it's inappropriate, but I just have to tell somebody, and I don't feel like I can say it to Anatole."

For a moment, she thinks he might cry, but he doesn't. He looks down at the plate he's holding. "Hey, can I offer you a shrimp? They're really good. This whole spread is amazing."

"You've done the right thing so many times for Anatole," she tells him. "You're a mensch. And your brother cherishes you. It means everything to him that you and Tabitha are here today. That's all that counts, isn't it? And yes, I'll take one of those shrimp. They do look yummy."

She's watched enough nature documentaries to know the comfort our primate cousins take in grooming each other.

The waiters are asking guests to begin moving to the banquet hall.

"Look who we found in the Grooms' Suite," Anatole announces as he wheels Mrs. Forman into the banquet hall. "Stashed among the other gifts. The bestest one of all!"

She clutches the arms of her wheelchair, stares ahead wild-eyed, helpless, as if terrified at having been plucked from her lair. But she's not mad; there's no dementia, the doctor says, just the confusion that comes with great old age.

It was a few years ago that she started using that phrase— "in my great old age"—to explain the various lapses that were becoming more and more noticeable.

*Be gentle*, Lydia wants to chide Anatole. *Remember how she gets around crowds.*

But then she sees how Anatole kneels beside the wheelchair, how he strokes her mom's arm, speaks intimately to her, how her mom suddenly beams, and Lydia's not jealous, nothing like that, she just sees once again that improbable bond those two established years ago and have never relinquished, and she's glad for them, she tells herself, she's glad for them both.

The guest register lies open and unattended. He's feeling so much like a ghost right now, it might be appropriate to leave no trace at all. But that would be churlish. He writes *Chris Havilland, Rumukoroshe R. A., Port Harcourt, Rivers, Nigeria*. He's in such an odd mood that it's all he can do not to walk out the front door of the clubhouse and disappear.

Instead he finds he's been seated at a table with Tom, Caleb, Craig, and his wife, whose name he never properly caught, and several other guests he doesn't know. Disappointingly, Lydia's not with them; she's at the grooms' table, seated with Rafa's sisters, and Miosotis and Mrs. Forman, and Anatole's brother and his wife.

He tells himself he welcomes Lydia's aggression; it feels real, even bracing. He's in the mood for a confrontation, and though she doesn't know it, she's been his wife for years. Isn't it appropriate that a husband should fight every once in a while with his ghost wife?

There was an album he used to like a lot—a David Byrne/ Brian Eno collaboration called *My Life in the Bush of Ghosts*. The title was the kind of fresh and original thing Byrne was always coming up with. It was only when Chris was in Nigeria that he discovered they'd lifted the title from a Nigerian novel. No doubt Byrne and Eno would say *sampled*. But Chris sees it now for exactly what it was. The same old tired unending story: Westerners ransacking the world and feeling good about it.

He's not political. He's just a guy who does jobs. An errand boy, as he's said. But errand boys notice things as they go about their errands.

He needs to slow down on the booze.

"Just so you know," Lydia tells Anatole—she's intercepted him before he can sit down—"Your brother's a little upset right now. You might want to speak with him when you get a chance."

"He's upset? But why?" He knows his mock astonishment won't fly with Lydia for an instant. "Oh. The prayer," he says contritely. He and Rafa had talked through the list and Rafa duly pointed out the omission, but he remained adamant.

"Yeah, that," Lydia confirms.

"What was I supposed to do? I'm not a bad person, but it's not something you get over."

"I'm not criticizing you," Lydia tells him. "I mean, your feelings are what they are. You can't help that. I'm just saying, is all."

"Ugh," Anatole says. "Family. There should be a law."

"And who just got married today? Who's planning to have children in the near future?"

"I know, I know, I know. I'll talk to him. Thanks for telling me. No, really. Don't look skeptical. I mean that."

"Anatole. You know I'm totally on your side."

"Doll, if there's one thing I know." He pecks her on the cheek. "That's why Rafa's sitting on one side of me and you on the other. But can I tell you something? I was such an idiot yesterday. I sort of mentioned to Chris about wanting kids and then I totally backtracked and told him it was a joke."

"Why'd you do that?"

"I panicked. I mean, his reaction was like, *What*? And so I got flustered. And you know what I do when I get flustered."

"You act like an idiot. You were flustered a lot last night."

"Do you think so?"

She pauses to think. "Yeah," she says. "Even Rafa noticed."

"What does that mean? *Even* Rafa. Look, we'll talk about this later, okay? I think we'd better take our seats. I get the feeling we're holding things up."

Conversation around the table is spasmodic, like the electricity in Port Harcourt. Epileptic, the Nigerians call those power fluctuations.

"Red wine or white?" asks the waiter. It's Quinn, whom he had admired earlier, and whose shapely wrist Chris further admires as he pours.

There's an African saying: The lion is only happy among gazelles. Chris watches as Quinn makes his way around the table, expertly dispensing red with one hand, white with the other.

Tom sits to Chris's right, but they ran out of things to say back on the patio. Caleb's on the other side of Tom, but he's not talking either, even though a blonde woman with an orange tanning salon complexion is trying mightily to engage him. The man who's presumably her husband peruses, with a frown, the marriage equality card that has been left by each place setting. Next to him two other couples, who seem on good terms with one another, form an exclusive conversational bloc, which leaves the fellow to Chris's left. Holding out a clammy hand for Chris to take, he introduces himself as Lanny. He's mid-fortyish, with dyed black hair, tweezered eyebrows, mannered sideburns. His suit is lemon yellow, his tie sky blue. He exudes the stench of cologne. Who on earth, Chris wonders, was in charge of the seating chart? Middle-aged gay men hold no interest for him whatsoever. In fact (he casts a look at Anatole and Rafa animatedly holding court at their table), they're probably his least favorite category of persons on the planet.

Waiters descend on the tables, delivering plates of mixed baby greens dressed with slivers of avocado, lobes of orange, crumbles of gorgonzola. Already stuffed with a wealth of hors d'oeuvres, the guests stalwartly tuck in as a silky, heavily miked voice wafts through the banquet hall.

"Welcome, everybody, to the celebration. My name's Marlon LeFevre, and I'm gonna be your special MC/DJ taking you through the happy events of this evening. I hope everybody's comfortable, hungry, feeling no pain. We got a lotta things to celebrate. And starting us off this evening is the lovely Lydia Daniels, who's gonna propose a toast to our handsome newlyweds."

Taking a deep breath, Lydia stands. She hates and also doesn't entirely hate being the center of the room's attention. "Okay, guys," she says in a too-loud voice. "I've been asked to give the toast. Why me, you might ask. Well, the simple answer is: without me, this grand day would never be taking place. I introduced these two. And now they're paying me back by making me speak in public, which is something I definitely don't like to do."

"Tell them how you introduced us," Rafa urges. "You'll all see how wicked clever she is."

Lydia beams; she can't help herself. "Well, I *was* rather clever, if I say so myself. I'd been trying to get Anatole to date for years, and I could tell I was starting to break down his defenses."

"She was starting to get on my nerves, is what she means," Anatole says.

"Yeah, well, that was all part of the plan. I had Rafa in mind for Anatole all along. I mean, how could I not, right? But I also knew Anatole, and I knew if I just introduced the two of them outright, no matter how dreamy Rafa was, he'd never go for it. So I set him up on a date with this other guy, who I knew would be a disaster."

"That he was," Anatole confirms.

The audience is loving it. It's like an intimate conversation shared among a hundred and fifty close friends. The waiters stand in the doorway, listening. Is this their first gay wedding? One boy barely suppresses hysterical giggles. The others are more circumspect. The beautiful one, "Quinn, is utterly impassive. Chris has seldom felt quite so alone.

"So after that spectacular fiasco," Lydia continues, "I came back to him with Rafa. And of course he said, Why would I want to do this again? I'm so over dating. It's the narrow single bed for me. You all know how dramatic Anatole can be. And so I told him, Try it once more. And if it doesn't work out, I'll stop."

"She should be a used car salesman," Anatole says.

"Preowned," Tom mutters, so only Chris can hear.

"And was I right?"

"It was like night and day," Anatole admits.

"So here's to my being right." Lydia lifts her champagne glass. "And here's to you guys being exactly right for each other. Definitely a match made in Heaven."

The clink of champagne flutes fills the room. Caleb looks around with surprise, but then realizes what that delicate, percussive sound is. He touches his own ginger ale-filled flute to the others lifted around the table, and as he does so he catches Chris's eye. He doesn't much like what he sees there: anger, disapproval, repulsion. He can't entirely rid himself of the feeling that his well-planned reproof of Chris has somehow backfired, that it reflects poorly on him. What if he really is only a spoiled American idiot who doesn't understand anything about the wider world? The Amnesty International chapter he's been so proud of starting at school—is it just stupid?

He was so looking forward to today. His Uncle Anatole's

big day. Now he just wants it to be over. He just wants to be practicing with the other guys from Modder Spook in Zach's basement; it's the only time he ever really feels happy, banging his heart out on those drums, feeling the percussive jolts in his wrists, his elbows, his shoulders, feeling alive and hearing and connected and normal.

*You self-righteous little shit*, Chris thinks, lifting his glass in an ironic toast not so much to the newlyweds as to this stupid deaf boy who's somehow bested him.

"Very nice toast," Lanny says. "Whatever else you might say about Lydia, she's one class act, that lady."

"That would seem to be the case," Chris says, unsure why he's feeling so hostile to everything at the moment.

Lanny doesn't seem to notice. "So," he continues between mouthfuls of salad. "Can I ask? How do you know Anatole and Rafa? I always find that so interesting. I mean, if you think of it, there're a hundred and fifty different answers to that question right here in this room."

"By the looks of it," Chris tells him, "about half of them would say, Because he does my hair."

"Well, that's true," Lanny concedes. "But I'd hazard a guess that you belong to the other half."

Chris sighs. Beyond the tall windows, the light of early evening blesses the empty expanse of the golf course. There's another African saying: solitude is the Devil's best friend.

"Anatole and I were friends ages ago. I just met Rafa last night."

"Whereas I knew Rafa first. We used to be an item. *Centuries* ago. Gosh, we were barely in our thirties. But Rafa likes to keep his exes close. There's a few of us here. Bernardo. Josh. I don't know why that is, exactly. But if it works for him, it works for me. Anatole's just the opposite, I gather. Once he's through with you, he's through. Since you're here, I gather you're not an ex?"

The last thing Chris wants to talk about is Anatole—Anatole isn't his to talk about anymore. He keeps his account as neutral as possible: how they were just casual friends, the kind who have a drink together now and then, maybe a meal; it was only for a couple of years, back in the mid-eighties, the Morning in America years, and then Chris moved away, his work took him elsewhere, they pretty much lost touch.

"What do you do?"

"I own a record store in Denver."

Lanny nods. "And now you're back here. I think weddings are great. The way they reconnect so many of the dots that get misplaced over time. It's a celebration of community in the best sense. I'm really quite the traditionalist when it comes to marriage. I mean, I think it's bedrock. And I definitely think it should be for everybody. Who knows? This might even be the night I meet Mr. Right."

"You never know," Chris tells him.

And if I had anything resembling a conscience, he thinks, I'd stand and declare to the room at large, a kind of counter-toast to Lydia's, *I have no right to be here* and then simply walk away. Into the green embrace of the Devil's best friend.

The entrées arrive: roast beef, chicken breast, or salmon, the holy trinity of American catered meals. The wait staff is impeccable; seldom is a plate set down in front of the wrong person. Only Caleb isn't served, which occasions a flurry of solicitude around the table—but then his plate arrives, everyone evinces great curiosity, it turns out to be an eggplant concoction that looks revolting. Of course, Chris thinks, Caleb would be the vegetarian among them.

"Fabulous meal," Lanny remarks between bites. "I happen to know the chef. Shea Mulligan. Old friend of the newlyweds. Trained at the CIA."

The last detail throws Chris, who's only half listening—what's the CIA got to do with any of this? Then he remembers:

Culinary Institute of America, just north of here. And he recalls the stale joke: How can you tell a CIA chef who graduated at the bottom of his class? He's opened a restaurant in—Poughkeepsie!

When Lanny's account of Shea's travails as a gay chef among his macho-and-brimstone colleagues at the CIA comes to an end, Chris says, since he's stuck with Lanny, "So I'm curious about something. What was the minister referring to in her sermon? The storm that threatened to bring down the house that Anatole and Rafa built."

"*It*," Lanny says with gusto, "was the so-called Dana Disaster. We even used to divide their relationship into BD and AD."

He lowers his voice; Chris has to lean in close to hear him. A miasma of cologne engulfs him.

"Dana was this cute little twink Anatole rescued from the gutter. Well, I'm exaggerating a bit, but not much. It's always been an open secret Anatole likes them young. We used to joke it was Rafa who converted him to adults. Anyway, before you knew it, Anatole was giving this kid private lessons in cosmetology."

"When did all this happen?" Chris asks.

"Maybe five years ago? He and Rafa were already like an old married couple. Anyway, before you knew it the child was working at Reflexion. I say child: he was probably nineteen or twenty. Apparently he was good. The ladies were all crazy about him. I'll give him this: he was gorgeous in his way. I'm not into twinks myself; I want a man with some heft and muscle. You know what I mean?

"Anyway, Rafa totally knew what was going on, but he didn't take it too seriously. He told me any number of times, Everybody gets to have a midlife crisis. I mean, really: sometimes you can be *too* laid back! I'm not saying Anatole was hooking up with Dana on a regular basis. How would I know? I only know what's public information. Which is this. Anatole had hired this Vietnamese girl to do nails. Monique was her name. She was apparently very nice but sort of naïve. Well, there was this one evening when she'd left work and then remembered she'd forgotten something, so she went back to get it and lo and behold, there was Anatole giving Dana a blowjob right there in the empty salon. She freaked, I think maybe she'd never suspected the first thing about her employer. Who knows? I mean, if she was so shocked she probably should have just quit. But she didn't. Can you imagine what it was like to have her show up for work the next day? Oh, hi, Anatole, hi Dana. Long time no see. You've got a little dribble on your chin there. Anyway, at least this is what I hear, she went on a secret campaign against them, telling customers what she'd seen.

"But then here's the real shocker. Anatole fired her and Dana both. What really happened, nobody's saying. Did Rafa finally put his foot down? I'd love to have been a fly on the wall for that! See what you've missed by not keeping in better touch?"

Chris can almost imagine this Dana. Isn't it Leigh all over again? And of course Anatole hasn't changed; nobody changes. They can go respectable and get married and promise to abstain from old habits and even mean to, but desire remains the same inconvenient, uncontrollable thing no matter what. The hypocrisy doesn't bother him in the least; he's almost heartened to learn that Anatole in middle age still wants what the Anatole he used to know once wanted.

He'll ask Lydia for her take on it all when he gets a chance. *If* he gets a chance. For now, he needs another cigarette.

What were Anatole and Rafa thinking, seating Chris next to Lanny? Lydia can see, from across the room, how he's trapped. Get Lanny going and there's no stopping him. Tom claims to get an allergic reaction in his presence, and to ward off that possibility, he's actually shifted in his seat so Lanny won't even

be visible out the corner of his eye. He's talking to—or at—
Caleb, who doesn't seem to be listening. She almost feels sorry
for Lanny's captive audience. Almost—but not quite. There are
some things you can't just shoot your way out of. She takes an
ignoble pleasure in this.

Anatole and Rafa rehearse their honeymoon plans for the
table's benefit. They're flying to Madrid tomorrow and plan
to spend two weeks walking the final leg of the medieval
pilgrimage route to the great church at Santiago de Compostela.

"We'll be roughing it," Rafa tells the table, as if they haven't
heard the details half a dozen times before. But he's excited,
and who can blame him? "We'll have our *credenciales*. We'll
stay in *refugios,* sleep in bunk beds in a room with ten or fifteen
complete strangers. We'll make friends along the way. We'll
have adventures. And when we get to the end of the *Camino*,
we'll be awarded a *compostela*. As one guide book says, 'The
*compostela* has been indulgenced since the Early Middle Ages.'
Don't you love that word? *Indulgenced.*"

"The church still does such things?" asks Miosotis, rolling
her eyes.

"You bet," Rafa tells her.

"And the, um, gay thing?" Nikauris asks, delicately,
earnestly. "Is that an issue?"

"Not an issue at all," Anatole is quick to assure him. "At
least I really hope not. Gay marriage has been legal in Spain
for a while now. Everything's cool. Rafa's been doing tons of
research. He's spent hours on the Internet."

"I always spend hours on the Internet. At least these weren't
*wasted* hours."

"Plus we've been getting in shape," Anatole adds. "I even
joined a gym this spring. Cardio, treadmill, all that boring stuff.
I'll probably drop dead from a heart attack the first day out. But
that's okay. I've already achieved my most important goal." He

pats Rafa's arm. "And anyway, I think if you die on the *Camino*, you go straight to Heaven, indulgenced or not."

She and Tom, on the other hand, honeymooned in the Poconos, staying at a surreally run-down resort they decided to find hilarious rather than depressing (it was either that or turn around and drive back to Poughkeepsie). They actually managed to have a pretty good time making fun of the champagne hot tub, the peeling wallpaper, the star lights above the bed that winked out halfway though sex. The next day they pretended they'd wandered into a horror movie (some of the guests and most of the management helped foster the suspicion that Rolling Hills Resort was actually the Bates Motel). In the midst of their goofy play-acting, she found herself remembering that afternoon when she and Leigh shroomed at the Vanderbilt mansion, then attached themselves to a DAR guided tour and Leigh kept her in stitches with his ribald commentary. And then later, after dark had fallen, they ventured onto the derelict train bridge, that moment of desperate madness she still remembers as one of the most shining experiences of her entire life.

Whatever happened to him?

"Barbadelo, Mercadoiro, Vilar de Remonde," Rafa recites melodiously. "Ribadiso da Baixo, Salceda, Lavacolla. Those are just some of the towns we'll be trekking through. Don't they sound wonderful?"

In some ways, they're still like kids, she thinks. She hopes the journey doesn't disappoint. She hopes Anatole, whose idea of roughing it is taking a flight of stairs rather than the elevator, doesn't complain too much. She hopes they stay safe.

It's not her concern. Caleb gives her enough to worry about. And Tom too, if she's perfectly honest with herself. Her mother, who's not paying any attention to the conversation, is fiddling with that piece of paper again.

"What *is* that?" Lydia asks her.

"It's nothing, really. You'll find out soon enough."

"Should I be worried?" Lydia says this more as a joke than anything else.

"Not in the least, daughter. Not in the least. You'll be very proud of your mother in her great old age."

Chris is surprised when his ghost wife joins him on the terrace. He offers her a cigarette, but of course she declines.

Dusk has begun to settle over the golf course, making it even more dreamlike than before. Clouds are moving in. The day's warmth dissipates. Strange, though: there're no fireflies. He points this out to Lydia.

"It must be the pesticides they drench the fairways with," she tells him, then exclaims, grasping his arm, "But look!"

"What?"

"Bats! Fantastic. Definitely a good omen."

Two black commas skitter about.

"And why's that?"

"Well, they're disappearing. They're dying off."

"Really? Tell that to equatorial Africa." Dusk's thick with them in Port Harcourt, they swarm the compound, they infest eaves and attics.

"We've got this thing here called white nose syndrome," Lydia says. "Scientists don't really understand it. Whole colonies are collapsing. Once it arrives in their hibernaculum, mortality's, like, ninety-nine percent. In the spring scientists go in and the cave floor's littered with dead bats. It's terrifying."

"Hibernaculum," Chris says. "What a great word."

"You're not taking this seriously," she accuses him.

"If I took everything I feel helpless about seriously, where would I be?"

"The Niger Delta," she says.

"Touché," he replies. Not ungenerously.

"Hey, sorry you had to be seated next to Lanny. Not sure what Anatole and Rafa were thinking. Lanny's nice enough, but a little tedious, as you've probably noticed."

"He's actually a very useful source of information. It all just comes tumbling out."

"Don't believe everything he tells you."

"But you see, he's exactly the type you *can* trust. He says he and Rafa were an item once upon a time."

"Hard to believe, I know, but that part's true."

"And then he told me about the Dana Disaster."

It's a long moment before Lydia responds. Chris contemplates the bats devouring unseen insects.

"Okay," she says. "What did he tell you, exactly?"

"Enough to make me wonder how good an idea this marriage is. Be honest." It occurs to him that if the pesticides have killed off the fireflies, then won't they have killed off the other insects as well? Maybe the bats are flying erratically because they're half crazed with hunger.

Lydia shrugs. "Look, they weathered that storm. Dana was just this hustler on the prowl. The world's full of hustlers. I'm probably in the minority here, but I prefer to think of Anatole as the victim, not the perpetrator. Anatole's always been a ripe target. You know that."

"You mean Leigh?"

She decides not to explain that she means Chris too.

"Anyway, he wasn't half so charming as Leigh," she says. "And nowhere near as beautiful."

"Our Boy of the Mall."

"You do agree he was beautiful?"

"Absolutely. Stunning."

"Just checking. We were so fucking ridiculous back then."

"And Anatole's still ridiculous?" It feels good to press that question. There are still pleasures to be had in a conversation with the ghost wife. He's missed her more than she can know.

She looks at him skeptically. "Why do you ask?"

Now it's his turn to shrug. "I don't know. I'm just trying to figure all this out. So in spite of Rafa and everything, Anatole still gets crushes on teenage boys. Am I right?"

"Dana wasn't technically a teenager anymore. Twenty-two, I think. Twenty-three."

"Ancient," Chris says. Then, feeling evil: "So, I have a question. Did you ever wonder what you'd do if Anatole got a crush on Caleb?"

"Talk about ridiculous," she says.

"I'm just trying to understand where things stand."

"I have no idea why you're so interested in this. Do *you* have a crush on my son?"

"Lydia, I don't get crushes. I think I've proved that to every-one's satisfaction. Anyway, Caleb clearly thinks I'm the worst thing since sliced bread. And if you want to know the truth, I think he's a little too certain about everything. I think he needs to allow a little more complexity in."

"His life's plenty complex. And he's done amazingly well. I'm incredibly proud of him."

"As well you should be. This is just about the most pointless conversation I've had since I used to try to explain to Iraqis why they couldn't loot the power station one day and complain there was no electricity the next."

"It's good to talk about all this. We needed to have more conversations like this back when we were friends. Instead of hiding everything while pretending we knew each other. And as for who do I think you are? I have no idea, Chris. I really have no idea."

"Well, if it's any consolation," Chris says, "neither do I. I sometimes think I'm just this drifting fragment of nullity. It's only through certain kinds of actions that I even manifest myself. I know that sounds silly and pretentious, but you think weird thoughts if you live the kind of life I do."

God, how she wishes she still smoked. She'd love to bum a cigarette from him right now, she'd love to have a tumbler of

ice cold gin in her hand, because this isn't a pleasant conversa
tion, far from it, but she's enjoying it so much. She hasn't had
this kind of conversation in ages.

"You don't have to put yourself through that kind of life,"
she tells him. "You're not getting any younger. You could come
back to America. You could be our friend again."

He looks at her with what might well be incredulity, though
in the fading light his features are too indistinct to read with
any accuracy. "You're suggesting I might want to live in Poughkeepsie? Lydia!"

"It's an idea. You said it yourself: you've made tons of
money doing whatever it is you do. You can retire anytime you
want."

"I'd just evaporate if I retired."

She shakes her head in exasperation. "This is all just so frustrating. I wish you were going to be here for a week or something. So we could get to know each other all over again."

"You don't really mean that. But it's nice of you to say so."

How very good it is, he thinks, for a husband and wife to
talk after all these years, even if they *are* just ghosts of who they
used to be.

"I hope you all enjoyed your wonderful meal," Marlon announces
in that silken voice of his. "The clock's a-ticking, it's time to be
moving on. We still got dessert, we still got that wedding cake,
we still got lots of shakin' and shimmyin' to do. But first, the
moment has come for sons to celebrate their mothers."

Light applause ripples through the room. Rafa takes Miosotis's hand, raises her to her feet, escorts her onto the dance floor.
She stands beside her son, her face austerely beautiful, her body
draped with scarves, bedecked with brooches and bracelets and
necklaces, her fingers covered in rings, turquoise and topaz and
silver. Even in her crocs she's got a couple of statuesque inches
on Rafa.

Marlon has started some dreamy strings playing softly.

"Mom," Rafa says, holding her right hand in both of his, gazing at her soulfully. "You've been the most incredible presence in my life. I couldn't ask for a better role model, somebody who's independent and free-spirited and loving and generous and stylish and just incredibly artistic." He holds his right hand aloft. "What about these fabulous wedding rings, huh? I wish everybody could see them up close, how beautiful they are. Anybody who wants a closer look, just ask. Don't be shy.

"Mom, it means so much to both me and Anatole that wherever we go, whatever happens, we'll always carry with us this physical symbol not only of our love for each other, but of your love for both of us. And I want to thank my sisters too. You've been champions, both of you. I couldn't have had it any better from the women in my life. And Lydia too. You'll always be my honorary sister, Bubbles!" He lets go Miosotis's hand, scampers to the head table, kisses quickly in turn Paloma, Chiara, Lydia, then dashes back, to appreciative laughter, to take his place beside his mother while Anatole rises to a suddenly hushed and expectant room. "Please, Mrs. Forman," he says. "If I can have the honor of your company."

She doesn't look surprised; she allows him to help her unsteadily to her feet. With chagrin, Lydia realizes they've planned this all along, just between the two of them.

"I think the wheelchair, dear," Mrs. Forman says. "Just to be on the safe side." But that too has been arranged; Craig's there to help ease her into it. "Okay," she says when she's settled, "Let's roll," and Anatole wheels her into position next to Rafa and Miosotis.

"First of all, thanks, New York State, for having done the right thing and finally granted marriage equality to everybody," Anatole begins. "Some of us have been waiting! And thanks to everybody here for all your love and patience and support through the years. I love you all more than you can know, and

I'm eternally grateful to each and every one of you. I only wish my parents could be here, I wish they could see how much love their son has been blessed with. As most of you know, they both died unreconciled to what they always referred to as my lifestyle choices. But I'm more grateful than I can ever put into words that my brother Declan, who tells me he doesn't believe in evolution, has evolved over the years on the issue of gay marriage and is here with his lovely wife, Tabitha."

He pauses, afraid he's only upsetting Declan further.

"I have to speak the truth," he says. "When I came out to my parents back in 1980 they ordered me out of the house and never spoke to me again. It grieves me to say this, but it's what happened. Maybe if they were still alive—but they're not. I guess that's part of my message here. While you're still alive, make sure you do the things you need to do. And that's as philosophical as I'm going to get. Because what I'm here to celebrate is my great good luck. See, I've been blessed with a second mom in my life. She may not be my biological mother, but she's definitely my logical mother. Mrs. Forman—"

"You don't have to call me that. I have a first name, you know."

"I've always called you Mrs. Forman. It's a sign of respect"— she makes a humorously dismissive gesture—"and I'm not about to stop now. This beautiful lady took me in like I was her own son. It didn't hurt that we had several things in common: our love for Lydia, our love of hairdressing. Mrs. Forman worked out of her basement, I had this fancy-schmancy joint down-town, but at heart we were total equals. I learned so much from her, and I hope she learned at least a little from me."

Another humorously dismissive gesture from Mrs. Forman. But then she turns serious.

"Anatole, may I speak? It's true, you've been a second son to me. I remember the first time I met you. What I've forgotten could fill the Manhattan phone book and then some, but meeting you I remember. It was Halloween. You and Lydia were going to a costume party, and you came to the house to pick her up. I can't remember what she was dressed as, but you I definitely remember. I was expecting a nice young man, a proper date for my daughter, and instead, there on my front stoop is standing a girl! Ravishing, let me tell you! In a miniskirt with long blond hair. And I say to Lydia, I thought this friend of yours was a man, and she says, But he is, and I look closer, and lo and behold! That's a first meeting someone doesn't soon forget!"

Anatole doesn't remember any of that; he's never in his life done drag, not even for Halloween; he wonders if she's somehow confused him with Daniel. But it doesn't matter; most of the guests think it's charming, exotic, titillating, though the long-suffering husbands of some of his devoted clients simply look confused.

"But enough of funny stories," Mrs. Forman tells them. Lydia hasn't seen her mother this engaged in years. "This is a serious occasion, and I have something very serious that I want to say, and it concerns each and every one of you." She pauses, pulls from her sweater pocket a piece of paper, rejects it, pulls out another, spends what seems an eternity unfolding it, frowns at it for a while, then turns it right side up and reads aloud, in a bold but shaky voice, "Please don't vote for Barack Hussein Obama in November. The president of the United States of America is a Muslim. This is a terrible thing but it's true. He's a sworn enemy of Israel. He was born in Kenya. He went to Muslim school in Indonesia. Everything about the man is a lie. He has one purpose only, to destroy Israel. Wake up, America, before it's too late. Victory to Israel against her enemies."

She crumples the piece of paper into a wad and tosses it onto the dance floor, the way someone might, five hundred years ago, have thrown down a gauntlet. She looks both satisfied and a little sheepish; a mischievous grin surfaces, then scuttles back into hiding as Miosotis barks, "That's complete nonsense and you know it!"

And Lydia's been worried Chris might turn out to be something of a wild card; it never occurred to her it was her mother she should be concerned about. Sitting alone in her room, swatting at flies, stewing about events she has no control over.

"Ah yes," Rafa says soothingly as his mother glares at Mrs. Forman. "Spats between the in-laws. It's bound to happen, folks. It's traditional at weddings. Don't worry. It's all in the script, somewhere! The video's recording all this, I hope! We'll sort it out later."

Anatole clutches his forehead. "Oy," he says, trying desperately for laughs. "And she's only my logical mother!"

"You!" Mrs. Forman says, shaking a finger in his direction. "To your room!"

And the guests, most of them, laugh gratefully, relieved that everyone—even Mrs. Forman!—is doing their best to turn this unexpected bit of ugliness into a lighthearted joke.

"Okaaay," Marlon purrs as The Commodores' "Three Times a Lady" swells. Rafa (who's responsible for this particular selection) takes a still volatile Miosotis in his arms and Anatole sways an impish-looking Mrs. Forman to and fro in her wheelchair, gently, gently, so as not to make her head swim.

Sons dance with their mothers.

And then, to the sweet strains of Neil Young's "Harvest Moon" (another Rafa pick), the two sons, lovers, newlyweds, castaways, husbands for life dance with each other—slow-dance, the way Anatole always dreamed in high school of slow-dancing with a boy. His face close to Rafa's, Anatole silently mouths the foolish words of Neil's crooning refrain, because despite the lapses, the irritations, the occasional boredom, he really is still in love.

Chris wonders if he's jealous, because he too used to be in love with Anatole a little—more, he realizes now, than he dared let himself feel at the time. And though Lydia prides herself on not being sentimental in the least, the sight of Anatole and Rafa clasping each other tightly, beaming magnificently, brings a tear to her eye. They've struggled, they've hung in there; they deserve every opulence.

As for her mother, whom she's more embarrassed by than proud of right now—sensible Craig has wheeled her outside for a cooling-off period. Lydia can see her out there on the terrace, furiously smoking a forbidden cigarette. Now, where did she get that from? She'll have to speak to Craig about this later.

Music makes the room come unstuck. Place cards no longer mean a thing. What had seemed ordained is dissolved. The dance floor fills. People circulate among tables, sitting anywhere they like; the whole room breathes differently. Chris is free to circulate as well, but who would he seek out?

The playlist is a compendium of eighties relics—New Order, The Cure, Psychedelic Furs, Style Council. So that's what Anatole meant last night. It's almost unbearably evocative; Chris could be back in Immaculate Blue, bantering with the high school kids who drift in after school to browse the bins; it was heavenly, really, just to be in the mix with them, and then there was the day Leigh showed up at the shop, the kid he'd vowed to keep his distance from, the one Anatole and Lydia were fighting over. He was brandishing a wad of cash—Anatole's, he cheerfully admitted. "Once a hustler, always a hustler," was the insouciant way he put it. He wanted to buy some albums to revive Anatole's boring record collection, but more important, it turned out, he just wanted to be Chris's friend. He just wanted to be—well, they teased that out over the next couple of hours, a boozy dinner at the Milanese, a confusing conversation that continued in the parking lot, a giddy sense of everything getting dangerous way too quickly.

In Naija, the Pidgin English of Nigeria, the word for *come to ruin* is *scatter*. Fela Kuti uses it to devastating effect in *Sorrow, Tears and Blood*.

Chris is surprised and pleased to see he's not the only one who's a bit drunk. Couples are dancing exuberantly. He's never been one for dancing, and besides, there's no one here for him to dance with. Sure, he'll dance with Lydia at some point, he'll no doubt dance with Anatole before the evening's over, but he watches it all from very far away. He imagines a dance floor where he and Caleb and Elian and Quinn are dancing, but that dance floor, as he knows all too well, doesn't exist. It's only in his lonesome mind. What happened to him that made him the way he is? That broke him so thoroughly, that ruined him for everything, scattered him completely.

He thinks of Jasper and Adam, those hustlers in Amsterdam who claim to be "real-life boyfriends." Certainly they fuck each other—per his instructions—with what looks to be unfeigned tenderness and passion, but for the prices they charge, why wouldn't they? He assumes they're drug addicts, but he's not going to spoil the pleasant charade by asking, and they're way too charming and canny ever to blemish a good thing by being truthful. Though when Jasper confesses his improbable ambition to compete at dressage, and Adam imparts the news, in his Birmingham accent, that he's just back from visiting "me mum in old Blighty," Chris cherishes these inadvertent honesties. That's always been half the thrill of the choreographed encounter.

The Adams and Jaspers come and go. Getting attached to them's not the point, and he never knows what happens to them afterward; they disappear into an abyss as big as the world.

Like Leigh.

Chris lets the familiar, never-to-be-forgotten music wash over him. Right now the crowd is slow-dancing to Frankie Goes to Hollywood's "The Power of Love." If he didn't know better, he'd almost suspect Anatole put together this playlist as a secret valentine to their shared past. But he knows that's just stupid. It's not even worth thinking about.

*Scatter.*

He goes to the still-open bar to order a double shot of vodka, but the bartender tells him, "Sorry, sir. No more shots."

Back in the banquet hall, as Marlon spins Tears for Fears's "Mad World," Lanny sidles up to him and says, "Feel like a dance?"

Before he can stop himself Chris has said, "Are you kidding?"

"Never hurts to ask," Lanny tells him, though he does look a little hurt, which Chris immediately regrets. He's got nothing against the Lannys of the world. They're just trying to survive like everybody else.

"You're right," he says. "It never hurts to ask. But no thanks all the same. I've got a bad back I'm nursing."

Two weeks ago he was helicoptering out to a rig in the Bay of Guinea with a few crack troops to take out some bad guys who'd tried to commandeer the platform. Really—his back's not the problem these days.

Uncommonly quiet throughout the meal, Declan and Tabitha haven't ventured out on the dance floor but instead remain seated at the otherwise emptied table. Taking a deep breath, Anatole approaches them, saying to his brother with a solicitude he's all too aware is disingenuous, "You seem out of sorts. Is everything okay?"

Declan avoids his gaze. "I have a headache is all. Sitting out in the sun this afternoon kind of got to me, I guess."

"It's something more," Anatole says. "Do I owe you an apology?"

"For what?"

"I don't know. For saying some things that you and I both know are true."

"Maybe *you* think they're true. But then you were always a little selfish, Anatole. You know that, don't you? Selfish and self-absorbed. You're no different now than you were back in high school. Swanning around. Mr. Personality. Do you have any idea what it was like to be your younger brother?"

*Swanning around.* Now, that hurts.

"Mom and Dad always loved you the best. Can't you see that? You were the special one, the golden boy. And then you went and broke their hearts. They were never the same afterward. You weren't there, of course. You didn't see what you'd done to them."

It occurs to Anatole that his brother's a little drunk.

"Um, excuse me. They were the ones who threw *me* out, not the other way around."

"You always go on about how they failed you as parents. But what you never consider is how you might have failed them as a son. You've never considered your own obligations."

"What on earth do you mean by that?" Anatole's conscious of Tabitha watching the two of them. He's never been able to read her; he has no idea what she's thinking. Lydia, who's always too honest, calls her "the brainless one."

"I'm sorry," Declan says. "I shouldn't have said any of that. But thanks for asking, as they say. Thanks for giving me the chance to get some things off my chest that I've needed to for a long time."

"And now you have," Anatole tells him more icily than he'd like. "We'll talk about this later, okay?"

This seems to be the weekend's refrain. Later, later, later—and yet at some point, which is coming for all of them with terrifying speed, there won't be any later.

"Forget everything I said," Declan tells him. "Like I told you, I have this splitting headache. I think Tabitha and I are going to make an early evening of it. Congratulations on getting married and everything. We wish you and Rafa the absolute best. And enjoy the rest of your special evening."

It sounds a little too much like *Enjoy the rest of your life* for Anatole to take any comfort in it.

He's been worried about this pilgrimage honeymoon he's heading off to tomorrow, but right now the idea of some penance, some soul cleansing, the clearing of a lifetime of not so good karma, doesn't seem like such a bad idea after all.

Dark handsome Elian dances with his dark beautiful sisters. Rangy Caleb dances with his stoutish mom, he dances with Rafa's slender sisters, he dances a threesome with Rafa and Anatole, then just with Anatole as Rafa spins off to dance with Tom, who eventually pairs up with Lanny, of all people, but then Tom's clearly more decent than Chris will ever be.

Chris regrets that he was once a nicer, more gracious, more civilized person. He left America rich in charm, good looks, youth; he's returned from the years abroad a complete pauper.

As if in recompense for that unwelcome insight, the universe apparently decides to reward him with one brief gift. Caleb and Elian are dancing. They're on the far side of the dance floor, his view of the pair's obstructed by thick middle-aged husbands cavorting with their thin wives. No one dances with anyone else for very long in this promiscuous free for all, and with a ludicrous sense of urgency (he's nothing more than a middle-aged pervert, after all) Chris threads his way through the crowd thronging the edge of the dance floor till he achieves a better vantage. Caleb's a clumsy, good natured dancer. A goofy grin lights his face. Elian completely outshines him, poised and flirty, polished and intense. The sight's a fierce pleasure.

The man has sidled up to him before Chris quite realizes it.

"You've been watching my son," he says quietly, almost casually.

"I beg your pardon?"

"I see you watching my son. All through this wedding. And now here. You were watching him dance."

Chris barks his Baghdad laugh. "That's absurd," he says. "I have no idea who your son even is."

Still, an invisible fist has appeared out of nowhere to squeeze his heart muscle quite unpleasantly.

"I see what I see. Okay? That's all I'm saying."

Chris says nothing, turns away, takes a few steps to distance himself from this unwanted presence. But he's rattled. It's not so much that he's been tricked into letting his guard down, but that for some reason he's made a conscious decision to. But why? Something's going on in him he can't quite put his finger on, and he doesn't like it.

A little later, when he steps outside for another cigarette, he finds Caleb on the terrace, standing alone, gazing off into the darkness. The deaf boy doesn't see him, and Chris's first instinct is to avoid him. But he's not a coward.

He startles Caleb by touching his shoulder.

"I take it the playlist isn't much to your taste?" Chris says companionably. "It must seem pretty old-fashioned to you."

"Too many sounds confuse the deaf boy."

"Out here, can you even hear the music?"

Caleb shakes his head. "I know it's happening. But I almost can't hear anything in the dark. Mostly I can only hear in the light."

The kid really is impaired. He makes it easy to forget, he compensates brilliantly—but the damage is there. It doesn't get entirely undone by technology or counseling or practice, and Chris feels a strange, unanticipated kinship. More than anything he'd like to put his arms around the deaf boy, hold him close, rock him gently. None of which, obviously, is an option.

"So you and Anatole are buddies," he says.

"I thought we were," Caleb says.

"Why do you say that?"

"Everybody pretends to take the deaf boy seriously, but they don't, not really. Oh, Modder Spook is so special. We really love what you do with Modder Spook. But the deaf boy hears what they're really saying."

Chris can't quite understand what he's talking about, but he can hear the hurt. Anatole's gone and done something. There's something so erotic about helpless teenage anger.

"Look, Anatole's a good person. I'm not saying he's a saint. Far from it. He can be stupid, he makes mistakes. That's the one thing I've learned in life. Everybody's stupid. You can't hate them for it. Maybe the only thing you can do is love them. I mean, we have to face the facts of who we are. Our brains got big because we stopped eating roots and started eating animals. We domesticated them so they'd be there for us to kill whenever we wanted to. We're really good at organizing our prey. Face it: we're a ruthless species, but we also make music and paint pictures and do higher mathematics and quantum physics and go into outer space—and that's all fantastic, it's almost unbelievable how smart we are when you consider that we were once just monkeys. We can try to deny who we are, try to pretend we're something better, we can stop eating meat and choose the eggplant entrée and stop drilling for oil and all that shit, but that's just withholding us from ourselves. I know I'm not making a whole lot of sense, I've had a few too many, probably, but then I'm finding this event very difficult, to be honest, and I don't even know what I'm trying to tell you. All I know is that I somehow want to tell you something."

Caleb stares at him blankly. Maybe it's true, he can only hear in the light and everything Chris has said to him has very much been said in the dark.

"Oh, fuck it. Can you even hear any of this? As you head out into the world, just try to stay alert, okay? Keep your eyes open. I'd say keep your ears open, but you know what I mean. Keep your brain open, I guess is what I'm saying. And that music of yours is pretty fucking cool. Definitely keep on doing that."

This is two nights in a row he's gotten way drunker than he intended. It really is time for him to get the hell out of America before it poisons him entirely.

Lydia's surprised to see her son and Chris out there talking. No, surprised isn't quite right. Wary and excited. What Chris wants has always been completely mysterious to her, and having drunken sex with him that one time didn't get her any closer to solving the mystery. But she's not concerned. Caleb's not gay, despite the worrying, sort of fabulous pink boy years, and Chris isn't gay either. She's always prided herself on her ability to read people that way, which was why she was always protective of Anatole when he was in the throes of his slow-motion crush on Chris, but also why, for all those years, she was baffled that Chris and Leigh seemed to have absconded together. At least that's been cleared up now; Chris's visit hasn't been for nothing after all.

She wonders what his life has been like. The army. Iraq. Nigeria. She always had the sense he'd done something terrible before they ever met him, that he was punishing himself. Everything she's heard this weekend suggests he's still somehow punishing himself. What she's learned over the years is that the ones who never show it are almost always the most damaged. Take the case of her dad, who blew his brains out in the bedroom one afternoon for no reason anybody could ever fathom. And yet her mother with all her debilitating phobias and anxieties just keeps going. As she's proved this evening.

She has to admit, now that the incident's safely behind them, that her mom's spasm of mischief has indeed made her daughter proud. Because face it: six months from now, the only thing anybody'll remember about this wedding is an old lady in a wheelchair excoriating the President of the United States for being an insufficient friend to Israel.

Noticing how stuffy it's getting inside with so many bodies in frenetic motion, she thinks maybe she'll open a window. She's got no particular desire to eavesdrop on Caleb and Chris; she wouldn't be able to hear a word over the throb of the music anyway. She only wants some fresh air. She tries the nearest window, but it's stuck. She tries its neighbor, and the one beyond that, till it becomes clear: the windows in the banquet hall don't open.

"Well, if this is what gay weddings are all about," Carole Braunschweig's husband says nervously, "I don't know what anybody has to be nervous about."

Mrs. Forman has made herself very popular with the Republican husbands. One after another comes up to thank her for having the courage to speak the truth. What they can't know is that she's the farthest thing from a Republican. It's just that she doesn't happen to trust this Democratic president on the only principle she holds sacred: the right of a people, forged out of unimaginable tragedy, hemmed in by enemies on every side, simply to exist.

She doesn't bother to correct her admirers. For a woman in her great old age to have admirers isn't to be taken lightly. And though all this crowd and noise and bustle is daunting, sometimes it's good to leave your room, to get out a little, like she used to do when she was young, and lived in New York, and worked at the Jet Messenger Service, and was seeing, in the evenings, a very fine, handsome, well-behaved young man who also worked in the office named Arnold Forman, who was putting himself through CCNY, who was going places, who she never in her wildest dreams imagined would soon—and on bended knee no less!—propose to her at the end of a lovely dinner at Gluckstern's on West Forty-Ninth Street.

Going places! Who knew it was to Poughkeepsie he'd be going? And that she'd still be here some sixty years later.

Whereas he took himself off to the Great Beyond for reasons unknown. *And so much you missed!* She wants to tell him. Your handsome successful son married to a woman who's not his match, but what can you do? Your wayward infuriating daughter married—who'd have ever guessed?—to *ein orntlekh goy, ein choshever mentsh.*

Maybe she'll die tonight. That's her secret prayer, every night.

*God answers every prayer,* Rabbi Schumann once told her, years ago. *Mostly His answer is "No."*

"Hey, Caleb." Anatole catches the boy's elbow as he moves past in that rush of teen energy he's always adored. "I've been wanting to talk to you all evening." He steers them into the relative quiet of the Grooms' Suite, now become a storehouse of gifts. "This is crazy, isn't it? Just one thing after another. But I wanted to say thank you. I got that video attachment you sent me. What can I say? I'm totally honored. Not quite sure what Spook Plumbbob means, I hope you'll explain it all to me at some point, but the music was just so strange and interesting, like all the music you guys do. Incredible stuff. You're going to have a record deal before you know it."

"Why isn't Modder Spook here?" Caleb asks.

Anatole isn't sure he's heard correctly.

"You mean your bandmates?"

"They weren't invited," Caleb points out.

It's Anatole's old nightmare: being ambushed by something he never saw coming. "But I don't *know* your bandmates. I mean, I've met them, I like them, they seem like great guys, and *very* talented, but I don't really know them, and I don't know their parents at all. So it'd be a little odd, don't you think, if I invited them but not their parents. It's complicated."

What he won't say: even in 2012, what would any normal parent think about a guy they don't even know inviting their teenage son to his gay wedding? You can never stop being careful. You can never stop assuming that people are going to think the worst of you. It's meant a lot to him to invite his loyal clients and their husbands; he relishes their witnessing how normal and conventional the faggot turns out to be, but at the same he's aware that it's all completely provisional, that the least misperception could turn things on a dime.

"They wish they were here," Caleb says. "They told me that. They really like you, and they're really disappointed. In fact, we were hoping we might get invited to do the music. Instead of this boring DJ stuff. We could've done something amazing. But we never heard a word from you."

"I never realized," Anatole says, but then stops. What's there to say? *Let's be realistic?* A live performance by Modder Spook would have been a disaster. Folks would flee in droves. How to convey to Caleb his utterly unrealistic ambitions? And yet those unrealistic ambitions are exactly what they've encouraged in him, admired him for. He wonders, not for the first time, if maybe their good intentions haven't inadvertently created a monster.

This is not a discussion he can imagine having with Lydia, but maybe, when he's back from Spain, it's one that'll have to happen.

"It's okay," Caleb says. "The deaf boy gets it. The deaf boy's having an education these last couple of days. He's learning lots. But I have to say, I don't like your friend Chris. He's not a good person. He's one of the ones who are making the world worse than it has to be."

"Well, Chris is a complicated one," Anatole tells him, realizing too late he's repeating himself.

Caleb grimaces. Adults seem to like that word. They use it to explain everything. It lets people get away with things they maybe shouldn't get away with.

Or is he missing something?

He doesn't like it that he feels attracted to Chris, the same way he feels attracted to his bandmate Zach. That odd, tingly, slightly unpleasant but still thrilling feeling—like hitting your funny bone.

Girls don't make him feel that way, at least not yet. He keeps waiting for it to happen. He's sure it *will* happen.

He lives in what he thinks of as his very weird head a lot. Probably too much. The question is, How to get out of it?

Very complicated.

Finally—*finally!*—the wedding cake's been cut. A lime-green, many-tiered monster of a confection surmounted, of course, by two tuxedoed groom figures. Now that Chris has had a few bites of its toxic sweetness, he figures he can at last respectably take his leave.

He waits till he can catch Anatole alone; he wants to slip away quietly. He has no stomach for goodbyes.

"Sorry I can't stay longer," he tells him, "but I've got a hellish day tomorrow. JFK to Paris to Abuja to Port Harcourt. Thirty hours, more or less"—so what if he exaggerates a little?—"and then I have to hit the ground running. Rust never sleeps. No telling what the bad guys have been up to."

Anatole looks stricken, though his eyes remain bright. His greatest fear has come to pass. Their broken, snatched, imperfect conversation on the front stoop yesterday is all he'll get. Because there's so much you need to say—the honest, emotional, truthful, scary stuff—but it's never the right time, the right time's always sometime else, and then suddenly that's it, there's no time left to have that conversation that would somehow make all the difference.

"Of course you can't stay," he says, trying to sound reasonable. "But at least let me walk you to your car." He links his arm through Chris's; it's almost as if they're progressing down the aisle toward some solemn moment, but it's only the parking lot. At the entrance, the waiter named Quinn is smoking a cigarette. His eyes meet Chris's, but only for a moment. Chris doesn't meet boys' eyes in the world he lives in. Once again he's disturbed by the brazen lapse. Just because a situation feels safe doesn't mean it isn't dangerous.

To the far west a nearly continuous drama of cloud-illuminating electricity is being staged, though the storm's still far enough off that there's no sound of thunder.

"Somebody over in Ulster County's getting pounded right now," Anatole says. "I'm just so glad the bad weather held off. It's really been a perfect day, and not just weather-wise. How did it seem to you? I can't believe it's over already. After all that planning."

Chris laughs his Baghdad laugh. "I don't have much to compare this with. But today seemed lovely"—not a word he'd ever be caught dead using with his security mates, except in jest, but he's not jesting here. At least not exactly. Though *bemusing* might be a better word choice. "What I mean to say is, you and Rafa seem happy. And the guests all loved it."

"You're the one I should've been marrying," Anatole can't help saying. Out here in the parking lot, away from the wedding crowd, with lightning stoking the thunderheads, it seems the perfect, honest, deathless thing to say.

"No," Chris says. "You're drunk. You and me and Lydia. I think we've all been a little drunk the last couple of days, but we can't quite figure out why. Maybe just being together again. Maybe it's as simple as that. Maybe we're all drunk on what we used to be and won't ever be again."

"I know, I know. I'm just being outrageous. But I could always be outrageous with you, right? That was what was so wonderful. Now I'm just a middle-aged married man indulging myself. It's fun, but it doesn't mean anything. Here, I'll pull myself together."

And suddenly he's in hysterics, sobbing and blubbering and

heaving as Chris, at once disconcerted and gratified, puts his arms around him. It's crazy, but Chris feels like sobbing too, though he hasn't cried in more than a quarter century, not since John Pembroke crashed his car into a bridge abutment outside Ithaca. He didn't even cry after he shot Gabir, three quick hits to the chest with a Beretta. He's not about to start crying now on a golf course at night outside Poughkeepsie, New York.

What he feels, instead, is the absurd, unruly stirring of his cock.

"So is this really it?" Anatole asks him, unaware of what he's provoked. "Come join us on the *Camino*. Meet us in Sarria. We'll do the pilgrimage together."

"I have no idea what you're even talking about," Chris tells him.

"Our honeymoon. Didn't I even get a chance to tell you? We're making a pilgrimage. In Spain. See? The time's all gone so quickly—and now it's over. This is so crazy bittersweet I can't stand it."

"We'll be in touch," Chris says, though he doesn't think it likely. "We won't go twenty-seven years before seeing each other again."

"Maybe we'll end up in the same nursing home. How would that be?"

"I don't imagine I'll last that long. I wouldn't want to even if I could."

"To be perfectly honest, I don't want to be around then either. Look at Mrs. Forman. She hates being so old. Forget the aches and pains, the worst of it is, it's just *boring*. That's what she complains about the most."

"Clearly it gives her way too much time to obsess about certain things."

"Oh, that," Anatole says. "I didn't mind that. Really. Lydia got all bent out of shape, but I thought it was just funny."

"I agree. Though if you ask me, Israel turned out to be just about the worst geopolitical mistake of the twentieth century."

"I wouldn't know anything about that. I'm just a hair stylist in Poughkeepsie. Politics was never my thing."

"Do you still dream about nuclear war?" Chris asks, remembering the chant *Anatole is dreaming, Anatole is dreaming.* "Caleb played me the Modder Spook song he and his guys did for you."

"My wedding present. Very thoughtful."

"He's a strange one."

"I guess so. If you don't know him all that well. Of course, I've known him his whole life. He's almost like a son. And I have to say, Lydia's been just an incredible mom. It can't have been easy."

Does Anatole have any inkling of the storm that seems brewing between him and Caleb? But that's not Chris's concern.

"Speaking of strange boys," he says. "I've been poking around a bit online. I don't think Leigh's gone far. I think he's living down in Newburgh."

"Really? That's so odd. I always figured he was long gone from the Hudson Valley."

"I have half a mind to try to get in touch with him before I leave."

Anatole doesn't respond immediately. They watch the approaching storm front. Lightning conjures thunderheads out of the dark, featureless sky—enormous ghostly presences suddenly visible before they vanish back into darkness.

He knows he shouldn't be away from the festivities up in the clubhouse for this long, so he finally says, "You should look him up. I *think*."

"You wouldn't if you were me."

"To tell you the truth, Chris, I got over Leigh a long

time ago. I never think about him. If there's anybody I think about…"

"It's Dana."

"Glad to see Lanny came through. I thought he would. That's why I sat you there. So now you know the worst of me. And, yes, to be honest, I'd love to be in touch with Dana right now, though I know I can't be if I'm going to be an adult. Still, I have my lapses. I stalk him on Facebook. Isn't that a hoot? He's very lax about his privacy settings. You should see the things he posts! There's this long, blurry video of him and some really cute friends stripped down to their briefs dancing to Lady Gaga songs. It's just out of this world. Listen to me. I'm totally sick, aren't I?"

"Totally," Chris says. "There's never been a pervert like you."

"Really?"

"Never in the history of the world. Everyone else I've ever met is completely normal."

"Lanny probably told you I fired Dana. Because that's what I told everybody. But I didn't. I begged him to stay. I told him I'd dump Rafa, I'd do anything to keep him. He said it wasn't right, he wasn't going to come between us. So he left. He withdrew. He was way too decent, if you ask me—not to sound selfish! Chris, I was so crazy about him. I was absolutely ready to leave Rafa for him. I realize now how badly I was behaving, but at the time… It's funny, I don't even really remember Leigh anymore; Dana just totally eclipsed him. But then I never gave Leigh a blowjob. We slept in the same bed for three months, and I never even got up the nerve to go down on him when he was asleep. How pathetic is that? At least I got to taste Dana's cum a few times. Big whoop-dee-doo. And so here I am. I'm married to Rafa. And it's where I should be. I feel totally happy. Well, not totally. I never feel totally anything. But you know what I mean. I'm just blathering here, because I really don't want you to go."

It comes to him, as he blathers here in the parking lot: there's something Leigh, Chris and Dana share, something as elusive as a scent, something at once insubstantial and totally alluring, but which Rafa, curiously, doesn't possess—which is maybe why, at the end of a long day, he can actually envision the two of them making a life together. Because let's face it, with the Leighs and Chrises and Danas of the world there's the obsession, the exhilaration, the despair, but there's no real, enduring life to be had. And Anatole, for better or worse, has chosen life.

He thanks Daniel for that.

"So tell everybody else goodbye for me," Chris is saying. "By which I guess I mean Lydia. And that very bland and nice-seeming husband who probably saved her life. As you know, I'm terrible at goodbyes."

"She'll be disappointed."

"I've never done anything but disappoint her. She'll get over it. But I do have one last evil question. Want to hear it?"

"Why not?" Anatole says, willing to do anything to prolong their goodbye. "You know you can ask me anything."

"Did you ever have a crush on that strange son of hers?"

"Chris! Oh my god! Not in the least. Why would you even think so?"

"Because I know your type," he says. *And because your type used to, at least, be uncannily like my type, which I never let you know, but which was why I always loved you in my way, because you didn't make me feel quite so alone in the world.*

"Not anymore you don't. I'm not that Anatole anymore. I'm really not. I changed. People do change, you know."

*No they don't,* Chris wants to say. *They may be able to hide their old selves for a while, but the ruined self never goes away. Dana proves that. And you're deluding yourself if you think it won't happen again.*

"Okay, I really am leaving now," Chris tells him. "You need to get back to the reception. I'm surprised they haven't sent a search party out looking for you."

"Thank you so much for being here. Are you sure you're fit to be on the road? Just one friend checking on another."

Chris snorts. "I've spent the last ten years on much worse roads than anything I could possibly encounter tonight."

"That makes me sad, somehow. But I'll have to trust you. No, don't give me a hug. I'll just start blubbering all over again, and my eyes are already red enough as it is. I'm an adult. I know I've got to let you go. So bye, honey." He touches his fingertips to his lips, kisses them lightly, consigns the airy result to oblivion. "Bye."

The ride home's been uncomfortably cramped, but she wouldn't have wanted Caleb to ride with Chris even if he hadn't bailed out early; he'd had way too much to drink, and she's a little annoyed that Anatole didn't take his keys away. But now everyone's finally settled. The house is quiet. Her mom and her son are tucked away in their respective bedrooms. She and her husband lie companionably side by side. Ravioli, who was supposed to be Caleb's dog, snores at the foot of their bed.

"Well, that sure was exhausting," Tom says. "I'm happy for Anatole and Rafa, but honestly, I thought it was never going to end."

"It did go on and on. Our own little wedding was much nicer, don't you think?"

"In every way," he says. "In every single way. And that's not meant to be homophobic."

"I'm not accusing you of a thing. You were very well behaved. You even danced with Lanny. *That* gets somebody a gold star, for sure."

"Hey, I may have my prejudices, but you can't call me a bigot. Besides, I danced with everybody."

"There were a lot of Republican husbands you didn't dance with."

He considers this. "True," he says. "And they didn't dance

with me. But I think I danced with every single one of the Republican ladies. Some turned out to be pretty damned good dancers once they were liquored up enough." He's thinking particularly of Carole Braunschweig, how she touched him freely, suggestively, in their few minutes together.

"And Caleb didn't do too badly, did he? Though he was in a bit of mood afterward. Did you notice? I'm not sure what that was about."

"Crowds are hard for him. And new situations," Tom reminds her. "Sometimes I think we underestimate." Still, he's so terrifically proud of Caleb. He used to worry, back in the pink boy phase; he has nothing against the gays, but let's face it, he'd take it pretty hard if Caleb turned out to be one of them.

"And my mother," Lydia says. "Sheesh!"

"Your mom was terrific. She was the high point of the whole event, if you ask me."

"Guess what she told me when I tucked her in tonight. She looked up at me with the sweetest smile, which always means she's either going to say something really nice or really nasty, and she said, 'You know what, daughter? Today was the kind of day that makes me feel very happy I'm still alive.'"

"Your mom. She can be a real pain in the butt, but honestly, sometimes I feel like the luckiest son-in-law in the world. And I'm not just saying that."

They nuzzle a little, they cuddle. She touches one of his earlobes, rubs between her fingers the hole where the plug used to be, a kind of empty reminder of his punk past. It's not sexy, in fact it always feels weird, but also fascinating: it's somehow the essence of him, much more than the tattoo. How strange—that what she loves most about him is something that's not even there anymore. The caress—a little obsessive, she'll be the first to admit—doesn't move them any closer to sex, but, of course, they're in their fifties, it's natural that they're slowing down.

"But the most amazing thing," Tom says, suddenly remembering, "was watching your friend Chris try to talk to Rafa's mom—what's her name?"

"Miosotis."

"Yeah. It was after the dancing started and people were milling around, and she was making the grand tour, going from table to table like some ocean liner calling at all the various ports. I have a feeling she was three sheets to the wind. Anyway, when she came to our table she was very nice to Caleb, I must say, and to me, and then when Chris invited her to sit down in Lanny's empty seat and stay for a while, she just looked at him—I mean, you should've seen that look, talk about totally staring through somebody. She didn't even say a word, just turned around and floated away." He laughs to recall the look on Chris's face. He really hasn't liked the guy very much at all, and he relishes the comeuppance. "Now, *that's* somebody who thinks very highly of herself. But then so does Chris, if you don't mind my saying."

She's sorry to hear Chris was ambushed yet again. He didn't have a particularly fun time, she suspects, but he's not exactly made himself an easy person to like. Leaving without saying goodbye, for instance. It's just like him to do that, but still, it's hardly endearing.

She wonders if she'd ever have liked him if Anatole's infatuation hadn't been so contagious.

"Anyway," Tom says, "have you ever noticed? All Rafa's relatives have such strange names. Well, not all of them, but a lot."

She feels it's her duty to elbow him in the ribs.

"Hey," he says. "I'm not being prejudiced or anything. I'm just noticing."

"Sometimes," she tells him, "the more you talk, the more trouble you get yourself into."

"You have any better ideas?"

She's still tracing the hole in his distended earlobe. "We could always have sex," she says.

"I'd love to," he tells her. "But can we wait till morning? Is that okay? I'm totally bushed. I've had too much to drink. And thanks for driving, by the way. I'm just not sure I could perform worth shit."

"I'm okay with that. I'm pretty bushed too."

"It's a date then. We'll have some nice Sunday-morning wake-up-and-smell-the-coffee sex, and then I'll get in the kitchen and make everybody French toast and scrambled eggs and bacon. The whole shebang. How does that sound?"

"Just remember, Mom doesn't like scrambled eggs. Poach one for her. And of course Caleb's not touching meat these days. But otherwise, yes, it sounds just perfect."

The clock's striking midnight as they arrive at the Millbrook Inn.

"Just in the nick of time," their chauffeur tells them. "It's not always so pleasant to be in the Rolls when it turns into a pumpkin. Gentleman, that's one heartache you've spared yourselves. I'd say you're definitely off on the right foot."

The checking in's already been done for them; their bags are stowed in their room, the covers of the king-size bed turned down, a single red rose and a square of chocolate adorning both pillows.

They don't have to worry about waking early; breakfast will be served whenever they're ready. And the chauffeur will return at two in a more sensible (and much thriftier) car to pick them up for the drive down to Newark International.

Gay weddings are going to be very good for the state's economy, though Anatole wonders whether they really *needed* to spend the night at an inn. Their own bedroom would have been perfectly fine—and he could have checked to see what damage Marley might have done to the garden.

For the second time today—though technically it's now tomorrow—they shower together, something Anatole tells himself they really should do more often. They're both exhausted but still flushed and giddy with everything that's happened. They luxuriate in the steamy downpour as, outside, the real downpour commences, complete with its exciting soundtrack of thunder.

"Wow," Anatole says as they snuggle naked beneath the sheets and a particularly prolonged eruption of close-up tympani shakes their cozy room. "I'm referencing that 'just you wait,' in case you don't remember. But you didn't warn me there'd be special effects involved." He takes a moment to peer out the window at the rain lashing the perennial borders, which look so attractive on the inn's website, and which he's eager to check out tomorrow by daylight. "I hope everybody's gotten wherever they're going okay. And I hope that stupid dog didn't destroy our garden. I was worrying about that all through the ceremony. It was like this irritating little mosquito buzzing inside my head the whole time."

"That's funny," Rafa replies. "Chris was telling me an African proverb along those lines."

"You talked to Chris? I'm so envious. I hardly had a chance to."

"Only briefly. You want to hear the proverb?"

"I guess. Sure."

"If you think you're too small to make a difference, try spending the night in a room with a mosquito. Not bad, huh? So are you glad he came?"

"Meaning, am I glad I faced down my demons? Then yes, I guess so. Seeing him after all this time, well, it was both different and more or less exactly what I imagined."

"Meaning?"

"Meaning, meaning," Anatole says. "Oh, I don't know. It's going to take me some time to think it all through. Which makes me glad we're going on this pilgrimage. Though I have to say we were laying it on a bit thick back there with all our hardship talk."

Because it's actually a package tour they're embarking on, with a private room in a two-star hotel at the end of each day's hike and luggage transfers from one hotel to the next.

"Oh, come on, Mr. Kitten." Rafa punches his arm. "They were loving it. And romance *always* involves a bit of deceit. You and I know all about deceit."

"Do we?"

"Well, we're adults after all. Isn't that part of being an adult? Like right now. I'm going to dim this light a bit. There. Now we both look a bit more attractive, don't you think?"

"I thought we looked okay in the shower this afternoon. For two old battle-scarred veterans."

"Was it only this afternoon? That feels like a million years ago. Surely we've aged a ton since then. Maybe I should turn the light completely out."

"You know, I actually wonder if we've gotten younger. I know I for one feel a new lease on life. Is that too corny to say?"

"Probably. You're a very corny guy sometimes. I've always liked that about you."

"Did you say *corny* or *horny*? Cause I'm maybe feeling a little bit of both."

"Well what do you know," Rafa says, his exploring hand having wandered down Anatole's chest, migrated around his sweet little pot belly to finally reach his groin. "You're already hard for me. What a pervert. If we were videotaping this, which thank God we aren't, unlike every other available second of today's ceremony, we could caption it Lovemaking Accompanied by Spooky Lightning and Loud Thunder. At least we don't have to worry about making too much noise."

"Will we ever watch even five minutes of those tapes?"

"Only if things go sour and we want to feel bitter. Let's hope they're a guarantee that won't ever happen."

"You know, Rafa, I don't see things going sour. I mean, we've tested our limits pretty thoroughly, don't you think? And it's not like we'll be getting randier over the next twenty-five years."

"Hey, you never know. I hear seventy's the new twenty-one. We'll both have boylets on the side by then."

"Boylets?"

"Mr. Kitten! You know what I mean. Men for me, boys for you. I'm well aware of our respective proclivities!"

"Speaking of proclivities, I think I'd like to suck your cock right now. How about that? For starters."

And it's a nice fat luscious cock, no doubt about that. He used to worship it for hours. Lately not so much, but what fond memories, rainy Saturday afternoons spent lazing in bed, living completely in the body, not a thought in the world, just pleasure and more pleasure, a slow delicious feasting, except that the agreeable hunger never entirely goes away.

"Ease off," Rafa tells him. "I don't want to come quite yet. It's my turn."

Slow and delicious turns heated and intense. They haven't made all-out love like this in a while. Not since their fierce reconciliations after the Dana Disaster, when the near crack-up of nearly nine years together seemed to rekindle a flame that had almost gone out but then burned with a renewed violence, a kind of blood ferocity that both enhanced them and took them aback. It didn't last; things eventually subsided to a more endurable and lasting pitch between them, but the episode nonetheless had the effect of a couple of lines of coke in the middle of a long evening of partying (remember those days?), a jolt that made possible a new purchase on the night and its enticements.

It's not quite the same tonight (and their coke days are long behind them), but two weeks' abstinence, the pleasant ordeal of the marriage ceremony, the prospect of the *Camino* all provoke new vigor in them. It's not the post-Dana urgency, it's something calmer, more deliberate, but all the deeper for it. Anatole's called them battle-scarred veterans, more as a joke than anything else, but somehow it's set the tone. They're no longer handsome in the way they used to be, they're sadder and more resigned and, let's face it, a bit less virile, but also saner and more content. Of course nothing that's happened today precludes future disasters, nor would either of them want to be completely inoculated (that's why it might have been nice to bunk with strangers in *albergues* along the *Camino*, Rafa thinks.) It's a cliché to say they drink deeply of each other, but that's what it feels like, at least to Anatole, this heavenly witching hour as they try to find their way into each other, the oldest, most primordial need of all. We're not impervious, we're not impenetrable. (With a groan of grateful surrender, Anatole allows Rafa inside him). God gave us orifices, God gave us wounds. He didn't mean us to stay pent up in ourselves, he meant us to sally forth, to retreat, to be invaded, occupied, eventually to resist, regroup, overturn the occupation (it's Anatole's turn to take Rafa, a conquest which, because it's achieved less frequently, is all the sweeter), while cannons boom and fireworks burst and nature sheds a happy tear for all the sullied, sacred, roiling, rollicking permutations the slow crawl out of the ooze has afforded. There are seven billion people in the world. Each the result of a several-billion-year pilgrimage converging in the here, the now...

They aren't alone in the room, of course. Not by any means.

Dana's here. He has to be. And Lanny and Bernardo and Josh, and Chris Havilland and Daniel, and Rafa's Jupiter, whom he hardly ever talks about, and Anatole's half-forgotten Leigh, whom he's never even mentioned to Rafa because why does it matter? But they all haunt the room, not as mosquitoes or ghosts or shadows or resentments or threat: more as plain, simple wonder. Anatole seldom feels a sense of the holy the way he used to, when the very light around a teenager with a perfect profile glimpsed out the window of Reflexion could suddenly seem transfigured, but it's possible, right now as lightning sparks and thunder cracks and rain thrashes and the earth receives, that something like holiness hovers close. And if Anatole, who sometimes accompanies Rafa to Mass, has a prayer—or not even a prayer, maybe just a wish—it might be this: *Fullness to the world. As much fullness as humanly possible.*

# NIGHT MUSIC

Once again he's lost. Following Lydia, he'd thought the route to Whispering Creek was pretty direct, but the dark masks landmarks, and the vast flickering wall of the approaching storm distracts his attention. He must have made a wrong turn just outside the entrance, or maybe failed to make a turn before reaching the main road, because now he finds himself on an unlit, sparsely settled, untrafficked country lane.

From the west comes a near continuous barrage of distant thunder, eerily like the sound of Spectre AC-130s pounding Sadr City he could hear nightly from The Mansion, only tonight the salvos are coming closer and closer.

A slow burn of irritation turns into panic. He's in a cold sweat, his heart's racing. All the PTSD symptoms are kicking in like crazy. Finding a narrow pull-off, he stops the car and tries to breathe deeply, evenly, calmly. It's not working. From the glove compartment he pulls out his emergency pint of vodka and sucks on it.

Not a good idea. He's already way too drunk as it is, and this only kicks him an unwelcome notch closer to debility. He shuts off the engine—its sound, the vehicle's vibration, is peculiarly irritating to him right now. He puts his head back against the headrest. He closes his eyes for a moment, trying to think the blankest thoughts he can.

He must have dozed for a bit, because it's well after midnight when he wakes. Rain drums on the rooftop and windshield like some Modder Spook outburst run amok. For a moment he doesn't know where he is. Lighting sparks, then the thunder detonates practically on top of him. Involuntarily he ducks for cover—but by then, if this were real life, it would be too late.

But it's not real life. It's just America.

Still, he's almost never just in one place anymore. He's either dreaming he's someplace or he's actually there and dreaming he's not.

It began routinely—as most everything disastrous does. Standard two-vehicle packet, pick up a couple of contractors at the BIAP, ferry them down Route Irish to the Green Zone. Easy as pie. As usual, they traveled covert profile, their vehicles a battered Opel and Nissan: Ian, Trevor, and Ali in the lead vehicle, Chris, Darby, and Saleh bringing up the rear.

Route Irish was the usual mad circus, six lanes bumper to bumper, cars and trucks traveling at 130 clicks weaving around donkey carts and pedestrians trying to get across and the occasional driver going the wrong way on the median. Along the shoulder, the nonstop grim reminder of burned-out, bullet-riddled auto carcasses, piles of garbage, dead animals, perfect places to hide a device, children playing or acting as lookouts for the insurgents up ahead with their fingers on the IED triggers. Ian was in constant radio contact, relaying possible threats—goat carcass to the left, garbage pile just beyond that, woman with two children standing on the flyover, maybe innocent, maybe not.

Pickup went fine, no problems there, but their clients, two good old boys from Houston, had been pretty rattled by their descent into BIAP; apparently nobody'd warned them that at the last minute, to evade the surface-to-air missile threat, the pilot would tip the plane ninety degrees and spiral down ten thousand feet in a couple heartbeats, to level out only seconds before the tires hit the runway.

Always a pleasure to see the bravura knocked out of those guys.

Heading back into the city center, they ended up in the wake of a Blackwater convoy, five high-profile 4x4s loaded up with guns and HF antennas, complete with signs in Arabic warning motorists to stay back one hundred meters. Now and again they'd let out a burst of weapons fire to remind everybody they were serious about their exclusion zone.

The Spartan packet was staying as far back as possible from the Blackwater folks; Blackwater's methods might be effective in preventing vehicle-borne IEDs, but their visibility made them a huge target for the remotely detonated ones.

Chris could tell his Texan, less than an hour in Iraq, was already wishing he'd signed up for the Backwater convoy. He loved it when he hated his clients.

Green Zone drop-off proceeded without a hitch. They showed their CPA passes, the Coalition guards waved them through. Another easy thousand bucks. They celebrated with burgers in the Burger King (this more as a treat for their Iraqi drivers than themselves).

It was returning to The Mansion that proved problematic. They'd just pulled off the main road, they were two blocks from their barricaded street and safety when traffic slowed, came to a standstill. Drivers leaned on their horns. They inched along in fits and starts; it was every covert packet's worst nightmare—stuck in a traffic jam.

"Some clowns have set up a checkpoint," Ian radioed back from the lead vehicle.

"Who the fuck are they? Why the fuck didn't we know about this?"

"Trying to figure that out."

"Where the hell are our guys?"

"Don't know."

It wouldn't be the Mahdi Army in this neck of the woods. More likely some local gang shaking down motorists for an hour or two, then folding shop before the police showed up (having been bribed to take their time). What was concerning was that their own guards were letting this happen so close to home.

"What are you getting from Ops?"

"Nothing. I'm trying."

That was even more concerning.

A couple of well-armed bearded guys wandered between cars, gesturing to the drivers to be patient, their overtures completely ignored.

"We've got to get the fuck out of here," Chris radioed.

"Obviously. How are you proposing to do that, exactly?"

A quick glance behind showed they were starting to get hemmed in.

"Fuck all," Chris said. "How do you feel about some ramming and jamming?"

That's when he saw Gabir. Chris knew instantly it was him; months of watching the kid as a kind of pastime meant he knew his movements by heart. He watched with a strange secret worshipfulness even now. Gabir walked among the stopped traffic, looking straight ahead toward the improvised chicane where the militia or gang were inspecting vehicles before allowing them to proceed, and for the briefest of instants Chris had an absurd thought: the kid was coming to rescue them. Our Boy of the Deadly Streets. Then in the next instant he registered a second thought. The skinny street kid he'd memorized wasn't wearing the Carlsberg T-shirt he always wore; he wore instead a loose-fitting yellow jacket. He met Chris's eye and in that instant everything came together.

Chris didn't hesitate. He didn't even think. He whipped his pistol from his vest and fired three quick shots through the car window. The first exploded Gabir's left cheekbone, the second drilled his throat, the third punched the center of his chest.

He leaped from the car and ran to the limp body. Gore had splattered everywhere. And the ripe odor of shit—that telltale smell of violent death. He didn't hesitate but plunged right in. Ripping open Gabir's jacket, he confirmed what his instincts had told him: the bulky vest strapped to his thin chest, its surface thick with taped-down nuts and bolts and screws. The wires. The detonator still clasped in his dead hand.

"What the fuck?" said Ian, instantly beside him. "Shit! Fuck me! That's one of ours."

People had ducked for cover, but were beginning to reemerge in the absence of any further gunfire. The commotion had drawn the attention of the armed guys up ahead, who were warily making their way down the line of cars and trucks, AK-47s at the ready. Meanwhile Trevor and Darby were scanning the street 360, their heavy weapons on hair-trigger alert. The Blackwater guys would have scoured the street with automatic weapons fire by now. Chris and his team prided themselves on their finesse.

It took him a few moments to realize exactly what had happened. The ringing in his ears deafened him, though in spite of that he could hear Ian's voice yelling, over and over, up close but as if from a tremendous distance, "Fuck, mate! Fuck, mate!"

The second bomber had detonated his payload some fifteen yards ahead of them. Their lead vehicle, while shielding them, had taken the brunt of the explosion. What remained of Trevor lay on the pavement beside the Opel; he'd lost an arm, a leg, most of his face. Ali sat behind the wheel, face and arms shriveling as flames licked about him. The street was full of screams. A severed hand wearing a large wedding ring lay on the hood of the Nissan. Bloodied families sat lifeless in window-shattered, shrapnel-riddled vehicles. A young girl staggered toward them, holding her spilled guts in her hands. From the checkpoint up ahead came a clatter of automatic weapons fire. And from some of the buildings on the street came gunfire as well—sniper fire. Chris was pretty sure it was directed at the white-eyes who'd been lured into this trap.

"You still with us, mate?" Ian asked, his face peppered with nicks and cuts. The long gash on his arm looked alarming.

"I've still got my balls," Chris said. "At least I think so." His hearing was gradually returning. There was a metallic taste in his mouth which, when he spit, he realized was blood. His nose was bleeding from both nostrils as well as back into his throat.

"Let's get the hell out of here."

Darby and Saleh were gathering as much of Trevor as they could into a duffel bag. They'd come back for Ali later—or not. Even burned out, the Opel would be stripped clean by scavengers in no time.

Drivers in the less damaged vehicles at the rear of the jam were reversing, fleeing, clearing an escape. Saleh confirmed that the Nissan was still operational. They loaded Trevor into the trunk and sped off, as much as that was possible driving on the rims of the two blown-out passenger-side tires.

"Spectre Zero, do you read?" Chris radioed ahead. "Spectre Ten here. Be advised. Situation red."

"Spectre Zero Ten acknowledged. Situation red here as well."

"We're heading in. Five minutes. Be ready."

They went the back way. The barricades at the end of the street were unmanned and disassembled. The Mansion was under full-scale attack. They roared into the courtyard as the gates swung shut behind them. Most of the remaining guards— several had fled or defected—had retreated to the roof and its stockpiled firepower. The attackers, outgunned, began losing steam, and soon the battle settled into a desultory exchange of shots, then subsided altogether.

Of course, that was the end of The Mansion. Chris and his team had been good neighbors, dependable employers, they'd kept the street safe. There comes a time when you realize you have to cut your losses and get the hell out. That may not be the pattern of everyone's life, but it's been the pattern of Chris's.

He's tried many times to puzzle it all out, but he can't. Gabir's family was dead, or at least that's what he'd been told, so there couldn't have been a financial incentive, no widowed mother or orphaned siblings receiving compensation. And he finds it hard to believe the kid had patiently infiltrated the Crusaders' outpost as an agent of—whom? The Mahdi Army? The fellaheen? Al Qaeda in Mesopotamia? Or was it all just about criminal gangs and turf wars? Questions on questions on questions.

What he can't forget is the look Gabir gave him, but neither can he read it, no matter how often he revisits it. Cold, estranged, determined, haunted—as if he both recognized Chris and at the same time it made no difference one way or the other.

What he always returns to is this: somebody must have paid him to do it. Not necessarily in cash; maybe just with the promise of paradise. But maybe that's just Chris. His own life's been a long, torturous calculation, a string of credits and debits whose final tally, indeed whose very purpose, is a mystery. No matter what happens, no matter where he finds himself, he's always just accruing more debt or paying it back. Everything's a transaction. Everything's bought or sold.

What's the difference between a mercenary and a whore?

The rain is lessening. Lightning and thunder are moving off into the distance toward rich, complacent Connecticut. Retracing his steps, he manages to find his way back to Whispering Creek's Welcome sign. Determining his mistake was to turn left rather than right on leaving the entrance, in a few minutes he's rewarded with the road back to Poughkeepsie.

It's after one when he arrives at the Inn at the Falls. As so often happens, his drunkenness has turned into something else: an energetic, hell-bent focus. It's how he manages these days. He's become adept at clicking his way around the Internet, especially since coming to Port Harcourt, where in the long evenings the connection, however epileptic, is a lifeline out of the stultifying compound. By the time he finds what he wants—a current phone number—it's nearly two. Part of him thinks, if this is the Leigh he's looking for (and it practically has to be), and if he's still the same Leigh, he'll be up at this hour.

But, of course, the last thirty or so hours have showed him that no one's still who they used to be.

It's better, he decides, not to risk voicemail. He'll send a text instead. But what to text? *This is a ghost from your past? Who you probably don't remember and if you do you'd probably rather forget?*

He settles on *Chris Havilland here. If that name rings a bell and you're interested, get in touch. I'm only in the area till early afternoon tomorrow, I mean today (Sunday).*

It's neither elegant nor eloquent, and he half hopes Leigh will just ignore it. In a way, that would make everything simpler. In a way, it would be a huge relief.

He hesitates, his finger over the Send button.

How many times has he pulled a trigger without thinking twice? And this he can't bring himself to do?

## CHAPTER THREE

S ugar Muffin," Pascal says. "You seem a little distracted this
morning. What's up with you?"

Pascal's got this uncanny ability to read him.

Morning light floods a kitchen that's too cramped for two
people to go about their tasks without occasionally jostling
each other, which they sometimes do on purpose, just for the
pleasure of contact. "It's so weird," Leigh tells him. He plucks
grapes from a luscious cluster and tosses them into a large bowl,
adds blueberries, blackberries, half-moon segments of clemen-
tines. "I got this text message. Sent very late last night. This
guy I knew, like, a million years ago. He's in the area today,
wants to see me."

"He's not that guy who used to stalk you, is he?"

"No, thank God. Somebody totally different. From when I
lived in Poughkeepsie." In goes a dollop of Greek yogurt, over
which he sprinkles some muesli.

"The rich guy?"

"No, not Ed. This guy named Chris. I don't think I've ever

even mentioned him. He's just somebody I knew. We never even hooked up. He was part of this crowd I got a little too involved with. And I know what you're planning to say, so don't even bother." A squeeze of lime finishes things off.

"You mean, 'You spent way too many years involved with crowds you didn't need to be involved with?'"

Leigh slaps him lightly on the forearm. "Sometimes you drive me crazy. You know that?"

"It's your favorite thing about me. So are you gonna see him?"

"I don't know. At first I thought I wasn't going to answer. But then I went ahead and texted him back. And now I haven't heard. So who knows what's up? But after all this time I'm sort of curious. He was really handsome. Full disclosure: I totally had a crush on him. Okay, even fuller, now totally embarrassing disclosure. I threw myself at him. And he turned me down." He doles the bowl's contents onto two chipped plates. "Breakfast is served."

It's their ritual Sunday morning healthy repast. Pascal's working the champagne cork.

"And now a million years later he comes looking for you? What's that supposed to mean?" He punctuates his question with a POP!

"I don't know. I don't even think he was gay. But who knows? Maybe he finally came out."

Pascal pours foaming golden liquid into the jelly jars that serve as glasses.

"That was when I still had my looks," Leigh adds.

"Your famous looks. You're better off without them. Didn't anyone ever tell you that? I mean, if you still had your famous looks, you'd never be with ugly ole me."

Pascal has this way of giggling—a sort of high-pitched whinny—when he thinks he's being transgressive. Leigh finds it goofy and adorable.

"I wonder what he wants," Leigh says. What he doesn't say is, What might have happened if things had gone differently between him and Chris Havilland. No Ed. No introduction into the Manhattan/Hamptons/Fire Island circuit. No years as the "it" boy. No crystal meth. No burnout, no breakdown, no slow climb back out of the abyss.

Leigh's apartment is tiny, Pascal's on the other side of town even tinier. They talk off and on about sharing an apartment, the money they could save, though neither really wants to. They've been together four years, but they both cherish their independence. It's an open relationship, as they say. Leigh especially doesn't like being hemmed in, not after all those years of being kept by one collector after another.

He tells himself, despite everything he's gone through, that he's still waiting for that big thing to happen to him, though he can't even begin to say what he thinks that might be.

Chris wakes feeling at peace. Birds warble outside the window. The little waterfall murmurs soothingly. He forgot to set an alarm—it's ten thirty, he's missed breakfast, but after yesterday's endless banquet he's not hungry. He's also, against all odds, not hungover—just a light reprimand behind his eyes.

He lazes in the deeply comfortable bed, gazing at the ceiling, feeling the way you do after a successful mission. That sense of having come through everything alive. Of not having embarrassed yourself professionally. And he hasn't embarrassed himself this weekend, he doesn't think, though he winces to remember Elian's father calling him out, and that completely unexpected snub from Rafa's mother, and... But enough of that.

When he sees himself as he must have appeared to Anatole and Lydia—boasting, truculent, aloof—he knows it's not pretty. He's not a loser, but he can see how, from their perspective, he might seem like one.

Then it comes back to him: the late-night text to Leigh.

He shouldn't have sent it, chances are it's not even the same Leigh, and even if it is, why should he remember something that happened so long ago?

His iPhone indicates he has two new text messages. The first is from Ian, a routine check-in.

The second makes his heart muscle clench.

*Chris Havilland! OMG! Blast from the Past! Where are you?! Do I have a chance to see you? That would be wild. Sunday's my lazy day. Nothing on the books that can't be changed. Eager eager eager.*

The breathlessness puts him off—was Leigh always like that? He can't remember. All he remembers is the boy's ethereal beauty.

He reminds himself the beautiful boy is now forty-something.

His peaceful mood's vanished, replaced by the feeling that the weekend's actually been pretty awful, so why's he proposing to make things even worse? On the other hand, what's to lose anymore? He paces around the room for a few minutes, then discipline kicks in. He drops to the carpeted floor, does his usual fifty push-ups followed by fifty sit-ups, but for once the routine doesn't steady him. He hates that you can't smoke indoors in America, so to calm himself he indulges in a luxury they haven't banned yet—a prolonged, steamy shower. He stands motionless under the promise of endless hot water, lets it soothe him as his brain replays, undimmed, that afternoon in 1985 when he and Leigh met up for late afternoon drinks at The Congress, deserted except for the bartender and a middle-aged man drinking alone and gazing up at the TV that was running those music videos that used to matter so much.

There'd been plenty of trouble brewing in his circle of friends, which he'd kept a cautious distance from as he watched, with a mix of wonder and schadenfreude, Leigh move methodically through Anatole and Lydia's friendship, apparently indifferent to the carnage. But that afternoon, over beers and whiskey chasers, it gradually dawned on Chris that the stupid drama he'd stayed clear of was taking the worst possible turn. It wasn't going to spare him after all, because for whatever mad, inscrutable reasons, Leigh was there to let it be known, with all the astonishing presumption of youth, that he was done with Anatole and Lydia both, that he was now Chris's for the taking.

Things get a little foggy after that. Blame, as always, the beer and whiskey. But Chris's refusal must have started there, in The Congress, to the soundtrack of Tears for Fears's "Everybody Wants to Rule the World," because Leigh, in a funk, at some point went to the bathroom to piss, and on his way back stopped to chat up the guy sitting at the bar, who sent a round of drinks to their table, and then joined them. He was exactly the kind of middle-aged queer on the make that Chris loathed, but he managed to coax Chris and Leigh to come back to his house—his mansion, as it turned out—and while he mixed drinks in his state-of-the-art kitchen, and a dazzled Leigh took in the vulgar opulence of the living room, Chris made a decision. He wasn't staying. If Leigh wanted to stay he'd have to make a decision as well.

Which is when Leigh uttered his ultimatum, those words Chris remembers exactly. *I'll leave but only if we can fuck.*

Beauty's everything and nothing. Chris already knew that, even then. It's what he paid teenage hustlers in that hotel on Lexington Avenue to demonstrate again and again. The truth's always been that he hates beauty just about exactly as much as he worships it. And he'd already made up his mind. Just because the kid had lucked into an angel's body, he wasn't going to fuck this hustler who'd already fucked over his two best friends.

He hasn't forgotten Leigh's forlorn *So you're saying you don't want me?*

Or his own careful, nonrefundable *No, Leigh, I don't want you.*

Or the look on Ed's face as he stood in the doorway with that tray of martinis, scarcely daring to believe his luck.

For years he jacked off quite reliably to the memory of that afternoon; sorrow of a certain kind's always been an aphrodisiac. He gives his cock a couple of perfunctory tugs now, but nothing's stirring.

He turns off the shower, shaves, dresses. The universe loves irony even more than it loves futility. In the long run, Leigh doesn't seem to have damaged Anatole or Lydia half as much as he damaged Chris, who never even allowed himself to be touched.

The birds chatter mindlessly, the brook chuckles like an idiot. Why is he doing this? Why not leave things exactly as they are? Sitting on the unmade bed, he texts Leigh back, saying he's in Poughkeepsie at the moment, asking when and where they might meet. The response is almost instantaneous. Leigh doesn't have a car; he hopes Chris does. How about the Funky Knickerbocker? It's a nice little café in downtown Newburgh. Say, one o'clock? Does Chris need directions or can he Google it?

He can Google it.

A sentence from the wedding ceremony has somehow wormed its way into his brain: *Now I know in part; then I shall know fully, even as I am fully known.* It's odd, he wasn't paying that much attention; he didn't even register it at the time, but now it's stuck there.

He's under no illusion their reunion won't be disillusioning. He's prepared for that—even, in a way, looking forward to it.

At least the traffic should be light on a Sunday morning.

"Hey, come with me." Leigh grabs Pascal's bony wrist. They've lolled about for a couple of hours, watched some meaningless TV, shared a joint, made out a little, finished the last dregs of the lukewarm champagne. Now they're about to part ways at the corner of South Street and DuBois.

"Why?"

Pascal is heading up to the gym at the College of Saint Mary's—his usual post-brunch destination on a Sunday afternoon. Cleanse the system he's just polluted, as he puts it. He recently finessed a pass due to some part-time instruction he does at the college. Leigh's welcome to come too, but the gym bores him to death, even though he knows he should keep in better shape—he's not fat these days, though he's not fit either. He doesn't live in his body the way Pascal does; nobody lives in their body the way dancers do, even dancers whose knee injuries have sidelined them from professional work and forced them to scramble for shit-paying teaching jobs.

"I'd just like you to be there when he shows up," Leigh says. "Then you can go."

"But *why*?"

"I don't really know why. Maybe so we can compare notes later?"

"This is a guy you've never even mentioned before, and now it's important for me to meet him?"

"Look, I'm having a strange reaction to all this. It's kind of out of the blue. But yeah, I think it's important for you to at least lay eyes on him."

"This is starting to get a little wacked, don't you think? Do you still have a crush on this dude?" Leigh can't quite tell whether Pascal's teasing or being serious. Their occasional infidelities, which aren't supposed to be an issue, sometimes can be.

To be on the safe side, he decides Pascal's not just teasing. "You can't really have a crush on somebody you haven't seen in—I don't know, how long has it been? I can't even count that high. But you're right, I've been thinking about him this morning. It's sort of put me in one of my moods."

"Your moods," Pascal says. "Almost as famous as your former good looks."

Leigh's having a hard time reading Pascal's tone.

"He's not something I've been keeping from you; it's more like something I've been keeping from myself. I just put it all in a box years ago and buried it and I haven't thought about any of it since."

Which isn't entirely true, but close enough.

Pascal's not mollified. "And now this dude comes and unburies the box and you finally just *have* to look inside."

Leigh caresses his boyfriend's thin arm. He rubs up against him the way a cat might. He knows how much Pascal thrives on simple physical contact. Pascal's wearing a sleeveless T-shirt, gym shorts, flip-flops, clothes he could so easily slither out of in an instant. That's maybe what Leigh loves most about him— that sex can happen anytime. With Pascal there's always this hint that paradise is just around the corner.

"It's probably a huge mistake," Leigh admits. "There's no good that can come of it. That's why I want you to be there when he shows up."

"I still don't get it. Why even bother to meet up with him? And what if it turns out he's had second thoughts after all these years? What're you going to say to that? I'm just trying to gauge your susceptibility here."

Leigh has to laugh. It's true: he's always thought of Chris as the big *If Only*.

They walk for a bit in a silence that's not so much tense as perplexed. Pascal's the one to break it.

"So, would you have sex with him? If it came to that?"

Leigh takes his time before answering. "If it came to that, would you be cool with it?"

Pascal shrugs. "You know me. I'm cool with everything."

"You'll sulk."

"We'll deal with that when the time comes. Just promise you'll tell me all the sordid details. You won't hold anything back."

"It's a deal."

"He'd fucking better be hot."

"But we're not going to have sex. That's just too crazy even to think about. Besides, he's got to be in his fifties by now."

Pascal nudges him. "As if Former Miss Sugar Daddy's Plaything of the Universe is going to have *any* trouble with that!"

"Oh, shut up!"

"See, you're already thinking about it."

"I'm just daydreaming. He didn't want me when I was pretty. He's certainly not going to want me now."

"You sure are going on about your looks this morning. You know that? It's not like you."

Leigh notes with satisfaction that they've both turned the corner and are walking down DuBois toward the Knickerbocker.

By force of habit he's early. Once he's reconnoitered the Funky Knickerbocker—an unprepossessing joint with a couple of forlorn al fresco tables set out on the sidewalk and a chalk menu board propped on a chair—he settles himself in a nearby park. From the little he's seen, Newburgh is Poughkeepsie's twin. Lots of abandoned, boarded-up buildings. Lots of parking lots and chain-link fences. Lots of glowering, heavyset nineteenth-century churches. It's still light years better than most of the places he's spent his life in.

Even though it's a beautiful Sunday, the park's deserted except for two old black men on a bench sharing a bottle and some small brown birds hectoring one another in the hedge. There's little traffic on the streets, even less on the sidewalks. A woman with enormous hips pushes a double stroller as if to say there's all the time in the world. An anorexic white jogger suggests the opposite. Along come a couple of middle-aged guys, one black, one white, too far away to see their faces, but it only takes a moment for him to register they're gay. Maybe it's the way the black one moves, a lightness of step, a sassy sway to the hips. The white guy's less obvious. But then he slides his arm around the black guy's waist, playfully bumps hips, there's no hiding it. Even at this distance Chris can hear a shriek of laughter, from which one he's not sure.

He's not wanted to admit this to himself; it's been haunting him all weekend, it's made him feel churlish and duplicitous and uncouth, but he finds something depressing about middle-aged gay couples. The whole farce of Anatole and Rafa's wedding, their craven attempt to mimic something that doesn't really belong to them, however much they and their many well-meaning friends try to pretend. Man up, he wants to tell them—but he never will, because he'll never see them again. If you're going to fall for men, or boys, then deal with the fact that you're going to be an outcast. It's not for the faint of heart, it's not for anybody hoping to be liked or respected or accepted or any of that bullshit. It takes courage, it takes armor and cunning and stealth and a fire burning you up inside. And it's going to be fucking lonely and probably lethal in the end. So get used to it.

The two guys are having a lively conversation; from this distance he can't hear what they're saying, but clearly they're into each other. The longer he gazes, the more clues reveal themselves. The white guy's wearing capri pants and espadrilles, for fuck's sake. He keeps touching the black guy, can't keep his hands off him. The black guy lights a cigarette, holds it theatrically aloft when the white guy tries to snatch it.

Chris imagines a sniper hidden in the park. It's a fantasy that often comes to him in Amsterdam or Berlin. A sniper watching, waiting. Finally deciding to take that pair out. Put them out of their misery.

Slot them, as his Rhodesian mates would say.

Those little brown birds keep fussing in the hedge, and he remembers—a stray, pointless memory; the important stuff vanishes, the stupid stuff remains—Gabir handling with great care one of those fat white pigeons Saleh used to keep in a cage in the courtyard of the compound in Karadah. The kid's long, gaunt, melancholy face as he held the bird at eye level, gravely pretending to converse with it in sweetly cadenced Arabic. Or maybe he really did converse, and the joke, as always, is on Chris.

Blue eyes thousands of years old.

Slotted.

The gay guys have passed nearly out of sight. Idly he makes as if to aim an invisible gun at them, pull a nonexistent trigger. Though instantly he's embarrassed by the meanness of the gesture. It's just that he's bored. He looks at his watch. Ten minutes to go. Still time to pull out, cut his losses. Something he's always been very good at doing.

The two gay guys are hanging out in front of the Funky Knickerbocker, both smoking cigarettes with attitude, and it suddenly comes to him like a punch in the gut: the white guy in the capri pants and espadrilles—he'd never have recognized Leigh if he just passed him on the street.

Leigh identifies Chris more readily. He smiles, tosses his cigarette aside, moves toward him while the black guy holds back. They don't embrace, they don't shake hands, they don't touch. They just stand there regarding each other. Leigh tilts his head a little to one side. Chris notices, on his left upper arm, peeking out from his short-sleeve shirt, one of those tribal tattoos all the young army guys in Iraq used to try to armor themselves with, talismans against bullets, bombs, terror, inadequacy. Did Leigh do a stint? Seems unlikely, but no more so than his own history.

"So," Leigh says. "Long time no see."

"Very long time. Thanks for agreeing to meet me."

"No problem. Thanks for being in touch. So I guess you found the place okay."

"No trouble at all. Exactly where Google said it would be."

"Ah, Google. How did we ever live without it? Badly, I guess. Oh, this is my partner, Pascal. I'm not too great at introductions."

Pascal comes forward, wipes his hand on his gym shorts before offering it limply to Chris. Though his eyes, set in an austere princely face, twinkle mischievously, almost as if to suggest he and Chris share a secret. His hair's braided in corn rows; from his left earlobe a delicate, leaf-shaped earring dangles.

"Nice to meet you," he says, flashing a wry smile as his grip momentarily tightens, then goes slack again.

"Same," Chris tells him.

He hasn't bargained on Leigh bringing backup. But why not? Always bring backup. He's spent the whole weekend outgunned.

"Look," Pascal says, "I'm just heading off to the gym. I'll leave you guys to it. Nice to meet you," he repeats, and Chris realizes he's grateful Pascal's been there for the beginning. The terrifying part will commence once the two of them are on their own.

"Feel free to join us," Chris hears himself saying. "Lunch is on me."

But Pascal's insistent. "Nope," he says. "I hear you boys have a lot of catching up to do. Have a fun time together. Call me later, kiddo," he tells Leigh, making that very American phone gesture, hand held to the ear, thumb and pinky extended, middle three fingers tucked away—the same pantomime those young GIs in the Green Zone deployed in their homemade Lady Gaga video.

"You bet," Leigh is saying to his boyfriend.

Chris watches Pascal walk, waft, swish away.

"Nice butt, don't you think?" Leigh observes, noticing the attention Chris is paying. He's gone for years without knowing whether men's butts mean anything to Chris; it's gratifying to think he finally knows.

But Chris's answer—"I'll take your word for it"—deflects him. He hasn't worked out in his mind exactly how he thinks this afternoon will unfold, or even how he wants it to. Now that Pascal's sort of on to him, is there really any reason to provoke the turbulence that's certain to follow if he indulges in some meaningless hanky-panky? Still, he's amazed at how little Chris has changed. His hair's cropped short, he's tanner, more sinewy. For a guy in his fifties, he's in superb shape. Plus he's lost none of his ability to withhold, that quality that made him so maddeningly irresistible.

"Even after four years I still can't take my eyes off him," Leigh says. "Sometimes he'll say, *Leigh, quit looking at me*. But he loves it. He's a born performer. Even now that his dance career's over. I'm just crazy about him. You know, I only started dating black guys in my thirties. I never even looked at them before, then one day I just started noticing how gorgeous they were. Is that racist—I mean, to be attracted to a type? Probably, but what you want is what you want, right? Your dick doesn't know fuck about political correctness, even if the rest of you is pretty well-versed."

Pascal danced with American Ballet Theatre—it doesn't get much better than that, professionally—but still his family won't speak to him, still he gets hassled up at the college (though he's got some powerful protectors there). Back when he had a car he used to get pulled over by the cops all the time for no reason. Driving while black, and all that. Leigh doesn't fetishize damage, but the older he gets the more he thinks it should at least be revered. Certain people, when they get damaged, don't become bitter: they become—how else to put it?—gentle and thoughtful and, well, exquisite.

"For a while I went after older guys. Or maybe I should say, I let *them* go after me. But you already know that. Then

I had my straight guy phase, which was fun and challenging and kind of crazy. Now this is where I am. It turns out to be true what everybody says. Once you go black, you never go back."

Chris has never actually heard anybody say this. But OK, he thinks. Fine. The door's closed. It ends even before it begins. Whatever *it* is. He even feels a certain relief.

"So this is a favorite hangout," Leigh tells him as they exchange the sidewalk's sunlight for the café's gloom. "Nothing fancy."

The place is empty except for a Bob Marley look-alike reading the newspaper. As his eyes adjust, Chris sees that the Funky Knickerbocker is at least funky enough to serve wine and beer. He's feeling flustered; his assessment is that things aren't going all that well. Leigh too seems ill at ease.

"You know what?" Chris barks his Baghdad laugh. "I could really use a drink. It's been a very long weekend. I'll tell you about it. Join me? I mean, it's already safely after noon."

It's a test—do they still have anything in common? (At least Leigh still smokes.) Most of their interactions back in the day were extremely well lubricated; in Chris's experience alcohol's always been the solution, never the problem.

"Hey, full disclosure," Leigh confesses. "I've already had half a bottle of bubbly this morning. It's our brunch thing. Don't get me wrong—we're not a couple of alkies. We only do this on Sundays. And the buzz is long gone, so sure, why not?"

Chris doesn't feel the need to tell him he's taken a couple of swigs of vodka on the way over. His own version of backup.

The Bob Marley look-alike turns out to be their waiter. He introduces himself as Malachi. He's got a lip piercing he seems unable to keep his tongue from toying with.

They order a bottle of white and peruse the menu.

"I'm trying not to eat meat these days," Leigh says, "but I'm a terrible backslider. Pascal's vegetarian, actually vegetarian trending toward vegan, so he pretty much keeps me in line, but the FKC makes an insanely delicious Reuben. Promise you won't tell on me, okay?"

What are the odds Chris will ever lay eyes on Pascal again? So what's Leigh worried about? Still, he's touched by this fiction that whatever begins this afternoon will somehow continue.

Though he's no longer as interested in Leigh as he was half an hour ago, he's still interested enough. "Don't worry," he says. "Your secrets are safe with me. So tell me everything. Why don't we start with the tattoo?" He can't keep his eyes off the ugly thing. It says, so sternly, *You don't know a thing about this person anymore.*

Leigh pushes his sleeve up so Chris can take in the whole design. It looks a bit incongruous on his thin arm; Chris is used to seeing tattoos like this flexed on considerably more pumped-up biceps.

"*The* tattoo," Leigh says. "It's not like it's the only one, you know."

Why should Chris care? But the news makes him queasy—like hearing someone's been in an accident. "How many?" he asks.

Leigh's laugh is bemused, almost philosophical. "Oh, I don't know. Seven or eight. You'd think I'd know the exact number. I try to keep them mostly out of sight. They're only for the people who get to know me really well."

Malachi interrupts to pour their wine, take their order: that forbidden Reuben for Leigh, a pulled pork sandwich for Chris (he got so sick of Green Zone pork in Baghdad, but now he finds he misses it in Port Harcourt).

"So, this one," Chris says, once they've clinked glasses, "the one I get to see. I'm just curious. To me it says military." He resists the urge to touch it.

Leigh laughs. "Hardly!"

"But I seem to remember you were a military brat. Like me. Isn't that right?"

"Reason enough to stay the hell away from all that."

"*I* didn't," Chris tells him.

"No way!"

Chris has promised himself not to rehearse his résumé. No replay of Friday's dinner with Anatole and Lydia. "Stupidest thing I ever did. I won't bore you."

"But that's awesome. I mean, it's fucked but it's awesome."

"Unfortunately, I couldn't put it better myself. But what about you? I want to hear what you've been up to."

"No. Wait. You have to tell me more. You can't just tell me you went military. I have so many questions. I gathered from your text you're not still living in Poughkeepsie. What brings you back?"

"Anatole got married. Remember him? Of course you do. I had to be stateside anyway, so I swung by the wedding."

"Let me guess. To what-was-her-name. Lydia. I knew it'd happen eventually. They weren't really fit for anybody except each other. But I didn't think it'd take *this* long."

"Don't be silly," Chris tells him. "You must've known Anatole better than that. He's married his fellow. Nice bland Dominican guy he's been with for ages. And Lydia's long since married. Has a kid in high school."

Leigh's not thought of these people in a very long time, and their sudden, conjured presence isn't exactly welcome. Anatole the borderline pedophile, Lydia a sad desperate cradle-robber. He's done some pretty atrocious stuff in his time, but sleeping with her was about the worst. So why did he do it? Well, because he could. Because he liked having the power to bewitch pathetic strangers. But also because he thought he was being kind, even though at the time he'd never even heard the phrase "mercy fuck." Let's face it: Anatole and Lydia were both mercy fucks. Though with Anatole, mercifully, the fuck never amounted to more than a couple of mutual jerkoffs. If even that.

None of this is worth remembering. He's being cruel, he realizes with some consternation. He wouldn't have slept with either one of them if he hadn't been attracted in some way.

He looks down at the table, traces a whorl of wood grain. "Well, I'm glad of all that," he tells Chris. "I'm glad for both of them."

Chris hears the careful neutrality.

"So if you're not in Poughkeepsie, then where?"

"Africa right now. Nigeria."

"Ooh. My idea of paradise. So what do you do there?"

"You've heard that old joke—If I told you, I'd have to kill you." Though he wonders whether that's exactly what he's become: a stale, unfunny joke.

"Ha ha ha," Leigh says drily. "That's perfect. I always thought that record shop of yours was a front. So now you can tell me the truth: was it drugs? Money laundering? I know: you were running a boy prostitute ring. But you forgot to recruit me. What were you thinking? No wonder you went out of business."

Chris tries to ignore the hint of hostility. "First off, I didn't go out of business. I closed. Second, I had a very loyal customer base. I actually did make a living selling high school kids the kind of music they wanted."

"And certain other useful paraphernalia," Leigh reminds him.

"Well, that too."

Leigh doesn't need to know about Dad's financial help. Nobody needs to know that, and nobody does. It doesn't prevent Chris, even now, from feeling inadequate and ashamed. Was making a mint in Iraq atonement or revenge?

Once again he's talking about himself way too much. "I want to hear about *you*," he tells Leigh. "I never imagined, when I decided to track you down, you'd only have moved a few miles downriver."

"It was a very roundabout move. Took me twenty years. And anyway, why *did* you decide to track me down? Sounds a little ominous, you know. Sort of like 'unfinished business.' You don't have it in for me for some reason, do you?"

Of course it's unfinished business—surely Leigh knows that as well as he. Or does he? Chris is having trouble getting his bearings; so far Leigh's a mix of exhibitionism, flirtatiousness, antagonism. There's no need to alarm him, so he says, "Oh, you know, this whole wedding thing, seeing Anatole and Lydia, it just got me thinking about the past. Not something I usually have much time for. In my line of work, I get shot at a lot. Not so much anymore. I've kicked myself upstairs. But when folks are trying to kill you, you tend to live minute by minute."

"I thought you weren't going to divulge what you do," Leigh kids him. "Now you tell me it involves folks trying to kill you. Does this mean you're going to have to kill me after all?"

"I do security work. I used to protect the guys doing power grid reconstruction in Iraq. Now I protect oil guys from getting kidnapped by local gangsters and revolutionary wannabes. Great fun, really, if you've got the chops for it. End of story."

"Okay," Leigh says. "Fine. And I work with LGBT kids in the Newburgh city schools. Maybe that's where the military-style tat comes from. Valor under fire. It's not what I'd have predicted for myself. I got a taste of all the other stuff. The shit I thought I wanted. So it's not like I never arrived. Anyway, I don't have a whole lot of illusions at this point. Which isn't such a bad place to be, given where I started out. I mean, do you remember the last time we saw each other?"

"Of course."

"Worst moment of my entire life."

"Surely that can't be true."

Chris has forgotten the challenging way Our Boy of the Mall could look at you.

"Are we going for polite," Leigh asks, "or are we going to try to be honest here?"

"Let's go for honest."

"Well that's refreshing."

"What's that supposed to mean?"

"I'm hoping to find out. Isn't that what this afternoon's all about? Otherwise we're just wasting each other's time."

So they *are* on the same page. Chris feels the kind of heady rush he gets when he prepares to head into a situation.

"You're certainly not wasting *my* time," he assures Leigh. "I'm the one who came looking for you, remember?"

"Okay. So you want honest? Here's honest. Ed fucked me that night. God, this is such ancient history. After you took off, he got me even drunker than I already was, and since you'd left me horned up and frustrated, I guess I was a pretty ripe target. I'd never gotten fucked before. I was really hoping you'd take care of that, but obviously you weren't interested. He had a huge cock and he knew how to use it. He practically destroyed me. And you know what? It hurt like hell but I fucking loved it. After you and Anatole and Lydia, all that fumbling around and ambivalence and confusion, he made me feel like something real was finally happening, like I was in the hands of somebody who knew exactly what he wanted. I was hooked. He just reeled me in, and I didn't even put up a fight. I mean, you'd just thrown me away. What else was I supposed to do? Is this too much to hear?"

"It hurts a little," Chris surprises himself by saying.

"Good. Maybe I want it to hurt a little."

Malachi sets their plates down, refills their glasses from the bottle chilling in a bucket of ice. They're the only customers in the joint, and Chris wonders if Malachi can hear every word they say.

Leigh's obviously got no such concerns; he talks right through their waiter's ministrations. "You know, I called you a bunch of times after that night. If anything, Ed just showed me even more how you were the one I really wanted. But you weren't answering."

"I'd left town."

"But why?"

"Because of everything. You and Anatole and Lydia. It was all too much like something I'd been through before. I was starting to have flashbacks. So this time I did what I should've done before. I extracted myself from the situation."

"And it didn't matter what happened to anybody else?"

"Given what I was dealing with—no, it didn't. I know that sounds like an asshole response, and probably it was. At the time I thought of it as the moral thing to do."

"And now what do you think about it? Throwing me away like you did."

"You keep using that phrase."

"Because that's exactly what it felt like. In a way I never got over it. Don't get me wrong. I picked myself up, I made the best of the situation. I mean, I was done with Anatole and Lydia. They were both needy jerks as far as I was concerned. I see now how that probably wasn't completely true, but at the time all I could think of was how they were using me."

"And, of course, they thought you were doing the same to them."

"I'm sure they did. That's how it works, right? You only see what you see, not what anybody else is seeing. So after that night I was with Ed for a while. Ed Dorgon. His friends all called him the Dragon. He treated me like royalty. Trips to the City. Five-hundred-dollar-a-night hotels. Amazing restaurants. Weekends in Miami, a week in Paris, a whole month in Rome. I don't know how he made his money; I didn't really care to know. I wasn't in love with him or anything like that—I was still in love with you, crazy shit that I was—but for a while I thought I was the luckiest guy in the world.

"He had this Cessna he'd take me up in; there was nothing the Dragon loved more than flying up and down the Hudson on a nice afternoon. I think he loved that a lot more than he loved me, which was fine; it made me feel a little less dishonest. And he was a very generous guy, paid for some courses at the community college, even paid for pilot's lessons, though I ended up never getting a license—or a degree either, for that matter.

"So that went on for a while, probably a couple of years, and then eventually he got bored with me. He didn't drop me, exactly. After a while he started sharing me with his friends, who were extremely grateful, both to him and to me. And eventually he just passed me on to them. There wasn't any one single moment when it happened, but one day I realized I wasn't in his life anymore. It didn't really matter. I was very popular for a while. The 'it' boy, people called me. Fire Island. Provincetown. I was never a whore, exactly, but I guess I came pretty close.

"I know this sounds really strange to say, but I was just way too pretty for my own good back then. It brought out the worst in people. The bad thing was, it made them expect things I just didn't have. The good thing was, they were willing to fork over a lot of cash to find out I didn't have what they wanted me to have. And to this day I'm not even sure what that was. Am I being too honest here? Have you lost whatever respect you ever might've had for me?"

"Go on," Chris says. "I need to hear this."

"Well, so eventually I wasn't the 'it' boy anymore. One day I woke up and I was thirty years old and the gorgeous hair that Anatole used to love to get his hands on was thinning, I'd put on weight and the world was suddenly full of dazzling new 'it' boys coming out of nowhere. Pretty soon I realized I didn't have a clue what I was going to do next. So yeah, that was a rough time. There was this guy Matty I got involved with who turned me on to meth, which was pretty fucking great at overcoming my self-doubt and punching my libido up a few notches, but three years of my life basically vanished. It's a wonder I never got AIDS. I don't even have herpes. The worst I ever got was hepatitis. Well, and gonorrhea. And anal warts. I know I'm oversharing, but what the hell? You tracked me down. Obviously there was something you wanted to know. Though probably not the timeline of my STDs."

He didn't really know till he laid eyes on Chris that he still wants the big *If Only*. Even after all this time. *Especially* after all this time. Chris hasn't changed a bit—only become more intensely himself. A distilled version of the unassailable man who threw him away.

Malachi has asked, "Is everything okay?"

"Peachy," Leigh tells him. "But it's not okay to eavesdrop."

Malachi doesn't miss a beat. "Wouldn't even think of it."

"Good. Then don't."

There's a sassiness to Leigh that Chris has forgotten, an edge that's a little aggressive and not entirely pleasant, particularly now that he's lost his beauty.

"I usually know the waiters here," Leigh explains. "This one must be new. We'll break him in soon enough. By the way, I need to piss. I have a tiny bladder. Liquid just runs right through me. Back in a sec, okay?"

It's not even that he's lost his beauty, Chris thinks as he watches Leigh flounce away. Has he gotten more effeminate over the years? He used to be androgynous in an unearthly sort of way; now he's got that self-advertising butt wiggle gay men of a certain type acquire.

Everybody likes to say beauty's only skin deep, but he's pretty sure they've got it all backward. Beauty's the very skin of the soul. And when a boy's beauty starts to fade—meaning, when the boy ages, as he always, always does—it's because his soul's fading too. It's the symptom we try not to notice, the symptom we like to pretend we don't believe in. Because, face it, the soul doesn't fare well in its transit through the world, and Chris is only really invested in souls still relatively untouched by the corruption. He can grieve for older souls, but that's a very different kind of investment. And love? He's not sure love's anything he's ever been particularly interested in. Longing, adoration, awe—sure. But love?

He recalls that night he and his friends first met Leigh, that night the kid fell into their clutches, and they brought him back to Anatole's apartment, and in some kind of inspired dementia Anatole and Lydia took crayons that had materialized out of nowhere and drew pictures on Leigh's white T-shirt as he sat there on the sofa, head thrown back, throat exposed, drifting in and out of alcoholic stupor. Graffiti, defacements, desecrations posing as tributes. But now it's Our Boy of the Mall who's vandalized himself. The reasons aren't so unfathomable, Chris thinks, unable to let go that phrase, so lightly spoken but so deeply melancholy: *Eventually I wasn't the "it" boy anymore.* Those hidden tattoos he's both dying and dreading to see: what are they but Leigh's way of having come to terms with that?

He's hungering for those tattoos. He needs to rip open the tunic and expose the bomb strapped to the chest of the slotted boy. That's what he pays those handsome young men in Amsterdam and Berlin so handsomely for. What do Leigh's finances look like these days? But of course that's stupid. The last thing he wants is to finally turn Leigh into a bona fide whore. Not when he's spent years paying whores to turn themselves into Leigh.

The other words he can't get out of his head: *He had a huge cock and he knew how to use it. He practically destroyed me.*

Leigh's back, smiling affably—even coquettishly.

"So," he says, "I was in there taking a thoughtful leak, catching up on the witty graffiti on the wall, when it occurred to me, okay, this is all just really weird. You come all the way from Africa, and it's obvious you don't want to talk about anything regarding what you've been up to, which is the same Chris I remember. But here's my basic question for you. Was that basically a booty call you put through to me last night?

"I'm just trying to imagine it. You've spent the day watching Anatole and his fellow get married, you're surrounded by all these gay friends of theirs, most of them are coupled off but maybe there're one or two cute ones who might be available. Everybody's been drinking, there's nothing like a wedding to get people thinking about sex, right, because what's a wedding except one long foreplay leading up to the honeymoon suite. I'm guessing that underneath your man-of-mystery pose you're not that different from the rest of us—no need to be embarrassed by that—so maybe you try to hit on one or two good-looking fellows, but nothing's popping, and you end up back in your hotel room frustrated and horned up and, like you say, you've been thinking about the past for obvious reasons, and lo and behold after a while here I come floating up to the surface, and you think, I wonder if he's still around by any chance? Am I anywhere close?"

"I didn't call you because I was looking to get laid."

"Then what *were* you looking for? See, I don't think you're being honest with me. Or even with yourself. I think maybe in spite of your best intentions you feel like you made a mistake a long time ago, and you've decided you want a do-over. Which, by the way, is more than fine with me. You're still a really sexy guy. I know a million things have happened since then, and it's a real shame we didn't get it on when we were still young, but we can at least get a sense of what we missed out on. You know, what might've been. If only. To tell you the truth, I'd take a do-over on just about everything I've ever done if I could."

Chris can see Malachi pretending to read the paper with

great concentration. His tongue worries that ring affixed to the side of his lip.

"We'll never know what might've been," Chris says. "And anyway, if it's any consolation, I never threw you away. I threw myself away. It's what I've spent years doing."

This hasn't occurred to Leigh. "What a waste, then," is all he can say, though what Chris has just told him clearly demands a more substantial response than that. With a shiver he feels he's suddenly looking right into Chris in a way that's never before been possible. "Look," he says, seizing the moment for whatever it is. "My apartment's only a few blocks from here. Let's ditch the Knickerbocker. Come back with me, okay? I'm not asking you to either do or undo anything. If it makes you feel any better, just pretend you're interested in seeing my tats."

The wine on top of the champagne's gone to Leigh's head, maybe that overdose of corned beef and Thousand Island dressing in the Reuben too, but he's enjoying himself. He knows he's tormenting Chris, but he thinks he's earned the right to. It took him a long time to learn how amazing it can feel when you've got nothing to lose. If anything's made the sorry journey worthwhile, it's been learning how to revel in a kind of abjection. He's tried to talk to Pascal about this, but they always end up in some kind of misunderstanding or argument. Which is OK. It's just part of being abject, knowing there's no way to justify yourself. You just have to be what you are. There've been some sweet moments when he feels he's achieved that. Now might be heading toward one of them.

"I know I'm not so pretty anymore," he says. "I know I've got this body covered in tattoos I can't ever undo. Some of them are pretty great, but some of them are hideous, like 'what on earth was I thinking?' hideous.

"When I was a kid I read this book, *The Illustrated Man*. I can't even remember who wrote it, but it was about this carnival guy, covered head to toe in tats, and under certain circumstances those pictures would come alive, they'd tell their stories. The book was all the different stories this guy's skin would tell. My tats don't come alive. They don't even tell stories. They're just, I don't know, markers of things that happened. Or places I was. Or how drunk I was at the time. They don't mean fuck. And yet there they are, I'm always carrying them around with me, people who get to see them think they communicate something important about me, something that's secret and that I'm revealing only to them, and I guess they do communicate something, though I have no idea what it is, and that's sort of been my life I guess. It's all just pretty random and scattered."

"So what about Pascal?"

"Pascal doesn't have anything to do with this. It's not like we live together or anything cozy and domesticated like that. I'm not like Anatole."

What's Chris supposed to say? I don't find forty-something-year-old men attractive? But, of course, this isn't just a forty-something-year-old man, it's a forty-something-year-old man who still carries within him the drowned ghost of an eighteen-year-old. Despite himself, that's someone Chris is still attracted to.

"No," he tells Leigh, and he's not lying, "you're not a bit like Anatole."

"Thanks. Anyway, I wonder who paid for the wedding. Isn't it supposed to be the father of the bottom? So that would be Anatole's dad, I guess."

Once again, that quick shift from thoughtful to vulgar that's one of Chris's memories of Leigh. "Both Anatole's parents are dead," he says, but Leigh's still traveling on his own train of thought.

"I guess that means my dad would have to pay for my wedding. Since his son turned out to be nothing but a big old piggy bottom. Now, *that'd* be fun to explain to the old man."

"Are you in touch?"

"Hardly. We were never really in touch, even when I was a kid. My mom was the one I was super close to."

"Past tense?"

"She died a long time ago. Before I even came to Pough-keepsie. I was still in high school."

"I don't remember you ever mentioning that."

"No, well, I wouldn't have. You're not the only one who doesn't talk about things. So, now that we're on the subject, can I ask another personal question?"

"Sure, go ahead," Chris says with a touch of *déjà vu* as the weekend keeps folding into itself.

"Top or bottom?"

Malachi's abandoned all pretense of perusing the news-paper.

"Neither."

"I understand how you can be *versatile*, but how can you be neither? I mean, what do you do? I hope you at least jack off. But what do you fantasize about? Do you think about women, or men, or, I don't know, camels? Look, I know you're not going to tell me whether you're gay or not. I totally respect that. I know stuff's complicated. Personally I prefer *queer* to *gay* these days. But if you don't fuck, then what do you do? And don't change the subject on me. Now that I've finally got you, I'm sure not letting you out of this one. And if that doesn't make you happy, well, you should've thought about that before you showed up. Because this is exactly what you showed up for. I'm pretty sure of that. Or am I just pissing you off right now?"

But Chris isn't pissed; he's reached exactly the place he's wanted to be—cornered, hemmed in, pinned down. His whole life's been about escape routes. It's a relief, for once, to see so few in sight.

"No," he admits. "You're right on the mark."

"Then we've just taken this huge step, haven't we? So please answer my question." Leigh used to practice making doe eyes in the mirror; he hasn't needed to do that in a while, but old techniques don't easily disappear. "*Please,*" he begs in a way certain guys have really liked over the years.

He's gratified to see he hasn't lost it entirely.

Chris hesitates, and for a moment Leigh's worried he's going to clam up, but then he says, slowly and deliberately, "Okay, just so you know. Just so there're no secrets. I pay boys and watch them fuck."

He scans Leigh's face for a reaction, but there's none, just that intense Our Boy of the Mall gaze. "I tell them what to do and then I watch them do it. It's like those dreams where you can control everything that happens."

"Gee, that never happens in *my* dreams."

"Well, it does in mine. And it's pretty wonderful when it does, but of course it's not real. You'd think the Internet would be some kind of paradise for a guy like me, but it's not. I guess I'm old-fashioned. I need to be in the same room with them, I need to touch the clothes they've taken off and I need to run my fingers through their hair and I need to smell their sweat. And then I like to take them out to a nice expensive dinner. I like to talk with them, get to know them a little. That is, if you can ever really get to know a whore. Probably what happens is, they make up stories and I make up stories right back, and we're all satisfied by the lies we tell each other. Sometimes I think I should've been a porn film director, though I really don't have any interest in sharing those moments, or making any kind of permanent record of anything. So instead I ended up as a private military contractor, getting paid obscene amounts of money to do as I'm told and ferry a bunch of clueless contractors while guys with AK-47s try to nail my ass. Which all makes perfect sense, I think, though I'm not even going to try to explain why."

"Okay," Leigh says. "So that's definitely clarifying in your usual mysterious way. So maybe you want to hire me and Pascal for the afternoon? We can put on a great show, the two of us. We'll have you creaming in your trousers in no time. And we could definitely use the money."

"You've got to be kidding."

"Hey, I'm serious. I'd love to have your cock up my ass. But if that ain't gonna happen, well, I'm happy to do whatever gets your rocks off." His voice drops to a murmur. "I still think so much about what if you'd just said yes to me. How we might've even ended up in a relationship, I mean not just sexual but a real relationship, with emotions and caring and all that. All the stuff you long for but never exactly find. God, I'd so love to have gotten married to you, I'd love to have had your baby and all that, and here we'd be still in love twenty-five years later. You'd never have had to go down the road you did. And I wouldn't have had to either."

"You know that's just fantasy."

"I know, I know. Maybe I'm just really jealous of Anatole right now, even though I think gay marriage is total bullshit."

"Well, at least we can agree on that."

"But what a fucking wonderful idea all the same, don't you think? You and me together for the rest of our lives, for better or worse, in sickness and in health, till death do us part, blah blah blah. Doesn't it give you a hard-on just to imagine it?"

His hand gropes Chris's crotch for confirmation.

"Look," Leigh says, "we should get out of here. Before our friend Malachi throws us out."

As if on cue, their waiter approaches. "Would you gentlemen care for dessert?" He beams at his cleverness. His tongue dances merrily around his lip piercing.

"I think we'll get dessert back at my place," Leigh tells him. "I seem to remember I have some leftover cherries in my fridge that desperately need to be popped."

Chris can say one thing for Malachi as he lays the check on the table: he's not easily daunted. "You gentleman have a memorable afternoon, then," he tells them with a supercilious bow.

"Oh, don't worry. We plan to," Leigh says; and then, to Chris, in a voice Malachi's sure to hear even as he moves off, "I hope you're gonna leave our Rasta man a *huge* tip. I mean, for everything we've put him through. Though on the other hand, maybe *he* should pay *us*."

Since Leigh's apartment is only a few blocks away, and the weather's so nice after last night's thunderstorms, they decide to hoof it. They walk in silence, both smoking furiously, neither of them quite sure what they've agreed to, but both understanding that something momentous and long-deferred is finally at hand.

Leigh's not worried in the least about Pascal. He'll pitch it as just another minor backslide, a meaningless romp in bed with some guy he's not likely to see again because, hey, the guy lives in fucking Africa. And Pascal, for his part, will lap up the details, it'll fuel some fun between them, and what Pascal doesn't know won't hurt him—though what would hurt him is what Pascal already suspects: that Chris isn't just some guy, and whatever's going to happen isn't exactly meaningless. The only reason you never mention a person's existence to your lover is because you don't want to diminish their secret power by putting it into words. He senses Pascal's already read him pretty thoroughly on this one.

Chris's confession has surprised him, though in a way it makes perfect sense. He was never somebody who liked to get dirty, though Leigh doesn't quite see how being a hired gun, which is basically what he gathers Chris is, keeps you from getting dirty. Of course, he stopped looking for any kind of consistency in other people around the time he discovered he couldn't manage to find any in himself.

When the silence becomes too oppressive he blurts out,

"God I love this stinking city. Just had to say that."

They're on a particularly shabby-looking block.

"And why's that?" Chris asks with that arch tone Leigh remembers, and in fact did his best for a while to imitate.

"Why did I have to say it, or why do I love it?"

"Both."

"Fuck, I don't know. I think it's only the failures I'm really able to love. I mean, they're the ones that need our love, right? I think that's what my life's taught me. Not that I was ever much of a student. Does that make any sense?"

"Sure. Why not? And *why* did you say it?"

"Because I fucking hate silence. It makes me so anxious. When people go silent, it means they're thinking, and when they're thinking, that's when they start to get really dangerous. So let's keep talking, okay? Tell me what it's like where you live now."

"Port Harcourt?" Chris is thoughtful for a minute, and Leigh wonders what various answers he's sorting through. He's not convinced, even now, that he'll ever get more than a carefully vetted presentation from Chris. But he's grateful even for that.

"I remember when I was a kid," Chris says haltingly, like somebody recovering half-forgotten things, "we went on vacation to Disneyland. It was divided into different sections, there was Frontierland, and I think something called Fantasyland, and then there was Tomorrowland. Sponsored by Monsanto, as I remember. There was this model City of the Future, complete with monorails and skyways and geodesic domes and parks and I don't remember what else. But you know what? They got it totally wrong. Port Harcourt's the real Tomorrowland. It's got its surreal downtown of Western-style, air-conditioned office buildings with backup generators for when the power goes out two or three times a day, and then there're the fortified residential compounds where all the foreigners live. And then the slums. Slums like you wouldn't fucking believe, miles and miles of them, and then out past the slums, that's where the delta begins, where the Niger fans out toward the Gulf of Guinea, hundreds of dark sluggish waterways that're laced with crude oil from accidental spills, criminally sloppy engineering, illegal bunkering, natural seepage, all of the above. It's a horror; people are living out there in all that muck even though the mangrove swamps are skeletons, the fish are all dead, the fishing boats have to go a half mile out to sea to find any fish at all these days, and the methane flares are like something out of Dante's inferno. Everywhere you go there's this seething roar, and at night the jungle's lit with this fierce orange glow. I don't kid myself. I'm just a cog in a machine that fuels the rest of the world, that keeps the lights on and the engines running and the batteries charged.

"I tried to tell this to Anatole and Lydia, but they weren't really interested. I mean, why should they be? Or maybe it's more accurate to say, how could they be? You can't really be thinking about the Niger Delta with any clarity while you're getting married on a manicured golf course in Dutchess County. Even if it's fucking gay married. I don't have any illusions about myself. I'm just an errand boy for the likes of Anatole and Lydia. And you and Pascal and everybody else in this amazing, oblivious, doomed country. And it's not just America. It's the whole fucking species. Homo sapiens, which as far as I can tell is only another way of saying weaponized chimpanzees who are hell-bent on tearing their cage apart without realizing it's not a cage, it's their fucking life support they're shredding.

"So you wanted to know what's it like where I live now? That's what it's like."

He has the disheartening feeling he's delivered this same rant to someone else this weekend—but to whom? In any event, his monologue's carried them to Leigh's building, a late nineteenth-century row house whose brick was covered over with white paint at some point, though the paint's now flaking.

Two boarded-up buildings of similar vintage flank it. Dingy stairs lead to the third-floor apartment. Chris smells stale pot smoke, incense, cat litter.

"Watch out for Matilda," Leigh warns. "You probably won't even see her. She hates humans. Except for me, of course. Pascal claims she doesn't even exist. My ghost cat. Anyway, she's been known to ambush the unsuspecting interloper."

The living room's tiny and messy and ill lit. An ashtray balances on a stack of magazines and newspapers. Leigh's tacked some vintage beefcake photos of black men to the walls. Besides Pascal, does Leigh have any regular friends? Hard to imagine anybody stopping by this place for drinks. Apart from the beefcake photos, there's been no attempt at decoration, though on the windowsill some potted geraniums struggle to bloom. It's not even student digs—more like a transient's room in an SRO.

Leigh moves immediately to put on music. He crouches fetchingly by an old-fashioned CD player preserved in a kind of cultural amber Chris finds himself grateful for. This particular soundtrack's unfamiliar—some kind of Afro-Caribbean band.

"So what music are you into these days?" Leigh asks him.

"None, really. I mean, you can't be in Africa and not hear music, but I don't really listen to it anymore."

At night, when the surrounding slums are blacked out, drumming replaces the usual overlay of car radios, radios from the little bars that serve homemade brew, radios blaring in the overcrowded courtyards of the compounds the Nigerians call Face-Me-I-Face-You.

"How strange," Leigh says. He settles comfortably onto the sofa next to Chris, closer than need be but not quite touching. "I thought music was your passion. I mean, Immaculate Blue, and all."

"Well, it's gone now. I don't know what happened."

"Hey, I'm sorry about that joke I made about your store.

I didn't really mean it. You had some amazing stuff there. I remember I picked out some albums for Anatole. He wanted to deepen his collection. I don't think he cared much for what I brought home, though."

Chris notes the way Leigh says "home" instead of "Anatole's apartment."

"You were into hardcore, if I remember right. Butthole Surfers, Black Flag, The Pixies. So what are we listening to?" Lilting, rippling, laid-back—whatever it is, it's definitely not hardcore.

"It's this band called Boukman Eksperyans. Aren't they great? They're from Port au Prince. Pascal turned me on to them. It's kind of voodoo meets reggae meets rock and roll. It's a whole crazy genre."

Leigh's enthusiasm takes Chris right back. Do people still think music can conjure some wished-for life into being?

"You should check out Lydia's kid's band on YouTube sometime," he tells Leigh. "I'm not too sure what to make of them. It's more like organized noise than music. Though there's definitely music in there somewhere."

"Sounds cool. Is the kid cute?"

"You know I'm not going to go there," Chris tells him. "They call themselves Modder Spook. M-O-D-D-E-R. You can see for yourself."

"Oh, good, another way to waste time later. Hey, by the way, can I offer you something to drink?"

"I'm fine," he tells Leigh. "I've got to head down to JFK in a couple of hours." What he doesn't say is that, astonishingly enough, he wants to be sober for this. Whatever this will be.

Leigh makes a sad face. "So little time," he says. "I guess I should show you my tats, then, since that's what you came back here for. I'm not even going to make the etchings joke."

Chris has already thought of it, anyway. He's on the verge of telling Leigh *No, I don't need to see your tats, we don't know each other well enough for that.* But if they don't know each other well enough, when will they ever?

"First," Leigh says, "I think I need a little weed, you know, get me in the mood to undress myself for a stranger. You sure you don't want a toke? Just one can't hurt."

Chris hasn't smoked weed in years. "I'm going to pass on that too," he says.

Leigh laughs that bemused, generous laugh of his. "Hey, I totally understand." He takes a couple of deep drags. They sit in silence. Chris can see why silence makes Leigh feel anxious. He's about to break it with something inane when Leigh says, "So, off comes the shirt." He unbuttons slowly, deliberately, staring at Chris, who forces himself to meet and hold his stare. Leigh wads up the shirt and tosses it across the room. Only reluctantly does Chris shift his gaze to the bared torso beside him.

Twin canaries decorate Leigh's unmuscular pecs.

"These babies were early on." Leigh blots them out with his palms. "Oh, well. That's what I want on my tombstone, by the way. *Oh, well.* Don't you think that's a pretty good epitaph for somebody like me?"

Over his heart is a bright-red heart broken in two, with MAT inscribed on one half, and TY on the other.

"Way too obvious, I know. But I was suffering. That guy I was telling you about. Totally straight, had a girlfriend the whole time he was banging me. Matty on crystal was a completely different animal than Matty sober. He just couldn't get enough of me. Then I'd go for weeks without hearing from him. I hear he's clean now, married, has a kid. Another *Oh, well.* Didn't you love it when Johnny Depp broke up with Winona Ryder and got his tattoo changed to read WINO?"

"I don't think that made the news in Africa."

"I guess not. There wasn't any way to change MATTY into anything except MATTY, and besides, that sort of repair work's really expensive. Anyway"—he touches his stomach—"this one I still like. This one goes with me to my grave."

In gothic lettering is inscribed, just over his shapely navel, NEVERLAND AT NIGHT.

"My Tragic Lost Boy phase. Disneyland never had a Neverland, did it? Leave it to Michael Jackson to build that one, and we know how that all turned out." Leigh opens his hands to offer himself for inspection. "You can touch them, you know. They're not like Matilda. They won't bite."

It's a used, worn, scrawled-on body he's being offered. He touches Leigh's slack belly, trails his fingertips over all this evidence of damage, waste, life lived. Leigh's closed his eyes, thrown his head back; he's savoring Chris's touch. Chris meanders unhurriedly across Leigh's chest, circles his nipples till they harden, feels a heart beating extra quick beneath the inked broken heart, dances across an exposed throat, jutting Adam's apple, the middle-aged stubble of chin and jaw. He rubs a finger across Leigh's closed lips, which open slightly. After a few seconds' hesitation he slides a finger in, just to the first joint. Leigh closes his lips around it. His tongue caresses the tip. He suckles gently. Slowly Chris feeds another half inch in, to the second joint. Just like that, they've crossed the invisible line. Just like that, they've committed themselves to something that can't be undone.

Reluctantly he withdraws his finger. Leigh looks at him with the moist eyes of the stoned. "You haven't even seen the main event," he says.

Putting a hand on Chris's knee for support, he hauls himself up from the sofa and turns so that Chris can see his naked back.

A crosshatched, serpentine tree trunk emerges from the waist of his Capri pants, at first centered on his spine, then curving to the right as if perched on a windblown cliff overlooking the ocean. It sends its delicately leafed-out branches back to the left like beseeching arms. A few blue leaves have detached themselves and scatter across his left shoulder blade. A couple of the farthest escaped leaves have turned into birds.

He unhitches his belt, lets his pants drop to his ankles, exposing the tree's shallow, spreading roots. A muscular tap root disappears into his butt crack.

"Cost me a fortune."

Nothing says ruin like this fantastical, intricately inked tree—though it's as much a dragon, really, now that Chris contemplates it, as a tree. Or maybe a gnarled, sorrowful old woman lamenting her children cast away one by one. Or—

"I'd been hearing about this guy up in New Paltz for a couple of years. Sort of a legend in local tat circles. He supposedly studied with some master in Japan. Everybody said he was a total recluse, impossible to know. But they all revered him. Showed me pictures of his work, which was impressive, but then I saw a couple of his tats in person and I just thought, wow. I mean, the way they seemed to live, like they were, I don't know, emanating from somewhere inside the person instead of just being these decorations on the surface. So that's when I started saving up. I'd heard he wouldn't do just anybody. You had to sort of be sponsored. Get an introduction from somebody he knew, arrange an interview. Supposedly he only took one out of five people who came to him. Anyway, I took the bus up to New Paltz and met with him. Big gruff bear, huge beer gut, this long gray beard he kept tied up in a twist with a rubber band. I never saw him wear anything but overalls, no shirt. Not a tattoo in sight.

"He grilled me pretty intensely. I was honest with him, and by the end I was fairly sure he couldn't stand my little faggot ass. He said he'd have to think about it and he'd get back to me. So a bunch of weeks went by and I thought, okay, fine, obviously I didn't make the grade.

"Then one day he called me out of the blue and said, did I

still want to put myself in his hands? That's the way he phrased it. His name was Harvey Dark, which wasn't his real name, it was his *nom de tattoo* as somebody called it, but anyway, I just decided okay, I'll do this, I'll put myself in your hands. The stipulation was, I wasn't allowed to even ask what design he was going to do. I had to trust him. All my friends thought I was insane. The guy I was going with at the time told me, You do this, it's the straw that breaks the camel's back, which it was, but that camel was on its last legs anyway.

"When I showed up for the first session, Harvey told me that what impressed him was that I kept my tats private. That's one of the main reasons he decided to take me on. Because I wasn't doing it to show off. That's supposedly how it's done in Japan, since tats there have such a long association with the yakuza gangs. So he freehanded the basic outline that first session, and then whenever I had a little money I'd come in and get the detail and shading and all that in installments. This was when I was busy trying to kick the meth habit, and in some strange way I think it sort of saved my life. I mean, it gave me something to look forward to that wasn't about me. For about eight months I was a work in progress. By the time Harvey was finally done with the tree, I was done with meth. Sounds a little too pat, I know, but for the most part that's the way it happened."

Chris has the oddest impression Leigh's not even talking to him, he's communing with himself; this recitation has happened any number of times before, and not necessarily when anyone else was even in attendance. But that's OK; he's content to gaze at the squandered, transmogrified back of the untouched kid he was once in awe of.

None of his scripted episodes with hustlers even come close to the reality that stands with its back turned to him.

"I really don't have any idea what it's supposed to represent," Leigh continues. "Harvey kept calling it the heaven tree. But growing out of my asshole? I've had some pretty big things shoved up there, but a tree? Please! When I asked Harvey, all he said was, 'Sometimes the heaven tree grows out of the ear, sometimes out of the mouth, sometimes out of the asshole.' Like, yeah, very enlightening. And of course I can't even really see the damned thing, except sort of, in a mirror. Harvey said that was the point. That I'd have to rely on other people to describe me to myself.

"Anyway, I'm just talking. Now you've definitely got me pegged as either crazy or a loser or both."

Leigh doesn't turn around; he continues to present Chris with the illuminated page of himself. And Chris, grateful he's had some time to take it in before being asked to pronounce judgment, feels aghast, desolated, moved, wishing there could be a single word to somehow convey all that. But since there isn't, he gets up from the sofa and without thinking any further puts his arms around Leigh in a tight embrace from behind. He presses himself against him—and grabbing his encircling arms, Leigh presses back. Chris kisses Leigh's neck, his shoulders, those leaves that have turned into birds. He moves slowly down that desecrated back. His mouth follows the branches to the trunk, traces the trunk to its roots. His tongue completes its journey where the root disappears into mystery. Leigh's smell is funky, this is wildly unhygienic and humiliating and absolutely necessary. He thinks of the dark, oil-fouled waterways of the delta, the mortally wounded mangrove swamps, the floating mats of dead fish, the seething gas flares.

Every action's a desecration. Hasn't most of his life been devoted to turning that insight into a kind of sacrament? He feels he's arrived at something like complete abjection. It feels very good to finally be there.

Leigh's leaned forward, hands braced on his knees, to make himself more available. Chris reaches around to grasp a modest erection. So this is what all the fuss was about. He strokes the smooth shaft unhurriedly. His tongue, lapping and burrowing, makes Our Boy of the Mall gasp.

"Let's move to the bedroom," Leigh suggests. "Don't worry, I've got everything we need."

The bedroom's as messy and claustrophobic as the rest of the apartment. The bed hasn't been made, a laundry basket overflows, half the drawers in the battered bureau hang open. Chris notices leather restraints attached to the bed posts. Who knew?

Leigh kicks a stray pair of jeans out of the way. "Pardon my housekeeping. I didn't really know what to expect from the afternoon. No, that's not true. I was playing a little game with myself. Like, if I tidy up, it'll be for no reason, but if I don't—well, I thought, I'll take a chance on embarrassing myself with a slovenly apartment. How's that for logic?"

His erection hasn't abated. He sports it like the randy teenager he once was. This is how he would've looked as he jumped into bed with Anatole, with Lydia, with countless other chosen souls. "Here," he says, "let me get you out of your things. It's always been this fantasy of mine, stripping a hot guy naked before he has his way with me. It's not every day I get to act that out."

It's jarring for Chris to hear himself referred to as a hot guy.

"Oh my gosh," Leigh prattles on as he unzips Chris's pants, "I always figured you'd have a big juicy sausage. Very nice."

The moment's fast losing its enchantment, but Leigh's on his knees and expertly rekindling Chris's cock. There's been a worrying tendency, lately, for him to lose his hard-on with the hustlers—not a problem when he's only a spectator. Fortunately Leigh's very adept at what he's doing; by the time Leigh rolls a condom down his length, Chris is feeling almost supernaturally robust.

Leigh's pleased with himself. His vanity's taken any number of hits in recent years; he's grown used to disappointments, but he still remembers how completely devastated he was when

Chris turned him down. So it's kind of delicious that it's all come full circle. It's like going back to his younger self and saying, See? It wasn't some deficiency in you; the problem all along was with Chris, he was the one who was fucked up; and even though it may have taken him a long time to realize the error of his ways, he's come to make amends whether he even realizes that's why he's here or not.

Be kind to those who are kind to you, and be kind to those who haven't been so kind. It's not much, but it's what Leigh's tried to live by all these long hard years.

He positions himself on the mattress on all fours, because for whatever reason he likes being taken, at least initially, from behind. It lets him privately commune with the tender agony of being impaled.

In a haze of disbelief, Chris grips Leigh's flanks and slowly slides his cock into Our Boy of the Mall. Leigh pushes back, opening up, accepting him, and Chris delivers slow, meditative thrusts, each of which Leigh meets with a guttural groan. If hearing Jimmy Somerville's falsetto that night at Anatole's was a time machine, this is something altogether different. Chris suspects that the universe we inhabit may not be the only universe, that there may be an infinity of universes, all lying alongside each other, or even curled up inside one another like an infinite regression of nesting dolls, and if that's true, then the unlived past he's glimpsing here is really, in some other universe, the life he's known fully. He tries to savor the astonishing moment, but even in the midst of doing so he can't really pretend this present-day Leigh excites him all that much. Try as he might to imagine it's the teenage Leigh he's penetrating, the insane inked heaven tree spreading across his back makes that sleight-of-thought impossible.

Is it possible to be aroused by nostalgia alone?

In desperation—he can't bear to look at that heaven tree anymore—he flips Leigh on his back. Their gazes lock. His thrusts pick up momentum; Leigh's groans turn to sharp, satisfying yelps. Isn't this what Chris always wanted? To wrest a sob from the beautiful, exquisite, untouchable boy?

"Harder," Leigh urges. "Yeah, fuck me."

And now he's got that sob in spades.

At the same time, Leigh's expression has gone slack; the light's disappeared from his eyes. "Go ahead," he gasps. "Hurt me, dude. Make me feel it."

There must have been a time, before Internet porn, when there wasn't a script. Nowadays, everybody knows exactly how sex is supposed to go. Chris notices it in the boys he hires. They used to be clumsy, tentative, touchingly unrehearsed. Now they all recite the same lines. He's a little disappointed Leigh's no different.

He doesn't want to hurt Leigh, despite Our Boy's rote pleas, despite the staccato punches he's delivering to Leigh's asshole. It's not any kind of revenge he's taking. Or if it is, it's only revenge on himself.

Besides, is what he's doing now any worse than what he didn't do back then?

"Oh God," Leigh cries, as if on cue, "I fucking love it. I love your big cock inside me."

He's had lots of cocks inside him over the years. He wishes Chris's felt a little more, well, transcendental, but let's face it, Chris doesn't possess a whole lot of finesse. No big surprise, considering the guy's peculiar practices. But that's OK, it's not about technique. Leigh's enjoyed plenty of technique in his time. Instead it's about—what, exactly? Why has he waited years for this, when it's just another rod of flesh poking around, and rather inexpertly at that, inside his hole? At the same time, he definitely does love the feeling of Chris inside him—or at least the *fact* of Chris inside him.

There's the solid world of marriage and family and ceremony—Chris glimpsed all that yesterday. Then there's this other world that feels like leaning very far out over an abyss, where there's only the infinite drop and the momentary, insanely gratifying experience of sheer *being*. All at once Chris thinks he understands the heaven tree that grows out of the ear or the mouth or the asshole, but then almost instantly that insight recedes, it doesn't even make any sense anymore; and yet he has that residual feeling he sometimes gets when he wakes from a dream—of having almost grasped something essential, without which life is just darkness, confusion, despair.

Then it comes to him—how you can't return to a place you've never been to, can't recapture what you never had. The chances you miss stay missed forever.

You can't fuck Our Boy of the Mall because in this universe, the only universe you get to live in, he no longer exists.

The thought's enough to make him lose his hard-on. Though he substitutes in quick succession images of Caleb, the waiter named Quinn, Adam, Jasper, Gabir, John Pembroke, it doesn't work.

"Well, what happened there?" Leigh asks. "I thought we were getting into a groove."

It's an excellent question. Chris is certainly not going to say, *Nothing personal—I just realized it was a ghost I was trying to fuck, not you.*

"Sorry" is all he can think of.

"Hey, not a problem. It's the thought that counts."

Leigh's disappointed, but he knows from experience—both bitter and hilarious—how that can happen with older guys (younger guys too, actually!). It hasn't yet begun to happen to him, but it's only a matter of time.

"So now what?" Chris asks. He doesn't see much prospect of regaining his erection.

"It's all good," Leigh tells him. "And anyway, I'm still rock hard. Want to make me come?"

Does he? It seems churlish to say no, though he's given up

any notion that he still craves this version of Leigh in any carnal way. "Let's put a condom on it first," he suggests.

Leigh's a little surprised, given the voluptuous precedent Chris's tongue set earlier (and which Chris is regretting), but as he's said, it's all good.

It turns out Chris gives a passable enough blowjob. Leigh looks down at him and thinks, this could've been ours. But it's a tricky fantasy to sustain, even as Chris's mouth edges him closer. He imagines coming while still in Chris's mouth—the totally unnecessary condom is ample protection, after all—but he worries that'll upset Chris, so he pulls out, slides the condom off, and with a groan more perfunctory than heartfelt squirts on the sheets. They need to be washed tomorrow, anyway.

The moment's merely squalid, Chris thinks, two inconveniently middle-aged men stranded together on a mattress in the middle of an aimless Sunday afternoon. He can't help but glance at his watch, dismayed there's still a good half hour left till he needs to make his exit.

That milky splatter on the sheets makes him unbearably sad, and he wonders, not for the first time, whether the whole point of orgasm isn't, somehow, unbearable sadness.

Despite or because of that, Leigh insists, wordlessly, on a postcoital cuddle. Cuddling's definitely not Chris's thing, but he acquiesces. They make a clumsy fit—Leigh curls an arm uncomfortably behind Chris's back, nuzzles his nose in Chris's armpit, and asks, "So, what's Anatole's husband like? On second thought, don't tell me. I don't really care. Does that make me a terrible person? I hope they're really happy together. That's all I have to say."

Chris tries to relax into a semblance of ordinary conversation. "It was the most conventional, middle-class, ghastly wedding you can imagine."

"I guess I'm not too surprised," Leigh replies. "Still, what I really liked about Anatole was his—I don't know what to call

it. Daringness? Aliveness? I know he was silly and manipulative and a lot of other not-so-great things. But I also thought
he had some kind of, I don't know, courage? And I saw how
that courage wasn't going to last, because there was this huge
terror there too, and I guessed that terror was probably going
to win out, and in the end he was going to opt for some kind
of safety. That's why, when you said he'd gotten married, I
honestly thought he'd married Lydia. Because both of them
were really conventional when you got right down to it. But
what did I know? I was this fucked-up kid. Not only had I just
lost my mom, I'd seen my best friend from high school who I
used to get stoned and trade blowjobs with die of some kind of
overdose. I mean literally, right in front of me. So I was freaked
out and susceptible to just about anything by the time I stumbled into Poughkeepsie. And Anatole and Lydia in their spider
webs just waiting for me. Not that I can really blame them.
They were just being who they were. And you know, Lydia
had some spunk as well. That night we shroomed and went out
on the train bridge. Crazy stuff. In her way she was even more
wacked than Anatole. I guess I have to give them both some
kind of credit. Sometimes what you depend on is other people
being even more wacked than you are."

They're just old friends reminiscing, conjuring a world
nobody really remembers anymore except them.

"Lydia and I went out on the Walkway yesterday," Chris
mentions. "Or was it the day before? This weekend's such a
fucking blur. Anyway, she told me about that night the two of
you ventured out there. I never had the courage."

"The Walkway Over the Hudson," Leigh says mockingly.
"I've never been. Never had any desire to go, now that just
anybody can. God, I wish it'd been you and me out on that old
wreck. Think of the things we could've gotten up to, if only we
hadn't both been such cowards."

"You were never a coward," Chris reminds him. "You were

being very brave. Just as I was trying, in my feeble way, to be ethical."

"Ethical schmethical." Leigh traces Chris's nipple with his fingertip. "You were just afraid of my awesome boy power."

"Being afraid isn't the same thing as being a coward, you know."

"Here," Leigh tells him. "Just relax and lie back. Enjoy."

His lips graze a fit chest, hard belly, toned thighs. Chris closes his eyes. He's fine with this; he thinks Leigh's more than earned the right, though he feels unmoved by these investigations. It all just seems empty and pointless.

Leigh feeds on an armpit, gently pushing Chris's right arm above his head; he follows with the left. He seems to have a thing for armpits. Chris feels a little exposed, the slightest reflex twinge of anxiety that kicks in whenever he's less than completely in control. Then he hears a click. Cold metal encloses his wrist. *Stupid boy*, he wants to say. *I've slotted guys for less.* But he doesn't say that. He doesn't say anything. He could resist, of course; he could so easily take Leigh out before the poor bastard even knew what hit him. But the damage has already been done, the weekend a stunning string of reversals. After so many dogged checks, this feels blessedly like checkmate.

He allows Leigh to cuff his other wrist.

"That was almost too easy," Leigh tells him, straddling his chest, watching him with that fond, vague smile of the stoned. "Should I be worried?"

To Chris's consternation and even disbelief, his cock has gone achingly hard.

"You're already a dead man," he tells Leigh.

In response, Leigh kisses him on the lips. "I actually think you're kind of liking this. Let me get your feet here, then we're good to go." Chris lies becalmed, an almost welcome resignation descended on him as his captor restrains his ankles. "Excellent," Leigh informs him. "Now we're talking."

Chris is pretty sure Leigh's not a maniac. Anyway, he's been fully complicit in this sudden turn of events. He noticed the restraints first thing on entering the room; he chose to ignore them, chose to proceed. He's never understood suicide bombers, finds it impossible to get inside their heads, but he's never been sure they were crazy—in fact he's always secretly envied them their resolve, their infernal, supernatural courage. He's never regretted slotting Gabir, he'd do it again in an instant, but he's always wondered whether Gabir, in that final instant of consciousness, regretted anything either.

Stroking Chris's resurrected cock, Leigh asks, "So what're you thinking about right now?"

"I'm thinking about a kid I blew away back in Iraq. Ugly story. I was thinking I'd do it again if I had to." He barks his Baghdad laugh. "I have absolutely no idea why I'm thinking about that right now. You're not going to make me miss my flight, are you?"

"You know, that might be the first completely honest thing you've ever said to me. Not about missing your flight. The other part. Even though there's a lot more there than I can even start to understand. And don't worry. I don't have any intention of blowing you away. Except maybe in a good way."

Chris isn't angry. He's not even upset. That's the most surprising thing. He sees how the whole weekend's been preparing him for exactly this. *Then I shall know in full, even as I am fully known.*

"Just relax." Leigh strokes Chris's chest calmingly. And Chris surprises himself by complying. "There now. Despite what you may think, I'm a gentleman. You can't go if you don't come."

His clever tongue flicks and teases and caresses; he gulps and gasps and gags; he demonstrates his considerable sword-swallowing skills. There's no need anymore to pretend it's Caleb or Quinn or Gabir or even Our Boy of the Mall. It's exactly who it is, Leigh Gerrard at forty-four, doing his strenuous best to pleasure a man who once caused him a great deal of unintended pain.

Leigh's fist takes over for the moment. He looks at Chris imploringly. Those doe eyes. "I want you to come in my mouth, okay?"

"It's not safe," Chris tells him.

"Why wouldn't it be? I mean, if you've been telling me the truth, there's no way you've got HIV, right?"

"You never know," Chris says.

"Well, it's a risk I'm willing to take. Indulge me here."

Chris doesn't have much choice. He remembers the first time he let John Pembroke blow him. It was late at night in that big old empty house they'd rented, and they'd been sitting close on the sofa, drinking and talking for hours, aimless talk that nonetheless had moved them inexorably to the moment that had been threatening for weeks if not months, till Chris said, with a sigh of doom and excitement and surrender, "So if you're planning to seduce me, which we both know is eventually going to happen, why don't you just go ahead and do it now, okay?" Handsome, smart John Pembroke, whom he may as well have slotted then and there, given how things turned out. He doesn't ever think about John, but now the thought of him brings an unexpected tear to his eye. He feels Leigh's fingertip find his butthole, linger there interrogatively, insert itself tentatively, then more boldly, all the way in, and somehow that not particularly welcome sensation gets mixed up with John Pembroke and the unexpected tear in his eye and before he can sort any of it out he's flooding Leigh's mouth.

Leigh laps gratefully. He's always thought, starting with Billy back in high school, that semen tastes like a cocktail of ocean water, coconut juice and freshly cut grass. Who knew Chris was carrying such a huge load. He must have been saving it up for months, even years.

"You don't need to kiss me," Chris warns as Leigh's face approaches. He doesn't particularly relish the prospect of a mouthful of himself, but then he's not the one in charge, and Leigh's going to do what Leigh wants to do, which is kiss him deeply and long, all muscular invasive tongue that Chris resists and then doesn't resist. His cum is salty and warm and viscous and sort of disgusting though he actually kind of loves what Leigh's doing to him and is a little sorry when finally he stops.

"I guess I should fuck you now, since I've got you all tied up," Leigh says, smiling and sitting back on his haunches. "And if this was a porn movie it's what the audience would be expecting, right? But I have this feeling getting fucked is about the last thing you want. And even if I thought I could crank it up again, I'm really not into fucking all that much, in fact I'm sort of philosophically against it. As opposed to getting fucked, of course. But obviously it takes all kinds."

Chris would like nothing more right now than for Leigh to fuck him, to break him in and make him hurt—but of course that's crazy, that's not what he wants in the least. Though it'd be fitting punishment for having fallen into Leigh's trap, which wasn't ever a trap.

Leigh's thoughts are moving along a different track. "You mentioned chimpanzees earlier," he says, fondling Chris's detumesced member. "You called us weaponized chimpanzees. Which is pretty good. But there's actually other monkeys we're even more closely related to. I was reading about this somewhere. Bonobos. The hippie chimps, some scientist called them. They're totally promiscuous, they use sex for everything, to comfort each other, to communicate, to reinforce the social hierarchy, to show gratitude for, I don't know, one of their buddies picking the nits out of their hair. I think some of us have more of the chimp genes, and others have more of the bonobo genes, but we've all got some of both, just in different proportions. I'm not sure why I'm saying all this. Maybe I'm just trying to make sense of where you've gone in the world, and what the two of us are doing together here. Because it feels kind of great having you here, being able to shoot the breeze like the old days when we knew so much less and had so much more to look forward to, and it's both totally crazy and completely sense-making that I've had to tie you down to make it happen. I mean, I'm hoping you find all this as fucking absurd as I do. And I mean absurd in a good way. In a sort of cosmic way."

"I have a feeling I need to be leaving very, very soon," Chris tells him. "As in right now. I really can't afford to miss my plane. I'm in charge of running these two Dutch engineers out to Bonny Island Tuesday afternoon."

As if in keeping with the skewed serendipity that's been the afternoon's dominant note, from one of those doleful churches he passed earlier a doleful bell spells out the hour. Four o'clock. He really does have to go.

"All good things come to an end," Leigh says, releasing Chris's ankles and wrists. "You're not too pissed off at me, I hope."

Chris sits up and pops him a fast one on the left cheekbone, not too hard but connecting with a solid thud.

"What the fuck?"

"Really sorry about that. But now I think we're even."

"I thought we'd already done a pretty good job of evening up the score."

"So maybe it starts all over again," Chris surprises himself by saying.

"Oww." Leigh touches his cheek. "That really hurt. Am I going to have a black eye?"

"Probably."

"Oh great. Well, whatever. God, this has all been so sleazy. I've loved it, though—really, I have. So thanks, Chris. Thanks. I say that with all my heart." Which he touches—or rather the cartoonish broken heart inked on his skin.

★ ★ ★

It's dark when he wakes from his nap. He hasn't realized how much the afternoon has taken out of him.

His cheekbone aches. He doesn't want to even think about looking in the mirror.

Chris must be on his plane by now, somewhere over the Atlantic, heading for Africa. Too strange to contemplate, so he doesn't.

He sees he's slept through a whole slew of phone messages from Pascal.

"So, did you fuck?" Pascal asks.

"Yeah, we did."

"That's cool."

"It was no big deal. It might've been once upon a time. But that time's long gone."

"Did he have a big cock?"

"I've seen plenty bigger. It was all kind of clumsy, to be honest. Not romantic in the least."

"Reunions never are."

"It wasn't even a reunion."

"Whatever. That hot guy was at the gym again."

"Did you talk to him?"

"You know me. I'm shy."

"You're not shy! Give me a break."

"Well, then, I like to take things slow. Besides, the best part's always the anticipation. Reality can be so disappointing."

"So when am I going to see you?"

"When do you want to see me?"

"Is tomorrow good?"

"Tomorrow's perfect. By the way, I scored some rad weed off that priest I was telling you about."

"Definitely bring it. We'll celebrate."

"And what're we celebrating?"

"I don't know." Leigh yawns, stretches contentedly. He's

not going to overthink things. "Life. Weirdness. Us. Something like that."

Malachi, their waiter this afternoon, was kind of cute, he thinks, in a Rasta sort of way. And Leigh's pretty sure the brother was digging his and Chris's conversation—Leigh even steered it in the direction he did at least partially for Malachi's sake. He's a little notorious for seducing the waiters there. He and Pascal have even turned it into a verb—knickerbockering. He thinks maybe he'll go knickerbockering later this week, see what this Malachi's up to.

Matilda has settled on his chest, purring possessively now that the intruder's been expelled. She's a really beautiful cat, affectionate, capricious, and mysterious.

His swollen cheekbone throbs. Not sure how he'll explain the black eye to Pascal. Blaming Matilda's not really an option.

In the long run, he suspects, it'll all come down to just him and Matilda. They're already practically an old married couple anyway.

It's perfect. It's everything that makes Nigeria Nigeria. They wait on the tarmac in Abuja for four hours without a word of explanation, which means the flying time he exaggerated to impress Anatole will turn out to be just about on the mark. Serves him right. The plane runs out of food, water, liquor, everything. The toilets overflow. A few passengers, then more, raise their voices in anger, demand to be let off. The flight attendants become defensive, petulant, aggressive. A fistfight breaks out in coach, though Chris is relatively insulated from that in business class. Airport security comes on board to remove the participants, which only incites a second insurrection from other passengers demanding to be removed as well. After a prolonged shouting match, the police withdraw with their lucky victims, leaving the rest of the passengers seething.

Chris always makes a point of not talking to his seatmate,

but it's hard to be stranded next to somebody for this long without communicating. In the aftermath of the hullaballoo he gives in to the stranger's periodic attempts to generate a conversation. Jaap's a Dutch chemical engineer, thirty-five or so, with a weak chin and thinning blondish hair. Very pale-skinned (the Yoruba word for whites is *oyinbo*, "peeled banana"). He speaks the precise, soulless English of the Dutch. He's coming off a stint in Qatar, he's never been to Africa before, he's not quite sure what to expect, but he's had all his shots, so what could go wrong? He's out for a six-month assignment at the Bonny Island refinery. Too late, Chris realizes he'll likely be providing security for the guy.

"The pay's amazing," Jaap tells him guilelessly. "But they told me not to bring my family. They didn't forbid it, they just strongly advised against it. I don't understand. They play up the safety of the Residential Areas, so I don't understand what the problem is."

"Trust me," Chris says. "This place is about to explode. Or implode. Or fucking tear itself apart. None of the options are very attractive. You really don't want your family out here when whatever happens happens."

"I'm very family oriented," Jaap confesses. "I have two terrific little boys. They're everything to me. Six months is a very long time."

*And you're never going to make it out here*, Chris thinks. The only ones who make it are the ones who've abandoned everything. Why they've done that—it doesn't matter. All that matters is that they have.

He's sorry he sucker punched Leigh. That wasn't called for, it wasn't fair. It wasn't just for the disconcerting turn the afternoon took, it was for the whole fucking weekend. Still, he'd like to think it did them both some good. But who can know?

There'll never be a real home in the world for the likes of him. He understands that. He can live with that.

Of course, there's always the question of money. Anatole's fine, but Lydia and Leigh could definitely use some help. Idly he explores the fantasy of astonishing them with a gift, but can't decide whether they'd be grateful or offended. It's something to think about.

He's pretty sure none of this has been the beginning of anything, though he wonders if maybe it's been an end to something.

At last the French pilot comes on to announce that unspecified mechanical difficulties are going to keep the plane indefinitely grounded in Abuja. There may be some seats available on the next Air France flight, due in fourteen hours or so. Those who choose to do so can transfer from Air France to Air Nigeria for the final leg of the journey to Port Harcourt.

"That's another thing you don't want to do," Chris says in answer to Jaap's question. "You really, really don't want to do that. Don't even think of flying anything but Air France or Lufthansa in Nigeria."

Once inside the chaotic terminal, he manages to slip away. That he's not taking his own advice will become apparent to Jaap soon enough. Maybe that'll put them on a more realistic footing the next time they meet.

Anyway, he's not worried. Discreetly but reliably weaponized, Ian will be at the airport to meet him. Chris can already hear the good-humored "bloody kaffirs!" that'll greet his account of his travel delays.

He's the only *oyinbo* on board. They've barely even risen to cruising altitude before the ancient Air Nigeria MD-80 hits tropical turbulence; rather than maneuvering around it, the pilot seems intent on riding out the rough patch all the way to its end. Nigerians are an exuberant lot. They whoop and shout and lament and pray as the plane bounces around the sullen sky. Clouds enclose them completely. They're flying blind. And over all the clamor from the passengers, seated alone in business class at the front of the plane, Chris can hear, because the door to the cockpit won't shut properly, the pilot singing robustly, fearlessly, in a magnificent baritone, *"How I love to fly Air Nigeria! Pleasure, pleasure! Go scatter! Scatter!"*

# ABOUT THE AUTHOR

 **PAUL RUSSELL** is the accomplished author of various works of both fiction and nonfiction, including several novels, anthologies, poems, short stories, essays, and book reviews.

For his outstanding accomplishments in literature, Russell has received many awards, grants, and fellowships, including the National Endowment for the Arts Creative Writers Fellowship in 1993.

His most recent title, *The Unreal Life of Sergey Nabokov*, published in 2011 by Cleis Press, won the Ferro-Grumley Award for Fiction in 2012. The same title received a silver medal for the Independent Publisher Book Award in the Literary Fiction category, and was a finalist for the Lambda Literary Award in 2012. He also received the Ferro-Grumley Award for fiction for his novel *The Coming Storm*, in 2000.

He attended Oberlin College and later studied at Cornell University, where he earned an MFA in creative writing and a PhD in English.

Russell has taught English at Vassar College and the University of Exeter, and is a professor of English at Vassar College. Among the courses he has taught are Gay Male Narratives in America after 1945, Queer Alphabets, Mormons in America, and James Joyce's *Ulysses*.

Other published novels include *The Salt Point, War Against the Animals*, *Sea of Tranquility,* and *Boys of Life*.

*Boys of Life* will be republished by Cleis Press in 2016.

A native of Memphis, Tennessee, Paul currently lives in upstate New York.

Read more about him at paul-russell.org.

Author photograph: Frank Bergon